FLESH OF THE BLOOD

A CALL TO ARMS

BY E.A. CHANNON

Flesh of the Blood
E.A. Channon
Cover art by Jason Behnke
ISBN-13: 978-1537589077
ISBN-10:1537589075
Copyright © 2016 by E.A. Channon
All Rights Reserved
This book or any portion thereof may not be reproduced or used in any manner whatsoever without the express written permission of the author except for the use of brief quotations in a book review.
For permissions, please use the contact form on:
www.EAChannon.com

Books by E A. Channon:
Ballad of a Bagpiper - Whatever Blows Up Your Kilt
Flesh of the Blood
Flesh of the Blood - Devastation
Flesh of the Blood - A Call to Arms

Prologue

There is a reason for everything, as all things have a beginning …

"If you are to understand the reason, my son, for the events in this world and why they are occurring … you must understand that, long ago, this world was a lot different — calmer, with only two known beings that lived in peace together, building a better world on Marn."

Meradoth had joined his father in the room where his father used to meditate. The group had been resting for a short time in his father's tower west of Bru Edin before continuing the journey to find the kidnapped Shermee. As Meradoth sat with his father, Nicolorr, the master of the mage tower, Nicolorr shared the history of Marn, a history only known to a few.

"A better world … how, Father?" Meradoth asked, putting a hand on his thigh and moving himself to look directly into his father's eyes.

"Before our people walked these lands … even before the Doro Amnach or elvenkind breathed the air of Marn, there lived two beings in this world." As Nicolorr spoke, the room that both he and Meradoth sat in began to shift around them. Meradoth noticed the walls disappear, and slowly, through a shift of light all around them, he began to see land, from mountains covered in snow to flowing waterfalls dropping down into glens. He was sure he could even smell grass.

"Marn before the eyes of both man and Doro Amnach observed it was one large land of flowing rivers, high mountains, long, wide plains and fields of grass. From the south, where the cold lived, to the north, where the wetness made life abundant, life in this world was peaceful."

"Father, I didn't know this." Meradoth stood up and turned around, taking in the scene that was around him as Nicolorr continued sitting on the bench that now stood in the middle of a grassy field filled with birds and other animals moving past them.

"My son, you must understand that one of the beings that lived upon Marn from when time began is now the most dreaded of all creatures that live upon the lands … but they were once peaceful and loving, such as you and I are!" Meradoth turned, looking down at his father, who still sat calmly upon the bench.

"Orcs?" His mouth opened in astonishment. "I thought that the gods …!" Meradoth whispered, looking up and seeing a group of beings laughing and playing some type of ball game on the field. Then he looked at his father, who smiled, nodding gently.

"They are known as the Orkani in their language, but yes, today we call them orcs, and together with the Gusfana, or the dwarven peoples, they lived peacefully on this world … so peacefully that nothing seemed to bother them … until …" Nicolorr looked down as he spoke the last word, making Meradoth turn to look at his father.

As he did, he noticed that a shadow was slowly forming on the far side of his father, making Meradoth tighten his face, wondering what would make a shadow. As he turned around, he noticed the sun far away, bursting out of the clouds and making long beams of light shine everywhere. But as Meradoth closed his eyes to enjoy the warm sunlight, he began to notice that the warmth was different.

"The world changed, my son, when the gods in the stars began to fight." Meradoth opened up his eyes as the warmth felt stronger, and he squinted slightly as he noticed an enormous dark shadow, larger than anything he had ever seen in the sky before, beginning to form, causing the sun to disappear. But he noticed that, in its place, clouds appeared, almost all of which were on fire.

"Father?" Meradoth whispered as he stepped back slightly. As the shadow grew darker, something began to take shape within — something dark, something so massive it obscured the lands as the edges of the clouds turned red, like fire was erupting inside them.

Suddenly the animals that were grazing burst into a hard run to escape, and he noticed the creatures had stopped playing and were all standing and looking up as well.

Turning to look at his father and then back up to the sky, Meradoth began to hear a high-pitched scream as the wind around the two mages began to swirl, making their robes flap hard around them.

Meradoth tried to concentrate on what was approaching, but the wind and screaming grew louder and louder, making him cover his ears. "FATHER, WHAT'S HAPPENING!" he screamed loudly as Nicolorr finally stood up to look in his son's eyes.

"This is when the world took a step towards evil!" His father's words crawled into Meradoth's mind as he looked up again, noticing that the shape within the dark clouds resembled a creature that he had only read about. He dropped his mouth, gasping and trying to stop the pain in his head, as the loud screaming of the wind made it hard to think.

The black image took shape within the clouds. "Oh, gods … It's a logikaar!" Meradoth screamed out over the high-pitched wind still making his robes flap around him.

The legends are true, Meradoth thought. *The elves brought dragons to Marn!* The clouds moved closer to where he and his father stood until, finally, they began to part, showing what was within them.

"Father!" Meradoth whispered as he stepped back, bringing his hands up. He wondered how he could defend himself against such a powerful being, which, according to legend, could destroy everything within its path.

As the clouds burst open, the two mages watched as a black-winged beast slowly moved out of the clouds and became enveloped in fire — fire that Meradoth could feel upon his skin, making the mage drop to his knees when he felt his father's hand on his shoulder.

"Watch, my son … and learn!" Nicolorr said again, calmly.

Meradoth did just that, but the fear of the dragon above seeing them made the mage shake under his robes. However, he did what his father said and continued to watch the beast, which he was sure was as large as all the lands around them. As the creature moved across the sky and the fires that surrounded it began to disperse, Meradoth saw small objects begin to burst out of the clouds.

His eyes followed the smaller objects, at first believing that they might be offspring of some type, but as they began slamming into the mountains nearby, causing the ground under their feet to shake, he considered that they might be something else altogether.

Looking at his father, who still acted calmly, Meradoth suddenly understood. As he observed the look upon his father's face, Meradoth realized that his father had seen this before. Standing up straight, he nodded to his father, who nodded once back. Looking up once again, he saw that the massive beast of a dragon was dropping hard from the sky as many objects, from long to short and small to large, flew everywhere, slamming into the ground hard, making the mountains burst open and causing the ground to continue to shake each time one hit.

"This is the gods? Why were they fighting, Father?" Meradoth asked, noticing that the wind had quieted down enough that he didn't have to scream now.

Nicolorr looked down to lay his eyes on his son's face. Then a slight smile formed on his lips as he nodded yes. "None know why … but all must make war upon the other … even the gods!" Nicolorr's words made Meradoth wonder about the why of all things … He looked back up just as the dragon beast dipped down, causing the land that they stood on to shake so hard that Meradoth was thrown down onto the grass field hard. He watched whole mountains being ripped apart as a boulder the size of a city flew into the sky and fell into the ocean beyond.

As they took in the scene, the sky instantly turned red as fires erupted and everything was uprooted before them.

"When the logikaar came down, it changed the very surface of Marn, bringing in the oceans to separate the one land mass into two. The power that was within it changed the two beings that lived upon Marn forever!" Nicolorr stated as the scene around the two changed to show a land ripped apart, rivers moving hard and fields that had been green now dark and dead. The mountains that Meradoth had seen earlier were now gone, as was any sign of life.

"The Orkani, who were the nearest to where the gods fell, were caught in the massive fires and energy waves, changing their very being down to the flesh of the blood, making them what you see today ... evil and bent on destruction." Meradoth's eyes moved across the field to see the group of orcs that had been playing transformed so that they were now covered in the familiar black robes that we see today. "They wear those to cover the hideous forms that are underneath, Son."

"What of the dwarven people that also lived on this world ... What happened to them, Father?" Meradoth almost knew the answer before Nicolorr spoke.

"The energy that the gods brought with them separated these people into two groups. The ones that were farther underground were not affected and are the ones that love the world today — the current dwarves. The other — the Qlorfana, or the dark dwarves, who are bent on hating everything, including themselves — were closer to the surface and succumbed to the powers of the gods." Nicolorr walked up, placing a hand on his son's arm and turning him slightly to look at him. "They have switched since then. Now the dark ones are deeper underground than the dwarves we know, and we do not see them much, if at all.

"Son ... the Doro Amnach and our people, the Vaca'nor ... We came here from another world. That beast you saw, Son, was a beast that the gods used to travel here, and it is what Methnorick seeks to power again. If he finds what he needs to power the gods' machine ... Marn will once again be changed."

"Then the legends are true ... Men and elves are not of Marn,"

Meradoth whispered as Nicolorr nodded yes in return.

"This very tower, Son, was once used by the gods. The power within it gives us — you and I ... our kind — the ability to do what we do. I know not why ... but those of our kind and many others have had abilities for many cycles."

"How do we stop Methnorick, Father? His power is ... I felt it when he entered Brigin'i City ... The things I saw him do!"

"Strength and cunning, Son ... They always win in the end, no matter what power your enemy has. Use that against him and you have a chance ... but you must stop him before he finds the devices to power the gods' machine."

Meradoth looked around, wondering where he was. He had never seen this part of Marn before, but before he could ask about it, the scene slowly turned to mist. Nicolorr turned and disappeared into the mist, leaving his son to look around as the mist turned back into the room that he and his father had been in since the beginning.

"Strength and cunning ... interesting!" Meradoth whispered.

Chapter One

Ruko sat at the edge of the water with his beloved fishing pole, enjoying the cool morning breeze that came off the bay before him. He closed his eyes and remembered his grandfather teaching him to fish for the first time when he was three winters old. He smiled at the memories of catching fish after fish with him.

His father had always been away on hunting trips, so his grandfather took him out and showed him fishing tricks. It didn't take him long to learn how to fish, and soon he was bringing fish home for his mother to cook for the family of five. His younger sisters and brothers were a handful, and their father was gone for the summers, so his mother loved the help.

Their village lay at the edge of a large bay. Village legends stated that when their people had arrived from across the waters those many seasons ago, they had seen a bright star above that shined on where the first hut was built. Now, many cycles later, the village had prospered to the point that the fields up beyond the trees grew all the food needed to sustain the village and the animals kept within the village were fat and full of life.

Life in the village of Trag was good. Ruko smiled as he considered how secure they were, even as rumors were spreading that creatures of darkness had been seen in the far-off south, beyond the mountains that surrounded Trag. Trag Bay on the east and the Trag Mountains to the west, south and north had always kept his people safe.

Ruko felt a fish grab the hook he had been using for the past hour to catch the five fish he had lying next to him. One more, he thought, and he could go home to help him mother with the family. A six-count of fish was good and should feed them all today and maybe even tomorrow.

He was also excited because one of the village scouts had returned, sharing word that his father had been seen and should be coming home today. For a while, the villagers of Trag believed, they were safe, but they took nothing to chance.

Since the passing of his grandfather last summer, Ruko had become the main source of food when their father went hunting for the food that would sustain the village through the winter season, and he was proud of the amount of food he had gathered since his father had left a few weeks back.

The fish bit the hook, and Ruko was able to reel it in with a sudden pull of the fishing pole. The fish landed on the ground next to him, jumping up and down, squirming to get back into the water. Ruko grabbed his small sword that, seasons before, his father had given him to use for this purpose, slamming the pommel down hard on the head of the fish, killing it instantly.

He stood up and put the last fish into the large pouch he carried with him and strung up his pole, looking out towards the bay, smiling as he watched fog move in slowly from across the land strip on the eastern side of the bay. Not that it was unusual for fog to come across the bay like it was, but it was unusual for this time of the day, Ruko thought. It should have come earlier.

Shaking his head, he turned to make his way from the beach to the village, which lay across a small river that was just north of where Ruko liked to fish.

As he stepped across the stones that lay in the river, he heard what sounded like waves hitting wood. He looked out again at the bay, but now the fog made it hard to see anything more than a few feet out. But he was sure he heard that sound again. Turning, he walked out to the edge of the beach and tried listening harder.

Why would a boat be out there in this weather? he wondered. He listened more intently but didn't hear the sound again, and shrugging his shoulders, he turned around and started walking back to the village again. As he came over a small rise that lay just south of the village perimeter, he heard the sound again. This time he heard what he thought was a grunt. He turned his head to look out towards the bay as his eyes caught sight of something moving slowly towards him. He started to see not just one boat but many boats slowly coming out of the fog.

Ruko was only twelve cycles old, but these boats coming towards him were different from any he had ever seen before, causing him to wonder if the tales told by the village elders of creatures that could harm the villagers if they knew of this place were true. He opened his mouth to scream a warning when suddenly his voice disappeared, turning into a cough as some unusual pain quickly formed in his chest, making him cough again.

Looking down to see what caused the pain, he saw a black-feathered arrow sticking out of his chest. He whimpered in both surprise and shock.

Raising his hand up, he tried to pull it out, but the pain made his knees give way, and he fell down hard, almost crying as pain shot through his body, making him weak. His fishing pole clattered to the ground, along with the pouch full of fish, which spilled everywhere, as boats slammed into the beach around him. Unknown creatures covered in black jumped out and ran past him, grunting a language that Ruko had never heard before. Ruko's eyes began to tear up as thoughts of his family moved through his mind. Then he saw a shadow move in front of him, causing him to look up as he felt his strength disappear. A pair of black leather boots stood in front of him. He raised his head slowly as the pain from his chest began to spread throughout his whole body. When his eyes saw what stood before him, he whimpered again.

Standing in front of him was a man — that is, Ruko was sure it looked like a man. This man wore clothing that covered him like armor. Ruko's eyes began to water up as the man stood, watching the creatures move past them both. The man looked down at Ruko, making his body shake like he was cold. Then Ruko saw under the hood what looked like a smile form.

As screams started emerging from the village, a larger and scarier man moved up and said something to the black-covered one, who responded in the same tongue, causing the other man to turn and run away quickly.

Then, catching Ruko by surprise, the man bent down and looked into Ruko's eyes, making the young boy start to cry.

Cocking his head, the man continued to look into the eyes of the young boy as he cried. Placing a gloved hand on the side of Ruko's face, he whispered something to the boy.

"Hmmmm, not to worry, boy … You will soon join your people … very soon …" the raspy voice stated to Ruko.

The black-clothed man laid his other hand on Ruko's shoulder and watched as, moments later, the boy stopped crying and the life in his eyes slowly faded. The man then laid Ruko's now-lifeless body on the ground as he stood up and looked over the scene in front of him.

Trag was fully in flames. Screams of its people finally began to disappear as black smoke rose high into the air, covering the sky. The black-clothed man looked around as more and more boats landed, soon crowding the beach behind him.

The man looked down at the body of the boy. Shrugging, he pulled out a small knife as he leaned down to stab a fish and then quickly cut its head off. When he whispered something, the fish caught on fire in his hand, instantly cooking it without burning his hand. He then took a deep bite of it, smiling with satisfaction at the taste of the cooked fish.

The large man who, moments earlier, had run off returned to give the man information. The dark-clothed man listened to the information and then spat out a command before turning back to walk towards the smoldering village.

"Yes, my lord, Methnorick," the large man said as he turned and ran off, leaving Methnorick smiling at the news he had just received. This village had been destroyed and the fields taken with no loss of his own, and the village's supplies had been found and were quickly being stored away. The fields beyond quickly turned black as his army began to form upon them and prepared to march out of the valley to the mountains beyond when their leader gave the order.

Methnorick smiled, placing both hands on his hips. So far his first move had been unnoticed, and that made him smile again.

* * *

Methnorick's army took two full days to get off the boats just west of the burnt village without being seen. He ordered his mages to have more fog roll in to mask his army, and they did very well at it. The whole area and valley beyond the now-burnt and dead village almost disappeared in the fog. If someone tried to find them, it would be hard.

So far his scouts had come back with news that nothing had been seen as yet. Only one villager that happened to be in the valley, trying to escape, was killed right away. This news made him smile as he thought of how his plan to land unnoticed had worked, and worked better than he had thought.

Now, sitting on top of his black horse, he watched as column after column marched past. The orcs grunted as they marched because his orders were no talking, cheering or even blowing horns to inform anyone or anything that they were here. The only sound he wanted to hear was marching feet.

After a few minutes of watching this, Methnorick turned the reins of his mount and rode past the large columns to the front of his army that was now marching its way up through the valley towards the pass that would let him break out to the lands beyond to the south.

As he rode and watched his armies, Methnorick thought of the plans that he had put into place and ones that were at this moment in play around the lands before him.

General Kaligor's army had made a perfect landing in the area, destroying the castle fortress of Stych, its town and the lands around it. From there, the cyclops had marched north-northwest through the land, killing and destroying everything he could. Villages, towns and even some small castles fell and were destroyed. He had gathered allies along the way, but not enough to change his plans. The cyclops had split his army into two, one continuing north as the other marched north and west towards Brigin'i City and its castle, where King Dia — Methnorick's first real victim of his war — reigned.

When Brigin'i fell, Kaligor marched back to the fortress castle of Bru Edin, cutting off the northern lands from the south and, in the process, destroying Brigin'i's only cavalry.

Blath 'Na was cut off and surrounded. The creatures made by the doctor Methnorick held captive had easily taken over the city. All this Methnorick considered with a smile as he rode his steed up the road to the pass high in the mountains above.

Only a few threats left, he thought, as he came to sit beside a stone post that had carvings in an old language that he could barely read.

He had not received any new information on the movements in the dwarven kingdom that lay below the mountains of Pilo'ach, but he knew they still were a treat to his plans.

The biggest threat, however, to his plans to conquer these lands was the elves. The elven army should have been destroyed with Bru Edin, but instead they retreated to their forest kingdom. He hoped they would stay where they were once they were back in their forest, but he could not count on that. He would prefer to wipe them off the map, but he still did not know where they were. Now that Brigin'i was destroyed, the elven army was bigger than anything in the northern lands.

As he sat, thinking of his goal of total annihilation and how it would have been so much easier with Shermee at his side (for she was the answer to everything, according to the writings, anyway) a scout came up to Methnorick. He informed Methnorick that he and the other scouts could see what could only be a human army marching their way from the western hills.

Methnorick looked back down into the glen, towards the burnt-out village and beyond to the seas. He knew that the army would take at least the better part of the day to get through the pass, and right now, if he were attacked, he could possibly lose the whole campaign in one quick battle, even if his army were ready.

Turning to one of his mages, he ordered the creature to make more mist to cover the entrance to the pass and make the mist move with his army as they traveled north. The mage nodded, and with a quick swipe of the hand, the mage disappeared, leaving nothing in his place, not even his horse.

Chapter Two

Nicolorr stood, explaining, "What you see here on the tapestry shows the city of Brigini'i."

As the group looked on, they saw the once-proud and mighty city of Brigin'i burning and smoking. They stood in the large chamber of the mage tower east of Bru Edin that was the source of power for mages such as Meradoth and Harbin.

"Yes … even though his city is gone, the king lives," the old mage continued.

"Dia's alive?" Amlora interrupted, jumping up.

"That's incredible that he lived through that," Kikor whispered as the tapestry moved, showing them the hundreds of victims of Kaligor's rage hanging high from the poles that the cyclops had put them on.

Kalion and his group stood, looking on without speaking as the image before them changed to show Bru Edin. The destruction of Bru Edin was just as complete, as the image showed hundreds of survivors in the city being lifted up to die on poles that the orcs had brought from the forests beyond.

Amlora alone was tearing up, as she couldn't believe that the city that once had been so beautiful and where she had laughed with a group of children not long ago was now a smoking ruin where orcs were killing all they found in the rubble.

Turning to look at Meradoth's father, Kalion sucked in a breath, hoping to hear good news. "If the king is alive … where is he? Is he a prisoner?"

Nicolorr turned and smiled at the ranger's question, hearing the desperation for hope in it. "No. In fact … King Dia is, as we speak, here …" The mage waved his hand at the tapestry, which turned to mist, and then, slowly, the picture switched to show a huge glen with high mountains on either side covered in snow. A huge river ran through the bottom of the glen, but it was the movement along the side of the river that made the group gasp as they took in what could only be a dream.

Hundreds, if not thousands, of spears, shields and banners gleamed in the sun, displaying the emblems of the elven realm. They saw the huge forms of ice giants, all carrying huge weapons on their shoulders, moving among the ranks of elven warriors. As the group began to understand that what they saw was not a dream, the image moved to show a group of armored elves standing at the top of a hill, along with a huge giant who wore a black fur cloak over his shoulders. Within this group stood a man wearing a green cloak over elven armor who looked smaller and older than the others.

"As you can see …" Nicolorr whispered.

"Dia!" the group almost said together as the once-mighty king of Brigin'i came into view.

"Who are those elves with him?" Kalion asked, walking up to stand next to Nicolorr. "I've never seen that emblem before."

"That, my friend, is the emblem of the high king of all the elven people throughout the lands: King Mass-Lorak," Kikor piped in, walking up to the ranger.

"If he truly is there with King Dia … then the north is finally moving to hopefully stop Methnorick and the evil he has brought to this land," Kikor added, looking at Meradoth's father. Nicolorr looked over at his son, who so far hadn't spoken a word since Nicolorr had begun speaking.

"Remember, Methnorick is searching for objects, of which I am not sure how many he has at this point … Where the next one might be, I can find out," Nicolorr said calmly as he moved to stand before the group. "These objects are the key reason why the evil has entered these lands."

"Do you know what the objects are for?" Kalion asked as he thought about what this creature might be looking for.

"No … maybe," the old man answered. "My eyes out there have been able to find no evidence of that, but whatever they are for, he is determined to find them, and in doing so, he will destroy everything." He looked at his son, Meradoth, who pressed his lips together as he looked back, not knowing what to say.

"Well, we cannot stop him; that is for sure … So I think we should get out of here and leave to fight something that we can kill!" Jebba's voice made the rest turn to look at the man leaning against a stone pillar not far away.

"Of course we can na kill that creature … but we might be able to slow 'em!" Holan said quickly before the others could answer.

"Jebba … not now, please!" Kalion looked at the warrior and then turned to ask Nicolorr a question, but before he could, Jebba interrupted him.

"Not now? No, now is the perfect time to speak, ranger. First you let Winsto get killed by creatures none of us have seen …"

"Exactly … none of us had any idea what they were or what they were capable of," Kikor said, jumping in to defend Kalion. "This is not Kalion's fault. Remember, he tried to stop Winsto, but Winsto was having none of that."

Dismissing the elf, Jebba continued, "Fulox … Zahnz … even Hrliger have died under your command … And don't let me get started on your betrayal of Birkita!" Jebba's voice rose so loud that it echoed through the chamber as the rest quickly jumped in to defend the ranger. Suddenly the chamber exploded in a loud, bright burst of light and sound, making the group quickly fall silent.

"You know we never really saw Winsto die!" Chansor piped in. "We saw him charge at them and disappear. He might not be dead." He looked at each of his friends.

Each member of the group looked over at him in astonishment, but none said anything.

"ENOUGH!" They turned to see Nicolorr, Meradoth and Harbin standing together at the edge of the chamber, all looking back at the group now gathered around Jebba.

"You will not fight here within my home … The fight is out there. You are on a mission to find the princess … Use this anger to find her!"

"Methnorick can't be stopped?" Kikor whispered.

"Yes, he can. He is mortal even though he has powers, but is Methnorick your mission?" Nicolorr asked, looking at Kikor. "We know that he does not have the princess currently, but you could slow him down by getting just one of the objects."

"Do you have an idea where Methnorick and his armies might be going?" Whelor, who hadn't joined in the argument, quietly asked the old mage, who turned to give the large man another suspicious look.

Slowly shaking his head no, Nicolorr looked at Kalion, who, just after the explosion, had let go of Jebba's collar to walk away and calm himself down. "Kalion … where do you plan on traveling from here?" Nicolorr nodded to the other two mages, who separated and walked away as Kalion tilted his head back for a moment to think.

"I believe we should make our way to Blath 'Na City … through Fuunidor." Kalion saw the look on Nicolorr's face, and he followed the mage's eyes over to land on Whelor, who was now leaning against a pillar, looking at the ground.

Nicolorr came back to the situation by blinking quickly. Then he turned and waved his hand at the tapestry, which had only been showing mist. As he did so, the tapestry slowly opened up to show the mighty walls of the port city that Kalion had spoken of moments before.

"Blath 'Na … There … there has been silence from the City of Ports for a while now," Nicolorr said quietly as the group gathered to look up at the city.

"Silence … What are you speaking about, Father?" Meradoth spoke up then as he slid off the table he was sitting on.

"My vision seems to be blocked somehow. I have heard nothing from our brothers that have lived in that city for a few days now … It makes me concerned, for my vision has never been blocked in this way before. I can't see beyond the walls of Blath 'Na." The mage gazed at his son with a look of sadness.

"With everything that you have told us the last few days, Father, I cannot believe that our brothers there would be silent unless something has happened to make them unable to speak, or worse." Meradoth stared at his father and then looked up at the tapestry that hadn't moved, only showing the walls of the city.

Nicolorr leaned back on the table behind him as he looked at the ground, thinking about how to answer his son.

"I believe some type of sickness has entered that city," he whispered.

"What was that?" Kikor turned to look down at the head of the mage. "Did you say 'sickness'?"

"What type of sickness could silence a whole city?" Amlora asked, as confused as the others were.

"I have seen only a few, but whatever you might want to call it, people caught with this … this sickness seem to die … but then return …" Nicolorr lifted his head to stare at his son, who returned a confused look.

"Return?" Bennak asked, confused as much as the others. *When you die … you die*, he thought.

"What would you call it when someone dies and seems to return to life and continue killing?" the old mage asked, speaking to the floor before him.

"Do you believe that by going to that city we might get sick?" Kalion asked, trying to figure out what to do if they couldn't get to the port city.

Meradoth looked at his friend and thought the same thing as he began to think of the words of a spell to gather his energy to travel to the city. His father stood up and stopped him, for he could see what his son was planning.

"Son … I know not what is in that city … but I feel that evil has entered it." Nicolorr's voice silenced Meradoth's mind as he looked at the sad face of his father.

Harbin moved over and waved his hand over the tapestry as he said a few words, trying to find the answer. Meradoth moved over to join him in speaking words quietly, lending his support to what Harbin was attempting to do.

The image on the tapestry moved across the top of the wall. They quickly saw smoke rising high into the air, as fires burned here and there across the buildings. When Harbin moved the image to display an area where he knew a mage tower stood, he gasped, as the image revealed collapsed rubble. There were smoke, fire and a few bodies of their brother mages. Suddenly the chamber was filled with such a high-pitched scream that everyone covered their ears. A few screamed from the pain as the tapestry above them erupted in flames and fell to the floor in ash. As it did, the scream quickly disappeared, leaving the group standing there in pain.

"Is this Methnorick's work?" Harbin asked loudly, looking over at Meradoth's father, who looked up, shrugging his shoulders slightly.

"I suspect it is. With the lands under the blade because of him … why wouldn't Blath 'Na be as well?" Nicolorr quietly said as Harbin turned his head to stare back at the ashes.

"Kalion … I know you believe that the princess might be in this city … but with everything I am seeing, how could she still be there … or even be alive?!" Harbin asked.

The ranger quickly answered, "She's alive, my friend … I have faith that she is!"

Nicolorr rose and placed his hand on the ranger's shoulder, smiling gently as he looked over, calming the ranger down.

"Then Blath 'Na is where we must go!" Meradoth said as he came to stand behind the ranger.

Jebba shook his head quietly, saying that he didn't agree, as Bennak just shrugged his shoulders, saying he would go wherever

Jebba traveled. Kikor looked over at Whelor, who stared back at the elven warrior, giving her a slight smile in return.

"We will go the city, Kalion." Kikor smiled at Kalion, who smiled back, nodding a thank you to her.

"There is one there who may have the answers you seek," Nicolorr stated.

"Who?" asked Kalion. *I thought Meradoth's father had the answers, but now …*

Nicolorr looked over at Meradoth with sad eyes. "Your mother, Tiffanori. She was in the city when things started to go wrong."

"What do you mean Mom is in the city?" Meradoth stared at his father.

"She was there conferring on matters that were occurring across the lands, and you know I can't leave the tower anymore, for my age will catch up with me."

"I know you can't go with us, Father, for the power within the tower is what keeps you alive," Meradoth calmly said, smiling at his father.

"Find your mother, my son!" Nicolorr whispered to Meradoth, who only nodded in answer as the group began to file out of the chamber. Grabbing his pack, the mage, followed by his father, made his way down the hall to the large door that opened to the outside. The door began to slide open, bringing in light and even a fresh breeze of air, which Kikor breathed in.

Nicolorr pointed to where the trail was as the mist outside lifted. The group moved past the mage, thanking him for his help. But as the last member of the group moved past, Nicolorr grabbed Kalion and Meradoth, motioning for them to wait for the rest to travel far enough away for him to speak without being interrupted.

"Keep an eye on that big man, Whelor … There is something about him I do not get, something that does not fit — something not quite human," Nicolorr said quietly as the other two looked at each other, confused.

"Whelor … I sense nothing wrong with him, but I will trust your judgement," Meradoth said, confused and almost laughing at the thought that Whelor was a problem.

Nicolorr placed his hand on Meradoth's shoulder. "Methnorick has experimented on a number of things and creatures, Son … Just be careful with him. I fear something is not right with him."

"Sir, I'm sure we will be fine with Whelor … but thank you for telling us, sir." Kalion smiled at the old mage, quickly thinking about Whelor and how he sometimes disappeared in the night and then acted a bit strange in the mornings.

Nicolorr watched the team walk down the trail as the mist closed in around them. He gently waved at Meradoth, who nodded back. Amlora smiled at the man, bringing a smile to the old man's face in return.

As the mist fell in around him, Chansor acted like always did: like a thief who was just on a fun adventure, looking for something to do. He bent down to grab a stick and used it to hit flowers that grew along the deer path they were using to travel down the mountain. He waited until everyone had passed him, most just smiling and shaking their heads at the thief, and then he stood still for a moment until he heard breathing along his neck.

"Masssterrr iss not happy, thieffff!" Elesha's voice rasped in his ear, making him close his eyes for a moment. He opened them quickly when he heard her voice to his right.

"What have you to say, thief?" Elesha's voice didn't send chills down his back as much as it used to, but it still made him nervous.

Turning, he stepped back in surprise when, thinking he was going to see a full-size creature, he instead saw a small creature that reminded him of creatures from legend.

"Do I scare youuu, thieffff?" she asked. He blinked as he noticed the creature's mouth didn't move. He slowly shook his head, trying to act strong and tough, when he saw her smiling back up at him.

Elesha, who had dark, almost purple, scales; legs holding deadly claws almost like daggers; and long tails that whipped around with what looked like a sword that probably could cut him in half if the creature wanted to, was only three feet tall and flapped a pair of batlike wings.

"No ... you just caught me by surprise," he whispered, trying to get his voice back after the shock of seeing what was hovering in front of him. He swallowed, remembering the question she had asked moments before.

"I ... mmm ... I haven't been able to report because I haven't been able get away since Bru Edin ... but the master should know what is happening with this group. Does he not?" Chansor's voice made the creature look at him more closely, squinting her eyes as she stopped flapping her wings. She dropped to stand on what could have been her hind legs and stared up at him.

Chansor continued. "Well, they just went down this path, friend. You can track them as easily as I can now. Why not just follow them?" Chansor's question sounded like an attack to the scaled creature, who hissed at him, making the thief step back, hoping that he hadn't angered her.

"Massster wantsss you tooo do yourrr tassskkk, thiefff ... Dooo it orrr I will whennn you are deaddd," Elesha said, flapping her wings. Chansor swallowed at hearing her threaten to kill him if he didn't do what he had originally been asked to do.

He opened his mouth to speak again, but she flapped her wings, and in a rush of wind that flew from behind him, blowing his hair into his face, the creature disappeared in a puff of mist, leaving the thief by himself suddenly. He was looking around for her when he heard the snap of a stick close behind, making him turn quickly around to see the smiling face of Kikor.

"Everything well, Chansor?" she asked calmly, giving no indication that she knew what had just happened.

Chansor quickly swallowed, put a smile on his face and laughed as best he could. He pretended to fumble with his trousers like he had just finished something.

Kikor shook her head. "Ahhh ... well, the rest are getting farther away, my friend, and I noticed you were missing, so ..."

Chansor walked up to her as she spoke. "Sorry, Kikor ... I guess that meal we had didn't go down well." He smiled again and rubbed his stomach, making the elven warrior laugh. She turned and followed the thief as they walked quickly to catch up to the rest of the group.

Chapter Three

Horns blew as the spears and shields of his army charged into humans that had been marching calmly in the valley when Methnorick's troops surprised them. Crashes of steel and bone and cries from horses, men and orcs echoed across the field. Sitting upon his mount at the top of a large mound of stone, Methnorick looked down at the battle going on below, using the banners that flew above the heads of his orcs to see where to send his reinforcements to push forward into another area. The yells and screams of pain and glory from both sides grew louder, as did the clangs of metal upon metal as shields and swords clashed, making him smile under his hood.

The sun to his right rose, starting to move higher over the mountains that lay far away. The sunlight reflected off of the helmets and shields of the cavalry that he had ordered to charge far right and then to swing around to attack the human forces on its left flank.

As the cavalry slammed into the men, a barrage of arrows from a hastily organized group of archers flew up into the air to fall and slam into Methnorick's troops. As he saw bodies fall back and get run over quickly by their comrades, he didn't give them a thought, for he had more to come when needed.

Cursing, he turned to his team of mages. "Block the sun!" he screamed.

The black-robed mages nodded back and then looked at each other and held hands. Mumbling could be heard coming from under their hoods. Methnorick saw a shadow move over him as he looked up to see the sun quickly being covered by a storm of darkness.

Across the fields, Methnorick saw that the humans were quickly breaking apart into smaller groups as his orcs moved through, killing whatever they could.

"No prisoners!" he rasped from under his breath as another

orc ran off to inform the generals who were conducting the battle. He continued to look on as he considered two things: one, the importance of no survivors leaving the field to tell others of his army, and two, what an opportunity this chance encounter with a small army offered to test his troops.

A huge Blingo'oblin standing just behind Methnorick grunted something to his lord. After Methnorick gave him a confirming nod, he turned and yelled to others that were waiting on the far side of the hill. Hearing this, they lifted up their massive weapons, all grunting in almost a cheer as they ran into the battle by circling the hill towards the front lines and slamming into a group of knights that had been able to hold off the orcs so far.

Quickly, five Blingo'oblins pushed themselves through, chopping three knights almost in half. One of the creatures cut the head off another knight and another stabbed upward from under the man's left arm, killing the knight instantly as the massive blade cut through the man's body and exploded out of his right shoulder. His blood shot over another knight, who died just as quickly as the creature in front of him slammed his blade through the knight's armor, cutting his spine in half.

Methnorick's creatures did what they were bred and made for, killing whatever they could quickly and effectively, causing the humans, who had been trying to form a defense, to scatter and run where ever they could.

Methnorick laughed and those around him cheered while watching those that tried to run die as orcs, now without a formed human line to stop them, massacred everything on the field. Screams echoed as the creatures that formed Methnorick's prized guard slashed and chopped humans that got in their way, quickly cutting them down with their blades.

Satisfied that his army had won the field, he turned his horse slowly and trotted back behind his lines. He got off the horse and stretched his back, but as he did so, he laughed out loud at the slaughter that was accruing. An orc servant ran up and offered him a wine jug. He grabbed it and took a large gulp, smiling as he looked up into the sky. Looking down, he observed the orc, who waited for his orders, and smiled again at him.

"Glorious, do you not think?" The orc nodded, quickly looking down at the ground, a bit scared of his lord who stood before him. The orc knew the power that the man held within his hands, and he didn't want to feel his lord's wrath for not doing his job.

Pouring some of the liquid into his mouth, Methnorick looked over to where his generals sat upon their own mounts, giving orders, pointing at his army and watching their orders being sent out by runners.

A few of his Blingo'oblin guards that didn't go into the battle stood at a distance, but close enough if needed by Methnorick. A few stood and watched the lake that was behind them as well as the mountains that were to Methnorick's right, keeping an eye out for anything that might harm their master, giving their lord a moment's rest and peace.

It didn't last long, as one of his lieutenants came riding up to inform Methnorick that the human army was finally broken and falling apart. He asked if Methnorick wanted warriors to finish the job and kill everything on the field, saying that some humans were quickly retreating and getting away.

Methnorick thought about what the lieutenant had just said as he walked over to look upon the large lake that lay about a mile from where he stood. Taking another drink from the wine jug, he said, "Take what is needed to finish the job. Have the human scum chased down ... no prisoners ... no mercy!" At that, the man bowed deeply on his saddle. Pulling his mount's reins to the right, he galloped off to inform the generals who were watching the movements of their army and the now-scattered humans before them.

Just as a spark from the sun shined on the ground in front of his boots, the ground began to shake under him, making Methnorick smile. He threw his jug at the orc, who tried but failed to catch it, spilling the wine all over himself. As the servant watched, his lord took a few steps, looking around, wondering and waiting for what was coming.

* * *

The dwarves slammed hard into each other again as screams echoed loudly in the caverns and tunnels deep in the dwarven kingdom under the Pilo'ach Mountains. Spears slammed hard into the shields, and a few slipped over the shields to rip into the helmets and chests of a few dwarves on either side. Some were lifted high into the air, screaming in pain as their enemy tossed them to the side.

Explosion after explosion erupted here and there, brightening the dark. Those not used the light screamed in pain and tried to cover their faces, only to die as the dwarves saw their chance to cut them down.

After the third charge of the dark dwarves, King Stokolma Finfilli of Chai'sell could finally see the desperation that was rising in his dwarven ranks. Whole groups of the dark dwarves had sacrificed themselves, hoping that their numbers could push his warriors back enough that his lines would collapse.

Luckily for now, the cavern floor was covered with more dark dwarven bodies than his own. He stood not far behind, screaming out orders about where spears and battle-axes were needed as he watched, finally catching sight of what his observers had been telling him: It was not just dark dwarves they faced, but dark elves as well.

Far in the rear of the cavern, almost hiding behind a stalactite, he could make out three dark elves commanding their allies into battle. The king caught sight of them as an explosion erupted, causing their black armor to shine slightly, revealing the dark elves' position.

"Got you!" he mumbled as he looked around, trying to find his best archers and a mage that could knock them out of this battle and hopefully change it into a full retreat of their cousins back into the deep darkness of the world.

∗ ∗ ∗

Kalion pulled back the string of his bow and released an arrow that rammed itself into the face of the orc that was trying to charge at him, killing the orc and knocking it back hard as Jebba, who stood nearby, also released an arrow, knocking back another orc not far to the ranger's right.

A few feet away, Harbin had put his hands together and then opened them up to release a huge wave of bright red lava that he had transported from the volcano not far away. It fell onto about eight orcs that screamed a moment and quickly disappeared, causing those that had thought this group of travelers would be an easy target to turn and run back into the darkness of the forest, leaving the small group alone.

"Interesting … That was quick, don't you think?" Meradoth smiled as his own hands, which had been glowing blue, slowly returned to his normal skin color. The rest slowly calmed down and looked at what was around them.

"Quick … but it might have gotten the attention of a larger group of orcs. We need to move," Kalion declared urgently as he stared at the orc he had just killed, seeing that it was still squirming, even with an arrow stuck in its face.

Not far away, Bennak walked up to stare at Harbin, who had crossed his arms as he stared at the now-cooled rock that he had made.

"If you're going to do that again, let me watch!" The big man smiled, showing off his missing teeth. Harbin smiled and nodded without looking at the half-orc warrior.

Kikor burst out of the bushes at that moment, whispering that, so far, nothing was moving behind them, but they should move. She replaced her blade, which the others could see was covered in black orc blood.

The rest of the day, here and there, the group encountered small groups of what could only be called patrols of orcs and goblins as they made their way off the mountain and into the heavy forest, continuing to travel along the road that would lead them to the elven kingdom that lay at that the eastern side of the Pilo'ach Mountain range.

By the end of the day, the group was exhausted from the quick attacks from the orcs. Chansor and Kikor went off in advance of the group and found a small grove that would give them an area to rest and hopefully gather themselves. As the group entered the grove, they sat and listened for a while for those that might be searching for them. No sound could be heard outside the grove, so they quickly fell asleep — all but Chansor, that is. He sat watching the others, thinking of the creature that had found him after they had left the tower and what she had said to him. He looked over at the group until his eyes fell on Whelor. He wondered why Methnorick wanted him dead.

Chapter Four

Kaligor sat at the top of what used to be the tower of counselors for Bru Edin, looking over what used to be the city that he had recently conquered. He had lost almost half of his troops in taking this city. A lingropand that had come out of the ground as his orcs were bursting through the final outer defenses of the city was helpful in breaking down the main gate that once had been boasted as being indestructible by the inhabitants of this city.

Even though they had made it through the outer walls with the help of the lingropand, his troops had had to fight even harder to get through the streets to make it up to farthest reaches of this city, where so far only light resistance — specifically, some caverns that were light in population — was being encountered.

He calmed his mount, which almost purred, when some type of explosion erupted in a building halfway into the city. He patted its neck a few times, letting it know he had seen the explosion and that it was fine.

A Blingo'oblin walked up and stood not far away, waiting so as not to disturb Kaligor's thoughts. Once he received a nod, the Blingo'oblin stated, "Methnorick, I'm told, has decided to leave his isle and join us!" Kaligor's eye winked at the creature upon hearing this.

"Where is Methnorick now?" Kaligor asked, trying to speak as an echo of orcish screams made it hard for them to hear each other for a moment.

Kaligor looked over to where the screams came from and saw that his orcs had been able to break down a barrier of final resistance that some humans had put up, which made him smile slightly.

"North of Blath 'Na City, I'm told … and I've received orders to join Methnorick as he marches south. As you are aware, his plan is to surround the elves."

Kaligor breathed in a huge amount of air, as he couldn't believe that Methnorick was coming now. *Hopefully he is here to join in for the fun and not something else*! he thought. *What has changed, I wonder?*

"Light this city ... I want the main battalions of warriors on the field within the hour to join those that already marched ahead to scout the area to the east. Then you can leave to join Methnorick," he calmly ordered the Blingo'oblin, who just nodded and bowed deeply before quickly leaving to carry out the orders. Kaligor could hear orders being yelled out within a few moments, and he watched orcs drop what they were doing and quickly make their ways down the streets and out of the city.

"On to victory!" Kaligor whispered to himself as he pulled the reins of his mount and made his way off the rubble and down the road to join his army, which was quickly forming below.

***

Kalion reached out to touch Shermee's face slowly. His hand passed right through her, but Shermee smiled back at him as he sucked in air, wondering what had just happened.

"My Kalion ..." Her voice seemed like a dream, like it was coming from inside a cave. "Kalion ... why do you not search for me?" Shermee's face turned to concern as she asked the question again.

Kalion stepped back for a moment and quickly thought of an answer but then threw it away as something else came into his mind.

"My love ... I ..." he whispered to the princess. "I am trying to find you, my love, but the quest is beginning to fall apart ..." He moved forward a few steps to get closer to the princess. "The orcs are ...!"

Shermee smiled again at the man in front of her. "I know you will find the way, my love. Please ... you need to get to me ... I am not sure I will live ..." Shermee seemed to float for a moment as she whispered to him. Kalion watched her move like she was on a cloud, and he moved quickly to get in front of her. He jumped in front of the princess, raising a hand to make her stop for a moment.

"Shermee ... Where are you, my love? I can't find you unless you can tell me more. Please ..." Kalion begged. He hoped she might be able to tell him something. "Not even the mages here know where you truly are!"

The princess lifted a hand and touched Kalion's face for a moment. He was sure he could see a tear forming on her face. He knew he was crying a little, as he was worried that she was being tortured, or worse.

"I am where you believe I would be, my love ... in the land where the morning sunrise begins." The princess got choked up as she spoke, and her image shifted for a moment, making Kalion jump closer, thinking he might be able to get to her.

"Find me, my love ... Find me soon ..." And as quickly as she had appeared, the princess and her image blinked and shifted as she disappeared from Kalion's sight.

"Noooo ... nooo ... noooo ..." Kalion called out, reaching out to grab the now-empty space where moments before the princess had stood, looking back at him. The tears that were on his face got heavier, so he wiped them off as he realized that she was gone.

"Noooooo!" He was shaken awake by Kikor, who had been near him, keeping an eye out for orcs, when the ranger began to moan and talk in his sleep. His voice carried, so she woke him.

"Kalion ... Kalion ... Wake up ... You're having a dream!" she whispered as she held his shoulders until his blinking stopped and he was staring up at her.

"What ... what happened?" he whispered.

Kikor smiled down at him as she leaned back, looking around at the others, who had been woken up by Kalion.

"You were having some dream ... something that made you scream out, my friend," she whispered loud enough for the group to hear.

"You probably brought the orcs down on us!" Jebba rasped

through his teeth as he lay on the ground not far away, holding his sword out and looking up over the edge of the hole they were using to rest in over the night.

"Jebba!" Kikor turned a hard look at the man, who just nodded and returned to looking over the edge, keeping an eye out.

"How long was I out?" Kalion whispered, grabbing his sword that lay near him and shaking his head to get the mist out of his eyes.

"Not long!" Whelor whispered. The big man knelt a few feet away from the ranger. Kalion nodded to the answer as he looked at Kikor.

The elf warrior leaned in as Kalion motioned to her that he wanted to talk just to her. "I was dreaming of the princess … She said something that I think might help!" He pulled back from her ear to look at her face for an answer.

Kikor's eyebrows rose up when she heard that he had been having a dream about the girl they were trying to find … and that she was speaking to him as well.

"What did she say?" she whispered back, indulging him because she was curious about this dream and why he was telling her and not one of the others about it.

"Something about how she was in an area where the sunrise begins," Kalion said quietly, realizing that her answer could mean almost anywhere in the east. He saw the same thought cross the elf's face as well.

"That could be anywhere, Kalion. Besides, that was just a dream, right? Why would you think it was anything else?"

"It was the way she spoke and how she said it. It reminded me of days gone by."

"We are already headed to Blath 'Na. We will get some answers there," Kikor whispered back, a bit annoyed.

"Nicolorr said that Methnorick held himself up on some island to the east and north … about a day's travel from the mainland … Maybe that is what she meant." Kalion was trying to understand many things that the mage master had told them while they had been in that tower earlier, but his description of where the Dark One was might be true.

Kikor just gave Kalion a look. "Kalion, a dream is not sufficient to change our plans. We will know more when we get to Blath 'Na. Now drop it!"

* * *

Far to the south, Kaligor's army marched away from the smoking and burning city that once had been called the "Shield of the North." Now it was just a shadow of its former self. He had clear orders to leave a message for those that might want to challenge him, even those that marched with the cyclops.

Along the edges of the now-destroyed and collapsed walls that had once proudly lined Bru Edin, his orcs had left men and women who had tried to fight, along with their children, hanging from poles, many still alive and screaming for mercy.

Kaligor ordered the heads of the generals and army leaders to be stuck on the tops of spears and placed at the top of the mountain. Their bodies were to be hacked into pieces and strung along the sides of the castle that had once stood at the top of the mighty city but was now a smoldering and smashed building with bodies lying everywhere, being fed upon by crows and other birds.

A few orcs stayed to drag bodies where Kaligor wanted them, piling them on pyres to be burned, leaving no trace of man within the conquered city. Soon huge fires ignited, and the skies above were filled with black smoke as those few orcs cheered in victory.

Kaligor had pulled himself to the side to watch his army march past. He was proud of these orcs and other creatures that had marched within it. Those men from the southern hills that had joined them all cheered him as they marched by. Not many of them were left, but enough to annoy him.

He looked back to see the skies black with smoke. He could just make out the city along the side of the once-powerful volcano.

Though his army had been cut in half by the men defending Bru Edin, he was confident that he could continue making war on the lands before him. Only a few of the war machines survived, he noticed, but why would he need them now? No castle that would have to be knocked down was ahead of this army, so as their engineers and giants were pulling them past him, he ordered them to be left behind. He wanted this army to move quickly.

The scouts had informed him that, so far, the roads ahead were clear. Patrols were finding survivors of the city within the forest, but none had survived the nights. However, he knew the farther they marched on this road east, the closer they would get to the elven homeland.

Would the elves march out and meet him? A few of the elves' patrols had been seen. Three had challenged his orcs, and though none of his warriors had survived, their bodies told him that the elves were ready for him.

Kaligor knew from legend that no man, orc or goblin had ever been within the borders of the elven homeland. It was so protected that not even Methnorick could see inside those lands. Kaligor remembered his dark lord speaking about it once before Kaligor had left the Black Isle, which seemed like cycles ago now.

Seeing the goblins march by in between his orcs, he shook his head. They had proven their worth, he thought. Small but strong, they had shown themselves to be worth having. They had been able to cut through the defenses a bit more easily than the larger orcs had.

As he waited for the army to pass, a scout runner rode up on a panting horse and handed him a rolled parchment. The scout only bowed quickly and then, pulling the reins back, rode off before Kaligor could say a word.

Seeing the mark of Methnorick on it, he shook his head slightly. *New orders*, he read, raising his eye slightly to see the rear detachment of his army slowly marching by. The dark elves smiled slightly as they nodded to their leader, soon leaving the cyclops alone on the road as he read the parchment just given to him.

Fuunidor! he thought, shaking his head again. *Methnorick ... No ... I'd best not counter what the Dark One has ordered. The last general that did now decorates the dark lord's ship that he used to conquer the Black Isle cycles ago.*

"Fuunidor it is ... Good ... Elves are too pompous to live in these lands anyway!" Kaligor whispered as he pulled his mount's reins to the right and kicked it, sending it running to catch up with his army, which was now marching down through a small gully.

As he approached the forefront of his army, he raised his armored hand and screamed out so all could hear, "TO FUUNIDOR!"

Instantly, the area erupted in cheers and screams, and songs began to echo behind Kaligor as he smiled, looking forward.

***

After leaving their hidden rest spot, the group cautiously ran through the rest of the forested area, hiding when they saw patrols or groups of orcs. Kikor led the group, signaling to the others, trying to be as quiet as possible. As the group approached the top of a rise, they stopped and looked around for any orcs that might be in the area. When none were seen, they knelt to keep their bodies as close to the ground as possible. Kikor came out of the brush not far away and quietly crept up on the others.

"What do you see?" Holan whispered, watching the elf warrior for a moment.

"No orc patrols around, as far as I can see and hear ... I think we got ahead of them ... That over there is Fuunidor Forest, though." She turned slightly and pointed to an area of large trees pushing high into the sky.

"How far would you say, Kikor?" Amlora piped in quietly as she knelt down. Since she was a bit smaller than the others in the group, she had to stand up a bit to peer out over the rest.

"Not far now!" Kikor said, smiling at her friend.

The mist and part of the mountain range still stood between the group and the forest, but Kikor quietly whispered that if luck was working for them, a day and a bed and they would be at the border of the elven kingdom.

"Any place we can rest for a bit?" Whelor asked, his tall frame still overshadowing the rest, even as he knelt next to Bennak, who was whispering to Jebba. Jebba listened to the elf but was also trying to figure out a plan of his own.

Kikor nodded slightly and pointed again to what looked like a gully not far ahead, whispering that inside that area, she believed, was a waterfall and a place to hide out for a bit.

Kalion nodded. Turning his head, he caught Jebba whispering to the half-orc. Jebba saw the ranger spying over and stopped his conversation with Bennak and nodded back.

"Let's make our way there as quickly as our feet can take us … I have a feeling that the orcs will be covering this area soon." Kalion stood up slowly, and placing his hand on Kikor's shoulder, he whispered to keep an eye on Jebba. She nodded and then turned and raced to get ahead of the group as they descended the hilltop, still not noticing that Chansor was leaving notes not far away.

* * *

The screams had quieted down for a moment, giving the dwarven warriors a moment's rest as they gathered themselves, pulling their wounded away from the front lines. They didn't have time to grab their dead at the moment, though, as doing so would give the dark dwarves a chance to kill more.

King Finfilli stood with two of his generals as they peered over a map that showed where his army was stationed and where the dark dwarves were probably placing themselves.

"You believe that these attacks of theirs might be a diversion of some kind?" Finfilli stood back, crossing his massive arms as he looked at the youngest general in his army, Aarik da'Firespear. Aarik was 65 cycles old, young compared to the king and General Hek Everhand, who at 98 cycles old was only a few cycles younger than the king.

Aarik stood nodding, his long grayish beard now placed in two ponytails being held together by small gold clasps. His armor was covered like General Everhand's in dark dwarven blood, as he had been at the front lines since the beginning of the battles.

"Look here, sir, how the main chamber that we've blocked off has two small entrances on the far right. If we do not block these off, they could somehow find a way to get small groups through them and get behind us here and here." Aarik pointed to where their forces were as the others peered down, seeing what Aarik was speaking about.

"If the dark dwarves do know that these two small tunnels are there … or if King Finfilli was correct in seeing a dark elf … those creatures could possibly be leading the dark dwarves."

"If we block those tunnels, though … how will we push them back, my friend?" Everhand's white and silverish beard almost shined in the torchlight in the room. His armor was dented from a few axe strikes, but luckily, the dwarf was smart enough to use a shield, unlike the younger dwarf.

"We know that they have come from somewhere north within the mountains … through tunnels, I'm sure. They have spent cycles digging to get to us here. My only idea, sir: Collapse the ceiling of the chamber on top of them when they attack next," Aarik said, confident his idea was the best.

Finfilli gasped slightly, surprised at the idea and standing back from the table to think about it. He listened to both generals go back and forth, talking about the pros and cons of destroying an area of his kingdom that had taken his father many cycles to build.

Finally he stepped forward, raising his hand to quiet the others as he decided what needed to be done. "Destroying that chamber is not what I want … I know our army can stop those things from getting into the main kingdom." Aarik's mouth opened. He was about to interrupt his king when Finfilli raised his hand again to stop the general.

"I am positing, my friends, that the Buwan Amnach must be helping our cousins. Otherwise, there is no way those creatures would have the will to do what they have been doing here. So I propose this …"

Leaning forward, he explained to his generals what he wanted to do. When he finished, the generals looked at each other and then back to the king, who nodded at both.

"Questions?" he quietly asked, seeing that both had their mouths open to ask, when they all heard the sound of boots running down the hallway. They turned and saw a warrior burst into the room, breathing hard from the quick run.

"My king … they are coming!" the dwarf declared, gasping slightly.

Finfilli nodded as the dwarf turned to get back to where his battalion had positioned itself. Finfilli leaned forward on the table to look at the generals, who returned his gaze.

"Get those mages here … Inform them of the plan and tell them to get themselves ready … Then tell the captains to get ready to retreat when I give the word."

"Yes, my king!" both generals said, turning and quickly walking out to return to the front. Everhand placed his hand on top of his friend's shoulder as they entered the main hallway that led to the chambers below.

"Your idea will work, but … you think our king's will?" he whispered, not wanting his voice to echo in the hallway.

Aarik pulled in a deep breath as he thought about their king's plan. He moved out of the way to let a few warriors run past.

"It will work … It has to work!"

***

Kalion sat on the trunk of a tree that had fallen as he watched Chansor stand up and casually walk over to chat with Kikor, which, of course, drove the elf to finally yell at the thief to leave her alone. He turned and watched as Meradoth quickly snapped his fingers to begin a fire while the others slowly sat down after getting their packs off to rest from the hard travel.

Meradoth leaned back against a tree as he watched the others quietly smile and talk about whatever they could to cheer themselves up. The mage drifted off with the thought that the world they knew might be burning, but his friends still wanted to smile at least. As he continued to drift off, he began dreaming about what his father had told him within the tower about his mother in Blath 'Na and about the images of the city.

The rest talked to each other quietly as Kalion stood up and looked back up the mountains to where the snow was lying on the peaks. He thought of their quest and what was becoming of it and the friends they had lost along the way. He started to think about their journey forward since he could no longer do anything for those they had lost. To get to the coast, they could travel along either the southern or the northern edge of the elven kingdom. Traveling along the southern edge of the elven kingdom meant traveling through the "Endless Bog" — a fitting name, as it seemed to go on forever. He had done it once, but it was a long journey. Most that entered it were never seen again. Traveling along the northern edge of the elven forest would take even longer, so traveling through the elven forest was by far the fastest way.

As Kalion sat thinking, Amlora, not far away, was talking to Harbin about his family when she looked over to the ranger. Seeing him deep in thought, she excused herself to walk over to catch his eye.

Kalion looked at the cleric, smiling. "Hello, Amlora, can I do something for you?" Kalion coughed for a moment as he looked at Amlora's face, knowing she was concerned about him.

"Well, yes, my friend … I was just wondering how you are." She walked up and placed a hand on Kalion's arm to let him know she meant well as she knelt down slowly to look at his face.

Kalion smiled back and scratched his chin for a moment, thinking of what to say to her. Since he had met the cleric, Amlora had become someone he could trust and speak to about certain things, and now he felt he could pour his feelings out to her.

Seeing her smile and give him a look of wonderment, he blew some air and explained his thoughts. "I was thinking of our possible ways to get to Blath 'Na. It seems that we have a few options for how to travel, and I am trying to figure out the quickest route." Kalion looked off in the distance as he talked. Amlora followed his gaze, knowing he was thinking of the princess from the look on his face.

When he finished giving her the options, Amlora squeezed his hand in hers and smiled at Kalion. "Kalion, of all the people on this quest, I believe you are the one man that will get us to the end. So I, for one, trust your judgment, for it sounds like you have already chosen the best route forward for us."

He walked past the cleric over towards the group that was eating some food and drinking a few pouches of wine that some had brought with them. A few giggled at a joke Chansor had just told, but they quickly got silent as the ranger came to sit next to the fire. He looked at the others as they looked at him.

"After some thought, my friends, and speaking with Amlora …" Kalion began, looking at the cleric, who came and sat down across from Kalion and listened to what Kalion was saying. Looking at each face being lit up by the fire, Kalion continued, "The quickest route is straight through Fuunidor Forest. Though we don't know what we will encounter there, we must get to Blath 'Na as fast as possible."

Soon most nodded and smiled at him, making the ranger smile in return. Only Jebba, who sat a bit away with Bennak, didn't say a word or give any indication that he was even listening, but Kalion just didn't care at this moment — they were too close. He stood up and grabbed his pack that lay nearby.

"Fuunidor here we come!"

Chapter Five

Methnorick kicked his horse to get it to move over to where a temporary tent had been placed for him to rest. Getting off it, he walked past the Blingo'oblin guards, who instantly stood stiff as their lord walked past them. Pushing the tent's flaps aside, he walked in and over to a table that had maps. Grabbing a jug filled with water, he took a deep drink and looked over the map that showed the ancient elven homeland's position in relation to his own. While Methnorick read reports, he began feeling like something was watching him. Putting the jug down, in one quick move, he turned and pointed his glowing-red hand at the darkest part of his tent, where he got the feeling from.

"Who is there?" he demanded. As the shadow moved and stepped out, he recognized the figure that was waiting for him.

"Blaaa ... announce yourself next time, mage!" He turned and tossed his blade on the wooden table. It made a loud clatter as it landed.

"My masssssterrrr, you asskkkkked me to come to you." It's voice made Methnorick's neck hairs stand up.

"Yes, yes, I did ask you here ... Where is your master, Sunorak?" he asked, leaning over the table, not looking at the black figure that stood just inside of the torch's light.

"Master, I attend you ... I have no knowledge of Sunorak's position." A thought came to Methnorick's mind as the black figure finished. Then, suddenly, a sickly feeling shot through Methnorick's body as he turned his head to look at another shadow just to his right. He squinted slightly as he looked into the dark and found the mindslayer standing in the other corner, looking back at him with its large, black, watery eyes.

"Where have you been, Sunorak? I requested your attendance

days ago, and you did not appear." Methnorick cocked his head slightly.

The mindslayer took a step forward into the fire light as the many arms that came out of his head moved around slightly. Quickly, he bent down to one knee and explained himself to his lord and master.

"My master, I carried your orders to the Buwan Amnach below ground, as you ordered … They are about to move and overwhelm their dwarven cousins." Sunorak looked at the feet of Methnorick as he waited for him to respond. "It should not be long before the dwarves are no longer a problem."

Methnorick stepped around the table and stood over the mindslayer, crossing his arms and smiling. "I am pleased." He turned around and took a drink, bending over the table and looking at a map of where the dwarven kingdom, Chai'sell, sat.

Standing back up, he crossed his arms and mumbled out loud again. "Now that the Buwan Amnach and Qlorfana will take care of the dwarves, I have my eye on the most ancient of all kingdoms in these lands.

"Have you been able to convince that thief creature to kill my experiment?" Methnorick asked, looking from the table up to the other figure standing in his tent.

"Massterrrr … the thieffff is resisting ourrr orrrderrrsss!" The black figure's voice sounded like razors for a moment, making Methnorick lean over and look directly at the face covered by its hood.

"I need that thing destroyed. Make sure the thief completes his orders, and soon!" Methnorick rose, his voice making the figure step back slightly and quickly bow.

"Yesss, masssssterrr … I am yourrrss to commandddd!" At that, the figure burst into a mist and quickly disappeared from Methnorick's sight, leaving Sunorak to stand up slightly as he crossed his arms and looked at Methnorick.

Methnorick looked at Sunorak, who stood almost like a statue.

"What of the elves?"

"Master … the elven king has somehow put a barrier around that forest that even I cannot break. The only way we will be able to find out what we face is to break through the defenses." Sunorak slowly advanced to stand at the table across from the Dark Lord, who leaned down and looked at the forest he wanted. "But with your forces coming from the north and Kaligor coming from the south, we have a strong chance of destroying them quickly. Once the dwarves are destroyed, my arm will move in from the east and joint you in destroying the elves."

"Hrrrrrrrr," Methnorick mumbled as he looked over at Sunorak and then back at the map. Pulling in a breath, he turned and walked over to a large chair that had been brought for him.

Quickly sitting down on the soft fabric, he looked over at Sunorak, who stood, looking back at him.

"Go back underground, my friend … and finish what I ordered you to do there. I want Chai'sell to be mine!" Methnorick said quietly as his head started to show signs of fatigue. Sunorak bowed deeply and left as quickly as he had appeared, leaving Methnorick to sit in his chair, looking at the map lying upon his table and wondering about his plans.

***

"You know that Kalion might track us down, my little friend," Bennak quietly said, looking over at Jebba, who was sitting in front of the fire he had just started. Jebba didn't show any sign that he heard Bennak's comment. He seemed to be in his own world, so Bennak shook his head and rubbed his hands together to keep them warm as he waited for his friend to speak.

Bennak had only known the small warrior since the beginning of the games, but in the time that they had been together, Jebba had become the best of friends to him. Bennak didn't speak or show anger as much as Jebba did. He really didn't have to, as Bennak's huge size was enough to make most quiet themselves before he even spoke a word.

Since they had left the tower and decided to make their own way, Bennak's thoughts of the others had kept him quiet most of the time, wondering if he had made the best of choices in leaving the others that had continued on the quest to find the princess.

Now that they knew King Dia was alive, Jebba's plan to return to that now-destroyed city seemed like a game being played by a helpless child. However, Jebba was determined, for his family was there. Bennak wasn't the smartest of humans, but he knew that Jebba and Kalion had never liked each other, and since Meradoth had mentioned to Bennak and others in passing that the two would fight it out someday, Bennak believed that leaving was the best option.

He watched the warrior for a while as the man pushed a stick in the fire, moving some of the coals around as he did so. Bennak squeezed his lips together tightly and wondered what the man was thinking. Then he looked up to the sky, watching the sun as it disappeared over the mountains that lay around them.

Jebba had told Bennak the basic route that they would be traveling a while earlier. If the reports that orcs were near the southern borders of the mountains and that the Hathorwic Forest and Levenori elves were around, then their travels might be easy, but if not ... things might become dangerous indeed.

By traveling along the tops of the mountains, they would only have to fight the cold, hopefully getting around any ice giants in case they met a tribe of the large monsters that didn't like men. Jebba had mentioned to him a while back that some ice giants just didn't like others at all and killed them without a thought. However, these thoughts didn't worry Bennak too much. He had fought against ice giants before, and though they were larger, even Bennak was smarter than they were. He was feeling proud of this as he pulled out some dried meat, took a bite of it and drank some mulled wine. As he did, he looked over to watch the others, who, like him and Jebba, had been told that they could rest for an hour before they had to move on.

A bit later, as the two continued on the trail, Jebba and Bennak hid behind a large snow bank as a small group of ice giants made their way past them on the trail, just below where the two sat, watching them. Jebba had seen the movement from the mountainside, so he and Bennak quickly tried to cover themselves with snow so they could blend in, making it harder for the giants to see them.

As the giants made their way past, Bennak whispered in Jebba's ear that he thought these giants were their friends and they should inform Kalion that they were near. Jebba raised a hand slowly as he saw one of the creatures look their way. He hoped the giant hadn't heard either one of them.

As they both stiffened up and watched, the giant turned and looked their way, but then turned to follow its companions. As it walked over the rise not far away, Jebba blew out some air, looking over to Bennak and giving the half-orc a look of relief, but also a warning not to speak so loudly. Bennak looked back and nodded, knowing it could have caused the giants to come their way.

The trail they took was going in the direction of Brigin'i, though neither really knew where it went, except that it was heading towards where the sun was moving, meaning west. Earlier they had caught and killed a mountain goat, getting some food into their bellies. Bennak had made a heavy cloak for Jebba from the fur since the man was more defenseless against the cold than Bennak.

Slowly, they made their way down the trail, leaving behind everything they had worked for and everyone they had been with for what seemed like cycles of time. Over the next few days, they saw ice giants, a few orcs and even some elven warriors, which must have been the winter elves Jebba had heard lived deep within these mountains. They even killed a group of orcs that had crossed the trail as the two made their way around a corner.

Quickly covering the bodies with brush and snow, they ran to get away from the area in case another patrol, or something worse, heard the sounds. As they worked their way through some small passes a few hours later, they had to stop and hide, as they observed a large group of elves and ice giants in a grove fight it out with a large group of orcs. Though the orcs had superior numbers, the ice giants had the greatest strength in size and weapons, and the elves had the greatest skills. Before either Jebba or Bennak had a chance to be entertained by jumping in, it quickly ended with only a few orcs scrabbling their way back into the mountains, leaving the elves victorious.

While the battle had been in full swing, Bennak had knelt behind a large boulder and watched. He thought back to the group he had in reality grown to like and even missed deeply now, but his friendship with Jebba, who knelt on the other side of the boulder, was more important now. He thought back to the only being in his life who had any meaning for him and who was the reason he was on this adventure: the girl that he had found while he was fishing in Brigin'i Lake a few cycles earlier.

She was the only being in the lands that understood the pain that the half-orc felt. She had been hurt cycles earlier by an orc attack on her village that once lay just on the northern edge of the massive lake. Her face had been cut, so she covered it with a hood most of the time. Bennak's face was also damaged, not by war but by heritage. However, this had brought the two closer. His orcish features made him shy, but Jebba, since joining the games and this adventure, hadn't been bothered by them. However, though it might not have been true, sometimes Bennak felt he saw looks from Kikor and a few others in the group.

It was Kalion that made him feel secure and even part of something, so leaving the ranger was hard for the large warrior. However, he had to get back to her, and with what they had found out about Brigin'i at the tower, he was even more sure of this.

Bennak's thoughts drifted from his love to the moment they left the group …

"Time to leave them, my friend!" Jebba's face showed both anger and something else that Bennak didn't understand.

"Now? … Here? … But they could die." Bennak looked over and

saw Amlora and Chansor, who had jumped on the back of an orc, fighting hard not far away.

"We can't just leave them, Jebba … not like this!" Bennak pleaded with the warrior as a burst of something erupted south of where they hid. Both knew that either Harbin or Meradoth had released something just then.

"I'm leaving them, my friend. They will be fine. But either stay with them or come with me. It is your choice!" Jebba's voice made it clear that he was serious about leaving. Bennak looked back and forth until, finally, his concern for the group was overruled by Jebba's words over the past few weeks.

"You're my friend, Jebba … Of course I will go with you … but I must tell Kalion!" Jebba shook his head at Bennak's answer when a scream made both turn. Quickly, Jebba blocked the descending blade of a giant orc that tried to kill the both of them as they hid behind the tree.

As Jebba's sword stopped the orc, Bennak, his anger rising suddenly, took the chance to quickly stab forward with his sword, almost cutting the orc's chest in half. As both watched the creature fall to the ground in a deathly surprise, Jebba turned and, ducking down slightly, ran to the north, leaving Bennak for a moment to look back at where Kalion was fighting off three orcs at once. Kikor herself was cutting through the defenses of two as she jumped over one and cut its head cleanly off.

Breathing hard, the half-orc turned and followed his friend to the north, staying as low as his big frame could go, hoping some orcs don't see them moving off. If Bennak had stayed watching for a moment longer, he would have seen Holan, who was the closest, observe them both run off into the darkness of the forest.

Before the dwarf could alert the others, though, he was body slammed hard against a tree by two orcs trying to cut through the dwarf's shield, hoping they had taken the dwarf by surprise. They had surprised him, but Holan recovered quickly and dispatched the two orcs instantly with some quick axe work.

Leaving the grove with its sounds of battle and screams of the dying behind them, they made their way onto a deer trail that wound itself up alongside a tall hill. From there they quietly made their way down the mountainside into a valley beyond that opened up onto a plain filled with swamps and empty of orcs and all sounds. As the two moved away, only Jebba was smiling, as Bennak kept himself quiet, thinking of his friends and what might lie ahead for them if they were ever caught by Kalion or Kikor.

Chapter Six

Methnorick closed his eyes and imagined how his army would march into the forest. He even envisioned the human, elven and dwarven armies standing up against him but then quickly falling back to finally be crushed under the weight of the numbers Methnorick brought forth onto these lands.

As he sat in his chair, lost in his dream, he didn't notice the glow coming from the wooden chest that sat on the floor to his right. He opened his eyes slowly in response to a feeling. Wondering what caused the feeling, he looked down and noticed the light peeking out from the cracks in the lid of the chest.

Standing up quickly, he walked over and opened the lid in one quick move. The light coming from box instantly blinded him, making him cover his face and curse for a moment.

Reaching with one hand, he pulled out two objects and walked over to the table, placing them on top. He turned around, taking his cloak off and placing it on his chair, and then turned back, as the glow from the light had gone down to the point where he could look at the objects.

"Why are you glowing, my friends?" Methnorick whispered out loud, staring at the metal objects lying before him. Suddenly he heard a loud voice erupt in his mind, making him yelp quietly and drop down to one knee in pain … Again he heard the voice come out of nowhere, making him look around quickly.

"Methnorickkkkk … the plannsssss?" The voice sounded like someone speaking through a long tunnel. It made Methnorick shake in his clothing as his nerves began to go crazy.

"My master …" he replied, slowly considering how he was going to answer. "The plan is working, master. The armies are marching south as we speak … Bru Edin is destroyed … Brigin'i is gone."

His nerves were causing him to shake so badly that his limbs were hurting. He felt as if his body was going to implode or shake apart as he gritted his teeth against the pain forming everywhere in his body.

"Gooooodddd ... Prepare yourself ... We will be joining you soon, Methnorick ... very SOON!" The voice boomed the last word, and suddenly the voice and pain began to subside along with the glow from the object. Methnorick pushed himself up off his knee, groaning from the pain that now shot through his body.

Walking over to his chair, he groaned again from the pain in his muscles and sat down. He screamed for water, wine or something, quickly. Instantly, the tent flap opened up, and a weak and nervous-looking orc ran in carrying a jug of wine, knowing his lord preferred wine to water. Running over, he knelt down and quickly poured the wine in a cup and gave it to Methnorick, looking at the ground the whole time until Methnorick took the cup.

"LEAVE ME!" Methnorick yelled out as the orcs whimpered and quickly left the tent while Methnorick thought about the words that still echoed deep in his mind.

"We are going to be joining you soon, Methnorick." Joining me ... all of the gods ... Whatever those objects are on the table, my masters wanted them badly ... so badly that they almost killed me! he thought, slamming his fist on the chair's arm, almost breaking it.

"I must break the elves before they approach these lands ... They will kill me if I don't complete this mission!" Methnorick screamed out. He sat, thinking of the creature he also wanted and needed dead. Somewhere the creature walked with a group trying to find the princess that he had thought would be with him now ... But somehow she had slipped away from his grasp. The thought of her escape made him slam his fist down again.

The princess had disappeared. Her father, that damned King Dia, had also disappeared. And that creature ... fighting now against him ... Methnorick's fortunes never worked out the way he wanted, but he would change that.

***

After the battle with those few orcs had ended, the group began gathering themselves when Amlora suddenly stopped and looked around. "Uhhh, Kalion, where are Jebba and Bennak?"

"I have not seen them since the battle started. Harbin, Meradoth, Kikor … have you seen them?" Kalion looked at each member of the group in turn, each shaking their head no in return.

Kalion turned to look at Harbin and Meradoth. "Can either of you locate them with your … mmm … skills?"

Harbin and Meradoth looked at each other. "Yes, but it might take some time," Meradoth responded. The two then stepped off to the side together and closed their eyes as the others all continued to look around the area for any sign of their two missing comrades.

After a few more minutes, they both opened their eyes and looked over at Kalion and then to the others in the group. Then Harbin said, "It seems they are high up in the mountains, heading west." He looked at Meradoth and fell silent.

Kalion looked back at the two of them and then turned away for a moment while the others looked at each other, wondering what would happen now. Suddenly Kalion turned around and looked at each member of the team. "Well, I guess they finally decided they could not continue on our path. I know that Jebba and I did not get on well, but I thought that Bennak was on the same page as the rest of us."

"Actually," Niallee spoke up, "Bennak mentioned his family back in the forest near Brigin'i a number of times. He had, over the last few days, been expressing concern about them after what we heard about the city, but I didn't think much of it because he was still with us."

"I guess you don't know people," Whelor piped in.

"I had the feeling that Bennak was enjoying our company, really … but who knows what the big man was thinking, yea!" Holan piped in quietly as he cleaned off his axe. The rest of the group quietly began to do the same while also trying to put things that had been scattered back into their packs. Slowly, the group got itself moving again.

＊＊

Jebba and Bennak watched the goblins as they sat around their small fire, laughing and eating cooked meat. They could see the group drink and eat themselves almost into a slumber, leaving their weapons on the ground next to them. The group would be easy prey for their swords … and that was what they wanted, or at least Bennak did, for he had been on the wrong side of many goblin attacks over the cycles. It took some arguing from the big man, but he finally convinced Jebba that they needed to kill them and get their food. He was getting hungry after having left their packs back with the group.

Hiding behind a rock, they watched the goblins laugh, eat and drink themselves slowly into such a drunken slumber that it wasn't going to be much of a fight. Nodding to each other as the last goblin literally fell over asleep, they broke off in different directions, coming down on different sides in case the goblins saw them and woke up to fight.

As he made his way into the camp, Bennak pulled out his smaller sword as quietly as he could. Even though the goblins were drunk and sleeping, one could try to raise the alarm if it saw or heard him and might even get away before he could kill it.

Standing over two drunk bodies, Bennak stabbed down hard into the chest of one of the goblins, killing him instantly. Using his foot for leverage, he pulled it out slowly and made his way to another group sleeping together and quietly did the same. Looking up, he saw that Jebba was doing likewise, quietly killing another small group of goblins lying either on the ground or against logs. Jebba, though, was getting closer to finishing than Bennak. He was also slicing through the goblins' throats, letting their dark blood spill down on the ground as he grinned up at the half-orc.

It didn't take long for the two to kill the eight goblins. As they finished, both whispered they were surprised that the goblins had been so careless as to not leave a guard. "They must be celebrating something," Bennak whispered. Jebba looked around, making sure they had finished off the goblins, as he searched for anything of value. He knelt to go through the meat lying on skin hides the goblins were using for plates when something on the large goblin that Bennak had dispatched at the beginning caught his eye. Leaning down, he saw it was a large pouch, so he began to rumble through it. Finding nothing but a few scraps of parchment, he opened one and tried to read it, but he couldn't understand it. Tossing the parchments on the ground, he found under some pieces of dried meat a smaller coin pouch, which he instantly stuffed in his jerkin. Dropping the pouch to the ground, he quickly patted their bodies for anything else that he might want to keep.

Bennak, meanwhile, grabbed and ripped through with his mouth the main pieces of deer the goblins were eating. He walked around the dead goblins, worried about why they had been celebrating. He stared at Jebba rummaging through a few goblins' dead bodies.

Suddenly he heard a rustle of movement to his right. Quickly bending down, he picked up his massive sword, which he had laid down to check the bodies. He scanned the area. Seeing that Jebba hadn't heard the sound as he was working himself around each body, Bennak slowly moved to where he thought he had heard it coming from. There he saw two goblins trying to crawl away. As he walked over, they both pleaded for mercy.

"Sorry!" he whispered as he dispatched them quickly, stabbing hard into their chests, ending the lives of the goblins. Bending down, he saw something under a bush not far away. It looked like the goblins had placed something there to hide it. As he pulled the branches up, he finally saw what they had been eating, or at least savoring. Covering his mouth quickly, he turned around and bent over, relieving the sudden pain that in his stomach as he vomited onto the ground before him, not believing what he saw.

Jebba looked over, saw what was happening and walked over, confused by the sight of the big man getting sick. He had never seen the big man act this way before. He watched the half-orc throwing up his innards. He walked over where Bennak had been a moment earlier and saw what had made the man so sick to his stomach: the goblins had been feasting not on animals of the wild but on human children.

"Oh, by the gods!" he moaned. Feeling sick himself, he turned and covered his mouth as the pain of sickness came up, but he was able to keep it down … just barely.

Hearing Bennak groaning again, he looked to the sky for a moment to center himself as he quietly spoke to his friend. "Bennak …" He waited for the man to look over at him. "Bennak, let us go … before more of these … more of these things come." Jebba felt the sickness again as he kicked the dead body of a goblin he had killed moments earlier.

Bennak nodded as he wiped his face clean and walked over to where Jebba waited for him. Neither said a word, but without speaking, Jebba pulled out the meat he had just gathered from beside the fire, dropping it on the ground as he motioned for them to leave.

Making their way up the trail, the two wiped their bloody swords on a dead goblin's cloak they found along the way and quickly left the area, both sick at what they had found and both being quiet about it as they wondered to themselves where the goblins had found those children … and what they might find farther down the trail.

Chapter Seven

Kalion, Meradoth and Kikor lay at the edge of the cliff, looking down, as the large group of orcs ran north underneath them. All three had seen them come out of the last mountain pass as they had finally gotten a look at the trees of the ancient elven homeland. Kikor whispered that the orcs were running below because her people were chasing them away from their forest, she was sure of it. She looked at Kalion and nodded towards two of the orcs, who were showing signs of being hurt. She could see arrows sticking out of their backs. Kalion nodded as he eyed them closely as well. The orcs numbered fifteen, so the elves must have killed a few as well.

Meradoth, who knelt next to the ranger, listened to Kikor whisper as his thoughts drifted back to what his father had told him in the tower's gardens just before they left. His father had told him that the gods were not gods and that more of the objects were in Fuunidor.

"Fuunidor," he whispered.

Kalion turned to crack a half-smile at his friend. "Are you well, my friend? Of course that's Fuunidor ... Have you not been listening?"

"Remember, there is an object that Methnorick searches for in Fuunidor," Meradoth told the others.

Kalion looked to Meradoth. "What do you suggest? We still have to get into the forest, right?" Kalion shook his head as he looked over to the elf on his left. "Do you believe your people have cut off all contact with the outside world?" He looked back to Kikor again as the orcs finally left their line of sight. They looked over to the trees before them and the road that wound along the edge of the tree line, which traveled from the south to the north.

"You think we should send in Chansor?" Kalion asked as he looked at the southern end of the forest, where the mountain pass would be. "He's good at being sneaky." Thinking of Chansor being sneaky made them all smile.

Kikor shook her head slowly, whispering that it was a place of sanctuary where they could get information, so being sneaky might not be the best way to approach. "Besides, a thief wouldn't last a moment in there!" she whispered.

This part of the land was under the protection of elven eyes, and since coming onto the plains, they had seen at least five groups of orcs and goblins, so the ranger wondered what might have happened within the forest. But Kikor was right. Sending in Chansor might not be the best way.

Kikor got up suddenly and moved back to where the rest of the group was waiting behind the stones of a once-large watchtower that had stood, watching over the fields and plains below, many cycles earlier. Grabbing her pack, she saw Kalion and Meradoth walking up, giving her looks of confusion.

"Kikor, what are you doing?" Kalion asked.

"I'm going down to speak to my people, Kalion!" She looked over at Niallee, who, seeing Kikor's nod, bent over and quickly gathered her pack as well while Kalion watched. The other elf walked up to join Kikor, pulling her pack onto her shoulder.

Meradoth placed his hand on Kalion's shoulder to stop him from speaking as the group watched the two elven warriors run off. "It is best that they both go … It is their people, after all." Meradoth watched the elves disappear into the woods. Kalion looked at the mage and smiled. He knew that it was best, but he had hoped that Kikor would have at least talked with him privately first. Two elves entering the forest might not raise alarm inside the forest, for they were kindred, unlike the rest of the group. However, he didn't like the idea of more of the group splitting off.

"I know … Thank you, my friend." Turning around, he walked back to the edge of the cliff to watch. He looked at the rest of the group, who looked back at him. "Let us wait for their return. We can all use a rest anyway. It has been a long few days." The rest nodded, knowing that Kikor and Niallee would do their best.

Kalion nodded to the group to keep an eye out, but to also rest. Whelor, who had been standing just north of their position, watched the elves enter the elven forest just beyond, wondering to himself if whatever was bothering him would put the group in danger when they entered that forest. He'd just have to chance it, he thought, as he looked over at the group kneeling and resting against a few trees as they waited … and waited.

* * *

The three attempts by the dwarven mages to collapse the ceiling of the chamber had failed. Each time they had tried, the ceiling had refused to crack and fall. Seeing the dark dwarves try to make their way through some smaller hallways, King Finfilli ordered that the small halls be destroyed in the hope that doing so would make it easier for his warriors to stop the assault by their dark cousins. If they only had one hall to deal with, then their forces would not be so spread out.

Quickly, the five halls were collapsed, cutting off the dark dwarves' attempt to destroy Chai'sell.

Many dark dwarves were killed as tons of rock fell onto them, giving Finfilli a moment's rest as he and his generals pulled their warriors back to the one tunnel left open: the main gate that led to the chamber the dark ones were moving into for a final assault.

Knowing that their cousin dwarves were being led by dark elves, who hid in the far rear of any assault the dark dwarves tried, Finfilli decided that, as soon as his warriors retreated and cleared the chamber, he would destroy the hallway that led down to this chamber. He and his general believed that doing so would give them a while to rest. The dark dwarves had brought engineers to work the rock, but it would be a long time before they got through, and that would give the Chai'sell dwarves time to get a better defense set up.

As soon as his warriors' shield wall had repelled the last charge of dark dwarves, they began to quickly retreat out of the chamber, seeing that the smoke the mages were throwing would give them cover and confuse the dark dwarves.

Finfilli stood on the side of the hallway his warriors were using to retreat out of the chamber. He nodded to those warriors that looked up at him, and they nodded back to their king. He patted many warriors on the shoulder as they passed him, giving them assurance that he was with them to the end.

Only the mages were left in the chamber, throwing out smoke to cover their escape, so when the last dwarf got out, he called loudly for them to move out. Slowly, the last three dwarves turned and stepped towards their king when a barrage of arrows flew out of the smoke and hit the stone floor and wall where Finfilli stood. He quickly ducked back into the hallway, calling out for the mages to move faster.

"Move your sorry bodies!" he screamed as the black arrowheads almost exploded around him. He saw one dwarf scream out and fall forward with two shafts sticking out of his back, making Finfilli shake his head and clench his teeth tightly as the other two quickly ran past him and down the hallway to safety. The king looked back and watched the dark dwarves. As the smoke began to clear up, he could just make out their helmets and blades moving towards him.

"Bastards!" he screamed out, angry that his generals' attempts to stop the assault had failed and he had to give the dark ones yet another section of his beloved kingdom. In return he heard screams and cheers and watched axes and spears being lifted as the dark dwarves suddenly realized the Chai'sell dwarves had retreated again. Finfilli shook his head, swearing to his gods that they would pay for what they had done.

As he turned to move down the hallway, his eye caught a flash of something appearing through the smoke, making him turn back around and squint to make out what it could be.

Seeing that the dark dwarves were marching slowly, not taking a chance that their cousins had pulled the wool over their eyes and were just waiting for them, Finfilli had a moment to look at the figure now standing at the rear of the armored dwarves moving towards him.

"In all the lands … gods, what have you brought to my kingdom?" he whispered as his eyes finally registered what he was looking at. Just then, another barrage of arrows began to fly through the smoke, making him turn quickly and run away.

As Finfilli ran down the hall, seeing that his warriors had put up a quick shield wall at other end, he thought quickly of what he had seen.

"So that's what is commanding their warriors … But it just can't be … Those things exist only in legends. Here … in my kingdom … a mindslayer?" Finfilli pushed himself past the wall as he turned back to look down the hall.

* * *

Niallee walked just behind Kikor as they made their way down the road and towards the ancient forest that held their people's most beloved, most honored and most ancient homeland. Kikor and Niallee continued to walk ahead slowly and in the open to show that they were not there to harm anyone, for the elves would be ready to attack anything, even one of their own, if they thought it was a threat.

Kikor made sure her hood was pulled back, as did Niallee, showing off their long, flowing hair and long ears. Kikor also made sure her bow was visible. As they approached an opening in the forest, they slowed down. The light from the sun quickly disappeared as they moved into the forest. Here and there the light from the sun sent streams through the branches of the trees around them, giving the place an eerie feel.

The silence was something neither had expected. They moved over fallen trees and branches, trotting up to a small creek that was running across the ground in front of them. Both expected to hear birds and other animals, but ... nothing.

Niallee looked around the trees, wondering why such a beautiful place would be silent now. Elven forests were by nature lively, and this silence bothered her. As a druid, she should have been able to feel the life here, but at the moment ... nothing.

Kikor slowly walked over, bending down and taking a drink of water from the creek, enjoying the freshness that came from it as it flowed past her slowly. She looked up when she heard a tiny crack of a branch not far from her. Reaching for a small knife, she looked and found standing in front of her an elven warrior holding a bow, with an arrow pointed directly at her chest.

Rising slowly, she watched the warrior carefully as he silently looked at her. Replacing her knife in its sheath as she stood up, she was about to whisper to Niallee, but out of the corner of her eye, she saw that the druid also had an arrow pointed at her.

"Why are you here?" the elf in front of Kikor asked her. The warrior's accent was hard for her to understand ... He was one of the "First." Those Doro Amnach that came from this forest were known in the elven lands as the "First Ones."

Holding her hands open to show she meant no harm, she responded quietly, explaining that she and Niallee were both part of a quest group in search of a human princess and that they had come to this place for information and to ask the elven high king for help.

The warrior's eyes squinted slightly. Before Kikor could say another word, she felt a quick pain in the back of her head as her vision darkened and then went completely black. As she fell to the ground, Kikor was just able to make out Niallee lying on the ground with another elven warrior standing over her before her world closed around her and she slept in the dark.

* * *

General Vana rode hard ahead of the warriors that he had

assembled back at the Father Gate to march south to where, according to reports, orcs had somehow gotten over the ravine and were causing havoc in the empire beyond the gate.

As they rode, finding only a few orcs here and there, nothing that would require more than twenty of his men, Vana was wondering if he should send back half of his warriors when a scout reported that movement had been seen about half a league away to the southeast.

The scout reported that the dust cloud he had seen meant a large band was moving in their direction. Working on a plan, Vana split his forces into two sections so they could come at the assaulting band from the sides. When they encountered what was coming at them, two assaulting teams would break them faster, he thought.

They had passed three villages so far that had showed signs of orc attacks. The orcs had left nothing, trying to destroy the lands entirely. Many of the buildings were still burning as his men moved quickly past. Vana tightened his fist on his reins as they rode up a hill where he could stop and look out.

When he got there, he lifted himself off his saddle and scanned the area quickly, trying to find out where the scout's report had been focused on. Quickly finding the dust cloud in the distance, he sat back down, looking at his men that were finally cresting the hill and seeing that he was lucky their hard march wouldn't cause them to slow down when they encountered the orcs, for none looked winded.

How in all the gods did they get past the gate? he wondered. The ravine ran east to west, with no point where it was narrow enough for man or beast to jump over, and it was at its widest near the Father Gate. The only place he could think of was near the coastline, but there was a tower there keeping an eye on things … unless?

"Scout … make your way to the coast tower … I need to know if it is still ours!" The scout nodded as he pulled his reins to the left and kicked his horse's hind. The man rushed past the general and headed north through the forest. The general knew the man would take at least a day to get there and back, but he had to know if these orcs they were tracking had come that way. His horse jumped at the sudden appearance of not a few orcs but what looked like hundreds, all charging out of the forest at his own men, who stopped in their boots.

Even without his orders, the men quickly moved out of the marching lines and rushed to make a heavy shield wall. If the orcs' numbers were what he could see at the moment, it should hold the creatures back.

Kicking his horse, Vana made his way to stand just behind his men, who, as one, lowered their spears at the charging orcs, which were now making their way up the slope of the hill. Vana shook his head slowly. *Charging up a hill. Never the best way to attack in battle*, he thought.

Seeing one of his cavalry men not far away ordering others to tighten up, Vana ordered the man to make his way up the hill and keep an eye out for movement from behind.

The man nodded, pulling his horse around and quickly riding back up the hill to stand just on the far side of the crest as he heard Vana scream words of encouragement to the men at the shield wall.

"MAKE READY!" Vana screamed out, lifting his sword out of it sheath as he saw that the orcs were going to hit the shield wall within moments. He could see they outnumbered his 800 men greatly, making the general again wonder where they had crossed without being seen.

"ARROWS!" he again screamed as loud as he could. Those archers standing behind the shield wall released what they could, causing the charge to collapse for a moment as orc after orc fell forward, each with a shaft sticking out of its chest or face. However, those behind quickly stepped onto the backs of the fallen, squashing them. The forward movement of the orcs couldn't be stopped. The orcs screamed the last few feet as they fell hard onto the spears. The orcs would use their massive numbers to break the spears and, in doing so, would cause the shield wall to collapse from the sheer weight of their bodies.

Luckily for the men behind the shield wall, the spearheads pierced the chest armor of the orcs and quickly broke their momentum, causing those orcs to fall onto the shields. Vana quickly ordered all spears to be weakened about halfway up with small cuts to the wood, allowing them to break with the heavy weight on them. He had been told that the elves had tried this once a cycle or two earlier and it had worked, stopping the assault of a group of orcs that had tried to enter one of their forest homes.

When their spears broke, the men dropped the shafts, pulled out their swords and began to stab through their shield cracks.

As Vana watched his men behind the wall fight back, his lieutenant rode back and forth, screaming out orders. Vana took in a long breath of relief as he saw that the orc numbers had finally stopped coming out of the forest.

One of Vana's men rode up to him. "Sir ... we must move back. The weight of the dead is causing the shield wall to strain, and it's giving those creatures the opportunity to jump over, sir!" Vana lifted himself up to look where the man was pointing.

Indeed, the man was right. The orcs were dying in such numbers from his archers' arrows and his warriors' swords that those orcs in the rear were using the bodies to climb up and over the shield wall.

"Order the movement!" Vana screamed back as the sounds of metal against metal and screams of death echoed loudly everywhere.

Quickly, the orders were passed along. Vana watched each section of warriors duck under their shields, and in one quick push, they lifted the orcs off their feet and quickly stepped back.

The orcs, thinking they were winning of course, charged harder at the wall, as Vana knew they would. His archers, in response, released wave after wave of arrows to keep those orcs back. Within three minutes, the wall had moved back about ten feet in total, giving the wall the relief it needed to hold back the onslaught.

Vana nodded, smiling at seeing his wall do a perfect job of keeping them back, when he heard movement rushing up behind him. As he turned his head, he saw the scout he had sent back to the top of the hill coming towards him. Vana then understood that these orcs were a diversion.

"Sir ... I've seen at least a battalion of orc warriors marching just over there, through those trees, sir." The man breathed hard at the urgency of what was going on.

"I knew it. Get back up there ... Be careful, but give me reports when you can, son!" The man swallowed, knowing he could be killed, but quickly, he turned around and rode back up the hill.

"Bad news always turns!" Vana whispered the ancient saying as he kicked his horse, steering it over to where a lieutenant stood, calling out as he rode up.

"We've got orcs in the forest behind us ... These were just a diversion until they were positioned. Get sections three and five ready to run up the hill and get in position!" Vana stated to his lieutenant as he attempted to hold his horse still.

When Vana finished giving his orders, he too turned and rode hard up the hill to where the scout had pointed. Vana could see that their numbers looked to be about the same as those of the orcs behind him now, and he quickly thought about how to counter their movement.

He didn't have the men to stop both ... and his warriors were now positioned at the top of the crest. They had limited options at this point

"Well then!" He smiled at the scout, who returned a look of confusion, probably wondering why his general was acting so ... calmly.

* * *

Kikor woke up slowly. She tried to open her eyes but then closed them as a light sent pain through her head. Holding her head with a hand, she felt the presence of someone close to her.

"Keep your eyes closed, my child," a soft and gentle voice

whispered. "I am sorry that the pain is hitting you like this. Sometimes, I know, my warriors are a bit … jumpy," the voice calmly said again.

Not recognizing the voice, Kikor moaned as she tried to sit up, stopping suddenly as she felt soft hands touch her arms, helping her get up. As soon as her body was upright, the hands let go. She tried opening her eyes again, letting the soft light in slowly. She felt a wet material touch her face, cooling her down and making her feel better for the moment.

Finally feeling able to speak, Kikor coughed for a moment. "Where am I?" she asked, coughing again as her voice cracked and strained from being dry.

"Here, my child … take this." Kikor's eyes could just make out a glass of water being brought up to her face. Grasping it, she took a long, deep drink of the water. Feeling better by the moment, she closed her eyes as the fresh liquid spread throughout her body.

She opened her eyes again, slowly registering where she was and who had been speaking to her. She coughed again, so she took another drink of water. As her eyes moved around the room, she saw an elf sitting in the chair next to the bed she was lying in.

This elf had long silverish hair and appeared to be of great age and experience from the look of his face. His skin was so cracked and thin she could almost see his bone underneath. He wore robes of highly rich blue material, but what caught her eye the most was what was hanging around his neck. A small chain with a small round shield showing the crest of the elven high king lay on his chest.

She cleared her mouth of water and quickly moved to get up, but the elf raised a hand and motioned for her to stay where she was. "Please sit, my child. All is fine for you. You are in a safe place." The elf's smile made Kikor feel better. He got up and walked over to an open window that looked out into the trees beyond, which Kikor could see standing tall. He slowly turned and looked at Kikor. She looked back at him, making him smile again.

"My child … where do you come from? It is dangerous in these lands now." The elf stood, looking at her as her thoughts raced while she considered how to respond to him. "Why are you here?"

"My … king …" She struggled to get her voice for a moment. "I am Kikor Ru'unn … born of the Eagle people, born into the Bright Spear clan." Seeing the elven king nod recognition of her family house, she continued. "I am part of a quest … a quest of different peoples in search of a princess that was kidnapped by a dark evil, Methnorick. Are you aware of what is going on in the world? Do you know of him?"

When Kikor finished, the door opened, and a few elven clerics walked in to check her forehead and then place another jug of water nearby on a table. Bowing to their king, they left as quietly as they had come in.

"My child … I know of your quest … and I understand that what you need is to continue on quickly." He walked over and sat quietly in front of her, smiling. "I can help your group to get to the east … but you rest for now. No one will or can harm you here." At that, he rose and walked over, bending down to kiss Kikor's forehead lightly. Standing back up, he smiled and looked down at her before turning and walking over to the door that had been closed by the clerics moments earlier.

As he opened the door, Kikor, who had fallen back onto her soft pillow, quickly looked over at the elven king. "My king," she said loudly. "My friend … Niallee … Where is she? And I must get back to the rest of my friends."

The king turned his head to her, smiling. "Kikor Ru'unn … your friend Niallee is recovering well, and as soon as tonight, you can meet with me at dinner if you like and we can speak more about this. But for now … rest!" At that, he walked through the door and closed it in a quiet move.

Kikor leaned back, feeling better at knowing that Niallee was recovering as well as she was. She slowly fell into a deep sleep, knowing things were better for the moment, but wondering why the king's eyes seemed … sad. The last thought that crossed her mind before she fell asleep was of her friends waiting in the forest.

Chapter Eight

Methnorick had been scanning the map of the northern lands. Seeing the banner they had been flying in battle, he realized that these men he was fighting small skirmishes with had come from the small principality of Blath 'Na. They couldn't have received orders from that city-state, though. He smiled when he looked at the mark on the map indicating the city-state, knowing that it had been destroyed. So this meant these were just a few escapees from the city and could be of no real importance.

Moving his eyes to the west of that city, Methnorick saw that the nearest and only threat to his plan for the northern lands was the ancient elven forest of Fuunidor, where, the elves believed, all their gods had once lived. They also believed that their high king was the voice and protector of their gods.

He traced his finger along the map. He knew that the pass that ran along the western and southern edge of Fuunidor Forest and the eastern edge of the Pilo'ach Mountains was watched by the elves. It would be a hard fight, but it was the only way.

Fuunidor and Chai'sell were the only kingdoms that had not been conquered prior to his landing. He leaned closer as he smiled at the mark that indicated Brigin'i. He loved the fact that the city-state was gone, but now he was enacting the most dangerous part of his plans.

He turned and sat down hard on his chair. He closed his eyes and thought of the one that would carry out his special orders. He called for that agent to come to him soon. In the past, the agent had showed up quickly when he called.

"My lord?" The voice made Methnorick smile as his eyes slowly opened up to see the black-robed death knight standing in front of him now. Instantly, the knight dropped to a knee, but stood up as Methnorick got up himself and motioned for him to rise.

"My friend … tell me!" Methnorick said calmly as he got up again to walk over to pour some wine from a jug sitting on top of a small table.

Lord U'Traa, a death knight, watched his lord as he walked to the map table and spoke about what he had found. "Lord Methnorick … we have found and destroyed villages of elves and of men. My servants are still searching for more, as you ordered."

Methnorick took a drink of the wine and then turned to look at the knight standing there, looking back at him. He couldn't tell if the eyes were really looking at him or at something else, but he knew the knight's attention was quick.

"Good … you have done well. But I need you for an important mission … one that is in need of your … skills." He stood over the map table as he spoke. He placed the wine glass on the table as he leaned over and pointed to the problem he was speaking of. The knight looked down at where his lord was pointing and then back at his face.

"I need you here." The knight looked down at where his lord was pointing to: Fuunidor Forest.

"In there, my lord … it will take more than just me," the knight said. Methnorick nodded at the knight and then at the map.

"You do what you do … I am marching towards that area." Methnorick looked at his map and thought of the march south. In just a few days, he would be at its borders. When he looked back to tell Lord U'Traa where to go, he found that the knight had disappeared as quietly as he had appeared.

A half-orc and half-human slave girl, who had been captured from a village in the north, moved over and helped him into his armor and clothing. He stood with his arms up as the slave girl took a damp towel and washed the few days' grime away. As she did so, another servant came in and handed him a few parchments with information on the army's status. He knew that the army that had landed a few days prior had totaled about 25,000. According to the numbers from his captains that he now read, the army now numbered around 23,000, still enough to take anything in these lands.

Reserves of orc bands were living within the Pilo'ach Mountains if he needed them, and there was Kaligor's army as well. Lord U'Traa, by destroying the elven and human resistance that lay within the mountains, seemed to have cleared the opening so that any orc trying to get to him could now.

* * *

"Baron!" On hearing his voice called loudly, the human fell down to the ground quickly and walked into Methnorick's tent. "Baron … you have much to answer for." Methnorick's voice echoed within the tent, making Baron Parnland shake, for the last man who had disappointed Methnorick was now outside in four pieces.

"You promised that if I landed my armies in the northern lands, no human, dwarven or elven army would confront me on the field … and now I have encountered resistance by armies on the field and even by small groups trying to slow me. And of all things … you lost the one man that I wanted to get revenge on. What is next, Baron?" Methnorick had lowered his voice slightly as he watched the baron get fidgety. He smiled as he observed the fat man kneeling in front of him.

He should just kill the fat man now and get rid of him, he thought. But plans were in the works, and he could help … maybe.

"Speak!" Methnorick boomed when the human didn't answer him as quickly as he wanted.

"My … my … my … my … my lord … I had no report of another army in the north. I was informed that all had been brought from the field to defend the fortresses and castles in the south. These men that you confronted, my lord, are just as much of a surprise to me as they were to you."

"To me?!" Methnorick slammed a fist hard on the chair, making Parnland jump. "Do not assume that you know me, Baron. But know this, Baron … if I meet any more on the field … you will feel my wrath!"

"As for King Dia, my lord … I had him in my hands. I was bringing him to you when I was surprised by elves, who attacked my group and killed them all … I was only just able to escape with my life!" Parnland whimpered as he tried to explain more about what had happened in the forest battle to Methnorick, who clenched his teeth as he listened.

The fat man had been found by Methnorick's forces that had been trying to fight off the last of the elves who were doing small attacks on the orcs that had been left in the now-ruined city. They had found him wandering through the forests just east of Brigin'i, almost in a trance, and upon receiving news that they were to send him quickly to their lord, they had tied him on top of a horse, with five dark elven guards.

The loss of Dia was one of the last things Methnorick wanted to be reminded of. However, he did not like to let those that failed him not face his wrath. His thoughts of taking his revenge on Dia for what he had done to him were almost complete when Parnland came in and reminded him that the old king had only been a finger's length away from being in chains.

"You, Baron, are on borrowed time. Leave me … my army marches on the elves as we speak, and I am leaving." Methnorick stood up when the tent flap opened and three orcs walked in to indicate that his mount was ready.

Methnorick walked by the kneeling baron, placing his hand on the man's shoulder and gripping it tightly as he looked at the horse beyond the opening of his tent. When he heard a tiny whimper again from the man below him, he bent down slightly and whispered in the man's ear.

"Fail me again, and this will happen to you!" Methnorick quickly sent an image to Parnland's mind that made the man gasp, as he instantly saw his body burning on top of a pole, screaming for mercy as he slowly slid down the pole.

When the image disappeared, he lay gasping for air as he realized he had been holding his breath while looking at the image.

"Yes ... yes ... yes, my lord ... I will not fail you again!" Parnland whimpered as tears rolled down his face.

Not looking back at the man, Methnorick walked out of his tent and quickly pulled himself up onto his mount as he scanned the field around him.

Orcs, goblins, giantkind and a few others were marching far to the south from where he and his guard now stood. The machines that he wanted to use in the upcoming battle were slowly moving not far away. Their giant engineers were pulling them with heavy ropes to get them across the ground.

"Onward!" Methnorick screamed as he kicked his horse's sides. Those around him returned his scream as, like a creature alive, the field rumbled with movement. Parnland walked out of the tent to watch what his lord had assembled, and smiled.

* * *

Vana's men had moved themselves to reorder the shield wall in two parts on top of the hill. He watched the orcs move themselves into four lines, lifting their shields up as they realized that their plan to encircle had failed. Their screams echoed in the general's ears.

As his men below finished off what was left of the orcs there, Vana, with one hand, held the reins of his horse, which stepped around nervously, wanting to leave. Vana didn't want to be here, either. Rather, he wanted to be sitting in front of a fire at his home back at the capital ... but ...

"Remember who you are defending this day!" he screamed, lifting his sword up high as the orcs across the field screamed loudly and rushed forward. His own men had fought off the orcs behind them easily, as the orcs had had to charge up a hill. This time, though, they were fighting on even ground against superior numbers. Vana made a silent prayer to his gods. "Give us the skill to end this!"

***

Whelor stood at the edge of the cliff, looking down at the elven forest below, waiting for the return of the two elves that had gone in. He was getting nervous that they had not returned. Had they been able to get in the forest and speak to those within it, or had they been killed like the orcs they had watched earlier?

He also was getting that feeling again. It moved through his body and made him shake slightly and swallow hard as he tried to suppress it. If his friends saw what was going on at the moment, they might do something they would regret, as he was finally beginning to understand what he was, and he was afraid he might hurt them. But he also needed answers, and staying with the group was the only way he felt he could get those answers, so he needed to try to hide his condition a bit longer from his friends.

He turned his head when he heard whispers not far from him. He saw Amlora and Holan looking down at the same forest, shaking their heads as well, probably wondering the same thing he was: Where were Kikor and Niallee?

Sitting on top of a small boulder at the far side of the tiny grove they all sat in was Chansor, who stared deeply at Whelor's back — or, rather, the back of the thing he was being ordered to kill. He rubbed his hands together, wondering how he could kill Whelor. The man was massive, and he … well, he was just tiny.

Chansor had a few ideas, but if he tried them, the others might come at him … and he didn't want to kill them.

"Do itttt!" he heard Elesha whisper. "Kill him, Chansorrrrr!" she repeated behind him, rasping a bit more as she said his name.

"I'm trying … I'm trying!" Chansor whispered back through his teeth. He had tried three times during their journey from the tower to this point to get Whelor away from the rest of the group so that he could dispatch him. However, every time one of the others came up behind him before he could make a move. Even during that forest excursion he had tried to get behind the giant man, but those orcs had gotten in the way before he could do what was needed.

As Chansor sat and tried to figure out how to kill the big man, Kalion stood, leaning against a tree as he thought back, trying to understand what had occurred since Jebba had left. That fight with that small band of orcs had been almost done when Bennak and Jebba had suddenly disappeared.

Pulling himself off the tree, he slowly walked over to the cliff to join Whelor, who still stood with his arms crossed, looking down at the elven forest. Kalion didn't say a word as he joined him; he didn't know what to say.

Nicolorr's warning about the man made him wonder, of course, but if anything, Whelor was an asset to their group, not a problem. As he looked down at the forest, he wondered, like the others, where Kikor and Niallee were.

* * *

"My king, our group is at the edge of your kingdom, wanting to enter and hoping they can get information," Kikor explained as she and Niallee stood before the elven high king and a few of his councilors in a small chamber in the elven capital city of Nakalor.

A number of the councilors in the camber started asking her numerous questions about the group and their quest. As these questions hit her, she lifted a hand to slow them down, which they did, but she tried to answer as many as she could.

Nakalor had stood long before man had crossed the eastern seas. Ages had passed since its first mighty tower had been raised by Mass-Lorak's people. Using the land animals for inspiration, the city soon began to form itself to look like a living, breathing creature of the forest. Even during the wars with man all those cycles ago, Nakalor had never been entered by force, having known nothing but peace. Kikor began to wonder if its people had become too proud, like the men of Bru Edin and even Brigin'i, thinking that the forest of Fuunidor and Nakalor could never be breached by the weapons that the orcs possessed.

"Our quest is a matter of honor for me and Niallee here, as we are Doro Amnach … We must continue, and we only ask for the safety of your kingdom to rest and get supplies and that you let us continue through to your eastern border," Kikor stated.

"How many are in your party?" one of the councilors sitting to the king's right asked.

"What do you seek from us?" another councilor asked before Kikor or Niallee could answer.

Kikor had started to answer when yet another councilor asked, "Where are you headed?"

King Mass-Lorak, king of kings of all the elven peoples of Marn, had ruled since he was a young elven warrior, longer than the lands had been there, or so the tales said. As he listened to the two elven warriors and his councilors, he leaned forward onto his fist and thought. He understood why the lands were turning darker and darker and the nightmares that he and some of his people were having. He was, indeed, worried about what was approaching.

Lifting a hand to calm the room down, he leaned back on his throne and smiled at the two. "I am sure you understand why my councilors are asking questions. I know who you are, my children. They are not questioning that you believe this quest you are on to be honorable; they are questioning our part in it. I will try to answer what questions I can." Kikor nodded slowly and smiled, knowing that the high king was there to help.

"But first, Niallee … would you please go to where your friends are and escort them back in? Guards … escort our sister here with two warriors. I want your friends within my borders." Mass-Lorak waved to the guards that stood along the wall not far away as the druid bowed down, giving Kikor a smile as she did. Slowly turning, she followed two elven guards out of the chamber, leaving her friend for the moment.

Watching her friend leave, Kikor turned to her king and started asking questions. "My king … do you know the movements of this Methnorick?" Kikor saw Mass-Lorak lift his hand up as if to stop her from asking too many questions at once.

"The Dark One, the one you speak of — Methnorick — has entered these lands himself with an army in the north. And now, as I am told, they march towards the only thing that is left in the north to stop him." King Mass-Lorak got up slowly, as did the councilors, as a sign of respect. Kikor bowed, understanding that he meant this kingdom. She watched the feet of the king as he passed her and walked over to a wall, where she saw a massive map that showed the whole of the continent.

"Our kingdom has stood against everything, from the ancient gods to man, over the cycles. It can withstand the attack of orcs easily. We have withstood attacks from other such creatures in the past. Even this mighty cyclops general they have that leads one of Methnorick's armies will not breach these forest walls." Mass-Lorak stood with his hands behind his back as he stared up at the tapestry that showed the forest, which, Kikor saw, was huge in comparison to the city of Blath 'Na that stood to its east and the mountains of Pilo'ach to the west. The mighty River Scannlomore, she saw, divided the forest in half as it moved from the north to the south.

As she looked at the map, she saw Mass-Lorak turn around to look at her, smiling.

"For now, child, rest yourself, get food if you like and wait for your friends to enter … I am sure they will be here soon. Then I will answer what I can." At that, Mass-Lorak waved his hand at the councilors, who followed the king out of the chamber, leaving Kikor and a few guards alone. One walked over, gently waving a hand towards another door, saying that within it was a rest chamber. As she walked in, she wondered how the king could stop Methnorick.

※ ※ ※

Vana's men fought hard against the orcs that charged across the field, trying to cut through the shield wall that he had been able to build. Not far away, two pairs of eyes watched from within the forest, on top of a large hill. The two people watched the battle, both wondering how it would end. They could see the men were being quickly surrounded, forcing them into a circle to keep the orcs from breaching their walls.

"Looks like those men are having a hard fight. Glad I'm not down there," the man said quietly.

"Me too, but as a warrior, why wouldn't you want to fight?" the other, softer, female voice answered.

Huffing a laugh, the man turned, smiling down at the face that had spoken to him. "Well, I am a warrior, but I have the liberty to pick and choose who I am to fight … or not fight!" The man looked back down at the battlefield below, hearing the familiar sounds of screams and cracks of weapons.

"Quinor … at the moment, you only fight for me, correct?" The woman looked up at the warrior, understanding his need to fight. Her face was showing signs of being tired, as she was sweating slightly from the miles they had walked since leaving the shoreline days earlier.

Huffing again, Quinor nodded and smiled back down at her. "Of course … I'm here to protect you and not rush into battle." Quinor looked past her to observe the forest they had entered earlier that morning, having walked for miles the day before and even more today. Shermee eyed the man as he continued to watch the battle before them, wondering if she was right to trust him or not. At this time, she would have to trust that he was able to protect her, but she was going to watch him still.

So far they had been able to get around anything that looked like it was a threat to the princess, and this battle below was something he seriously didn't want to get her any closer to. However, she had been the one to rush to the edge of the forest when she heard the far-off sounds.

"We'd better leave in case something sees us," Shermee whispered as she looked around behind them. The deer trail they were using made its way down the hill towards a grouping of trees and beyond.

"Orcs can't see us this far away … can they? Besides, the trees cover us." Quinor's question made Shermee tightened her face as she looked at the battle, seeing orcs trying to jump over the shield walls and the three men on top of horses directing the men.

"Are those soldiers from the empire?" she asked, seeing the surcoats of the three men. Even in the dust that was gathering around the scene, she could make out the bright colors of the men. Quinor looked back down, squinting slightly as he looked at the same men.

Nodding slightly, Quinor replied, "Yes … those surcoats even say that those men are high in the ranks of the empire's army." Squinting a bit more, Quinor saw that one of them even had what looked a gold crest of something hanging from his neck. The slight surprise he showed made Shermee look down, wondering what he was seeing.

"What … you recognize one of them?" she asked, staring down again at the men on the horses, wondering if they were anyone special.

"No … I don't know them, but I recognize the surcoats. That man there on the big horse … He's a general of the army. I believe the others are probably lieutenants … but that man has to be a general. I can see he knows what he's doing … But we need to leave here, Shermee … now!" Quinor rasped the last words as he saw what had to be orcs moving through the trees down the hill.

Both turned as Quinor put his hand on her shoulder. They almost ran down the hill towards the thick trees, away from the battle. As they entered the denser forest and moved down the deer trail, the sounds of battle slowly quieted down to leave both thinking about what they had seen.

Quinor again walked in front of the princess, placing his left hand on the pommel of his sword that, luckily, they had found lying against a house they had come across earlier. Quietly stealing it, Quinor had smiled at the princess, satisfied that at least he had something to protect her with as his other sword had broken the day earlier when he used it to try to cut through a branch to gather wood for a fire to warm them up.

Feeling like a fool for doing that, Quinor had been quiet most of their trek through the lands of the empire. The warrior knew that he had to get the princess back to Brigin'i, for she had been insistent on getting home, but he could feel her gaze on his back, and he knew she wasn't trusting him yet.

As the trail moved around some thick trees, Shermee was almost enjoying the hike. Time seemed to stand still until they had traveled some distance from the battlefield. She was in a land she had never been in. She had only heard of the empire — the beauty of it, the peaceful people, the history of its beginning, the food the people here enjoyed making — from her brothers and father, who had once visited it.

Food, she thought … Wow, she thought about it again as her stomach suddenly roared to life, telling her that she was in need of food. The nuts and berries that Quinor had given her for breakfast had worn away, and having only a sword, it was hard for him to trap or catch an animal for meat, having tried twice and failed both times to capture a rabbit. He had explained that he was better with a bow and arrow, but that didn't help her hunger.

As she thought of that rabbit, her nose caught the smell of what had to be rabbit. She sniffed a few times and then stopped, lifting her nose up to take in another sniff.

"Quinor … you smell that?" she whispered loud enough for him to hear. He stopped and looked back at her, tilting his head slightly as he also sniffed the air.

"Deer … no, rabbit, I believe … and a juicy one, I think." Quinor smiled at the princess, who smiled back, both thinking the same thing. Whoever was cooking a rabbit might, hopefully, share it with them … or Quinor could take it if they were orcs or something darker.

Following his nose, Quinor bent down and quietly stepped through the brush, leaving the princess, who gently followed not far behind, not wanting to step on something and alert whoever was cooking the food of their arrival.

As Quinor moved slowly, he began to see what looked like a clearing up ahead. As the smell got stronger, he could see the flames of the fire under what looked like a kettle.

Kneeling down, he raised his hand to Shermee, motioning for her to do the same. She knelt down slowly as he peered through the branches of the trees, catching sight of movement behind the fire and seeing that the fire was just inside the opening of what looked a cave of some kind.

Looking back at Shermee, he put his finger to his lips, telling her to be quiet as he then mouthed the words "Don't move!" He then slowly got up and stepped out of the forest, coming face to face with a surprised woman, who dropped the large spoon she held with one hand.

"No, wait … wait, I'm not here to harm you!" he said quickly as he replaced his sword, raising both hands up to show he meant no harm.

"I am not going to harm you … Please, my lady!" Quinor said, trying to say it gently so as not to scare the frightened woman any more. As he looked at her, he wondered how long she had lived out in the woods.

She looked at least 50 cycles of age, with long white and grey hair held together with a rope as it fell behind her back. She stooped over slightly, and her clothing had once been something of class but now was worn from cycles of being out in the forest. He looked over her camp, seeing no one else. He didn't move as she stared back at him, blinking a few times. She looked from him to the forest, where Shermee hid, and back.

"Who … who are you?" she whispered, breathing frightenedly.

"My name ... Well, I am Quinor. I'm not going to harm you ... believe me!" He smiled gently, as he could see that her body was not shaking anymore.

"Who is your friend, then?" she asked as Quinor returned a slightly confused look, wondering how in the names of all the gods she knew he was with someone, when he heard a snap of a branch right behind him. He cursed the princess for approaching without his telling her it was safe to come forward.

Turning his head slightly, he saw Shermee smiling as she walked out, opening her hands and raising them like Quinor had to show she meant no harm as well. "This is Shermee, my lady," he said, turning his head back to the old lady.

"And who are you, lady? I feel defenseless in giving you our names without getting yours in return," Quinor said calmly again.

The old lady's eyes darted back and forth a few times. Quinor could see she was thinking. "They call me Qushe, warrior man." Her voice sounded more settled, Quinor thought, as he nodded.

"Qushe ... she and I are traveling to the west, and we only came here because we smelled your wonderful food being cooked. The two of us have been traveling hard ... and are very hungry." Quinor lowered his hands slowly as he nodded at the black pot full of food.

"We were just wondering, my lady, if you would be interested in sharing a little of it," Shermee said gently as she walked to stand next to Quinor, for she was thinking the same thing as Quinor.

"Share?" Qushe looked back at her pot that was cooking the rabbit she had caught this morning as she eyed the two, seeing that, indeed, they were showing signs of being very hungry.

Nodding gently, Qushe smiled at them. "Of course ... it's too much food for me anyway!" Quinor smiled back, as did Shermee, who walked up and thanked the lady for letting them join her.

As they sat down, neither caught the look in Qushe's eyes. As she watched the two gather logs to sit on, she almost smiled. "Thank you!" she whispered gently to herself.

Chapter Nine

Amlora was searching a berry bush for something to nibble on when she heard something snort near her. She raised her head up to see that Whelor had moved closer to the edge of the cliff and had a hand on his sword pommel, and she noticed he was looking down more intently now.

Standing up, she slowly stepped over to the big man, thinking he was watching some orcs marching by below. When she looked down over the edge of the cliff, she could see the treetops below and the field and road in the distance, but nothing else. She was about to ask the warrior what he was watching when she caught sight of something shining in the sunlight as it walked out of the forest. Squinting her eyes, she tried to see what or who it was, noticing that there were now three figures. Two, she could see, were elven warriors holding their bow staves towards the north and south, keeping an eye out for orcs, but the middle figure made her smile as she saw that it was Niallee, who was waving up at both her and Whelor.

"It's Niallee!" she gasped. Whelor answered with a grunt, smiling down at Amlora when she looked up at him.

"It's Niallee … She's returned!" Amlora turned and excitedly yelled out to the rest of the group, who quickly jumped up and ran to the cliffside to look down, seeing the three elves standing at the edge of the elven forest.

"Why doesn't she come up?" Chansor gasped, quickly seeing that they weren't moving to come up towards the group.

"Probably don't want to leave the security of the forest," Meradoth said, nodding north, where he could see movement coming over the crest of the hill beyond which the road disappeared.

As all looked that way, Kalion whispered loudly that they should quickly gather their weapons and scuffle down the hill to join

Niallee, who now, along with her two guards, saw the movement coming closer.

As the group made their way onto the field, which was cut in half by the road, they began to hear the movement of heavy boots marching on the road.

Up above, Chansor was still in his daze, speaking to Elesha, when he heard a familiar voice call out his name again, bringing him back to where he was.

"Come on, Chansor, we do not want to be caught out in the open!" Kalion slapped Chansor's shoulder as the ranger ran by. Chansor returned his vision to the creature's gaze, nodding just once as he ran to join the others, knowing he had to complete his mission soon.

✳ ✳ ✳

It didn't take Methnorick's massive army, which had stretched itself along the north-south road, long to reach the northern edges of the elven forest after leaving the borders of the Northern Reaches. As the scouts entered the Esponori Valley, which lay between the eastern ends of the Pilo'ach Mountains and the western edge of Fuunidor, word was sent back to Methnorick that there had been no resistance from the elves to stop or slow them down.

As the orc and goblin scouts ran out in search of any threats along the edges of the valley, those few dark elves that were in the lead of the marching army moved forward through the valley, where they became the first of Methnorick's minions to place eyes on their prize: the elven forest of Fuunidor.

The three dark elves rode beasts, which cried out as they came to a stop, stomping the ground as the two elves pulled their reins to return and inform Methnorick that the forest was open for the taking. The third elf sat on his saddle, holding his reins as he scanned the forest and the road beyond, watching for anything.

The beast between his legs huffed a few times as it slowly sat down. The dark elf didn't stop it from doing so, as he had other things to think about, so his mount lowered its head as well and waited.

Before leaving the Black Isle, Methnorick had given each of his people that wanted one a beast like his. It was black with long fur and a tail that ended in what could have been a sword, as it looked and acted like one in battle. Its long but muscular legs were covered in leather armor and ended with massive claws that gleamed in the light, making them look like daggers. When it opened its mouth to yawn and stretch out, it displayed huge teeth, each about the width of a man's arm.

The dark elf smiled under his hood as the sky behind him grew darker by the moment. He felt strength in knowing that Methnorick was bringing even the weather to bear in his war in these lands.

The sound of thunder caught the elf's ears, causing him to turn his head and see the orcs begin to move towards him like a river opening up from a ravine as they made their way through the valley towards the forest of Fuunidor.

As they spread and ran past the dark elf, his mount jumped up on its feet and roared in excitement, believing it was joining in the charge, only to be stopped as the elf pulled back on the reins. The army ended up stopping themselves not far ahead, seeing the same thing he did: the forest of Fuunidor sitting peacefully, like it had been for cycles of time before.

✳ ✳ ✳

Vana held his reins tightly, swiping down with his sword to cut an orc's head in half as he charged by his men, who were breaking out of the circle, cutting into the orcs that had been surprised by the sudden rush attack, slaughtering them quickly. When he and his men finished rushing through the group of orcs, they turned to charge back up the slope and found that their comrades were surrounded by hundreds of orcs. Still, they continued up the hill, rushing into the orcs, slashing and hacking as they moved back towards their lines. The shield wall broke open just long enough to let them through and then quickly closed ranks again.

Arrows flew up from the few archers that the orcs had, and once in a while, they would find their mark, causing a man to fall. The orcs tried to get an edge by pushing more orcs into the space left by these fallen men and making the openings wider, but they weren't fast enough, as Vana's men were able to close the openings fast.

Vana had been able to see from his mount that their losses would, if they weren't given assistance soon, allow the orcs to charge over the top of their shield wall. For he had seen five men die within a few seconds from either an arrow or a spear that had been thrust through a shield.

Moving his horse in the encirclement became harder too, as the circle grew smaller by the moment. He was thinking it would be only a matter of minutes before his men would be cut down when he heard the familiar sound of hope.

His men, hearing the same thing, cheered from behind their shields and experienced a sudden surge of resistance against the orcs who were trying to use their bodies and mass to push the shield wall apart.

Pulling his reins to make his mount rear back on its hind legs, Vana looked over and smiled as he saw men charging hard to attack the orcs from behind.

"Now … show these things who we are!" he screamed as his horse landed hard on the ground with its front hooves, whining as it did. In return, his men roared in defiance and pushed hard at the orcs, causing many to collapse and fall back as they saw that now they were the ones becoming surrounded. The orcs quickly fell apart and tried to run away, only to be cut down and killed by those that, moments before, had thought they were about to die under the orcs' swords.

As Vana slammed his blade hard into another orc's helmet, cutting its head in half, he pulled on his mount, stopping and turning it so he could watch his men assemble. His men formed their ranks and then rammed their shields hard into the ground to make a tight wall surrounding those that were wounded or dying. Others moved out in small groups and slaughtered the retreating orcs.

When the scene had quieted down enough that he could walk around and check on those that had been wounded, he found that, out of the 800 men he had had in these two skirmishes, over 250 were either dead or wounded. "Many of the wounded, sir, will be unable to hold a sword or shield," the three clerics traveling with him told him.

Nodding at the last comment, Vana walked around slowly, bending down to speak to those that were dying to ease their pain as he took in the number of orcs that his men had fought against.

Walking up to his one remaining lieutenant — the other having died when an arrow found his open neck, killing him almost instantly — he joined the younger man, who was bent down, examining the corpse of one of the orcs. When he saw the general approaching, the lieutenant stood back up and waited for the older man to look at what he had been checking out: the clothing.

"Have you ever seen these garments before, sir?" The younger man, who had only been in the imperial army for a few cycles now, was looking at the black-robed orc that all men were used to seeing in these lands. But it was the clothing under the robe that was puzzling.

Vana knelt down and looked at this orc and then many around it. They were each wearing a reddish, almost gold, surcoat under their robes — not the clothing that orcs normally wore.

Standing up, Vana shook his head no.

"Have the men check those that they can. I want to know how many of these things are wearing this type of clothing. It could be a new tribe … but I need to know. Understand, Lieutenant?" Vana looked directly into the man's eyes as he saluted while backing away.

Vana crossed his arms as he surveyed the field, wondering what orc would wear something like what he had been looking at.

Methnorick's orcs? he wondered, for he had not heard if Methnorick had uniformed his army. *Orcs normally wear their tribe's clothing, not someone else's,* he thought again.

* * *

Far to the north of where Vana stood, across spans of mountain ranges and fields, the largest armies of evil marched hard southeast as the word reached Methnorick's ears that Fuunidor was now within striking distance.

Screaming a victory cry, which was repeated loudly by orcs and others within range of his voice, Methnorick kicked his horse hard, whispering something that made the horse suddenly ignite in flames, causing many around him jump back as he yelled for the horse to move forward.

Those within his army that could muster the courage saw Methnorick, like a flame from a torch, move quickly down the field past his army, for he wanted to be the first one seen by the watchful eyes of the elves he knew would be waiting for his army.

His scouts were joined by the forefront of his army, which included a battalion of giantkind, who, when the word was passed to them, decided to run hard to get there before the rest. As the valley opening became crowded, the orders were sent forward as Methnorick galloped hard to reach the point of his army and begin marching.

Cheers erupted from the orcs as they poured out of the valley and marched in rows of twenty towards Fuunidor Forest. Each imagining the glory of slaughtering the elves that lived deep within the forest that soon covered their vision, they soon moved over the top of the hill and out of the Esponori Valley with their banners flying in the wind. The sky above slowly turned dark as lightning ignited the tops of the mountain range to the west and the forests to the east.

It didn't take Methnorick long to reach his destination due to an interesting travel spell he had given his horse, which allowed it to move more quickly than anything on the land. He had considered moving his entire army this way, but the power that would take was beyond even him. As he approached, the flames slowly extinguished, leaving his horse in its fearsome black armor. Methnorick smiled as he trotted forward to look down at the treetops and the road moving south along Fuunidor's western edge.

As his army marched slowly past, opening itself to move around him, Methnorick held his mount's reins tightly. He squinted his eyes and looked around, waiting and wondering what the elves had in store for him, when he caught sight of something familiar moving across the road far to the south. He stood up slightly in his saddle as he tried to figure out what it was. Then suddenly …

"YOU!!!" he rasped through his teeth.

Chapter Ten

With the surprise appearance of Sunorak within the tunnels of Chai'sell, the battle suddenly reversed against the dwarves, who had been close to stopping the assault of their dark cousins from the deep.

Finfilli tried hard to defend his kingdom, but after two days of heavy fighting, he saw that nothing could stop the attack.

His scouts were now reporting that orcs were gathering at the main gate. Meanwhile, large numbers of dark elves had been seen moving towards the last means of escape for Finfilli's warriors.

"What am I to do? Those things are winning my kingdom with … with the help of creatures I despise. I should have realized that someday they would be here!" Finfilli whispered to himself as he eyed his proud warriors. From the wounded to the dying, he knew they would fight if he commanded.

Putting his hands behind his back, the proud king smiled and nodded at the faces that looked up at him as he passed by; he could see the worry on their faces as well. Chai'sell could be seeing its last sunrise soon.

* * *

The rest of the group was headed towards Niallee and her elven companions when Kalion noticed the big man wasn't moving. He stared into the distance as if something was drawing him.

"Whelor, the elves are waiting for us. What are you looking at?" Kalion asked. As he moved to see what was in Whelor's line of sight, he saw a figure upon a horse come into view.

"By the gods!" Kalion gasped as he recognized the man sitting on the horse. "Methnorick!" he moaned through his teeth as he felt a chill run down his back.

"Methnorick!" Whelor repeated the name, a feeling of familiarity growing stronger within him.

"We must leave this place!" Whelor whispered fearfully.

"I know … Come with me, my friend!" Kalion placed his hand on Whelor's arm.

Whelor's body was shaking as Kalion literally dragged him towards the forest border. They had just crossed into the forest when they both stopped in their tracks as a booming voice reached them.

"Whelor … Come with me now, and I will spare your protectors. Disobey me, and they will all die … by your hand."

Methnorick's scream diminished, as if even sound was buffered by the magic.

"You'll not be dying today," the warrior next to Kalion said as they passed the trees that guarded the elven kingdom. Kalion shook his head a few times and blinked hard to clear his head as they passed two pillars that had once held gates. Kalion could see a statue of a deer on top of each pillar as both walked through the entrance.

Kalion recognized the footprints in the dirt from Holan's and Amlora's boots, and he could see the rest of the group up ahead. Knowing that his friends were safe, he turned to Whelor. The look on Whelor's face told Kalion that he had already guessed Kalion's question.

"You wish to know how Methnorick knows me, do you not?" Whelor laughed mirthlessly and looked away. "I honestly do not know." With that, he turned to follow the path and the others.

※ ※ ※

"Kikor!!!" Chansor's voice echoed throughout the courtyard as the young thief jumped up from his chair and ran over to the elf, who gave him a tight hug. "Where have you been, Kikor? We've been waiting here for a while." He let go of Kikor and gave Niallee a hug as well, as both watched the group rise from their own seats, smiling and welcoming the two elves back. The group had been within the elven kingdom for a while now and had not seen Kikor since they had arrived. Niallee had disappeared not long after they had arrived as well.

Accompanying Kikor and Niallee was an older elf, who watched the group with a slight smile as the two female elves tried to calm their comrades down.

After Kikor and Niallee introduced the elven high king, Mass-Lorak, to the group, he waved his hand, and a few servants brought out spirits and water along with some food as the old elf explained what he knew. They all listened, with the exception of Chansor, who dived into the food, moaning that he hadn't eaten for a day.

"My friends, your companions here …" the king said as he looked at Kikor and Niallee and then continued, "explained your quest. Here is what I am willing to do for you.

"At the edge of this mighty city of my people, you will find horses, food and enough equipment to get you to Blath 'Na City, which lies four days' travel from here along the Blath 'Na Road." Kalion, who sat next to the king, nodded in approval at this news, as he had been concerned about their dwindling supplies. He knew that it was considered bad form to question royalty directly, but he still needed answers.

"Your Highness, what do you know of what has happened with Blath 'Na … or the forces that are outside your borders?" Kalion asked.

"The force outside is nothing for you to worry about, but we are aware," Mass-Lorak replied, coughing suddenly as he spoke. "I understand you have many questions. However, I do not have the answers you seek. Hopefully, Blath 'Na will have those answers."

Meradoth stood up slowly at that moment to stretch his legs. Mass-Lorak paused for a moment as he watched the mage.

"Before you begin this journey, let my people entertain you and feed you. You are welcome to stay until you are all rested."

Mass-Lorak closed his eyes slightly as he watched his guests. He could tell that each was thinking of something besides what he was offering.

"Tonight dine well and get a restful sleep, as nothing will harm you here. Tomorrow all will be taken care of!" Standing up, Mass-Lorak nodded to an elven warrior, who walked quietly into the courtyard, looking for the king.

"I have some business to take care of … Please enjoy yourselves!" He smiled at the group, who bowed their heads, thanking the elf as he turned to follow the elven warrior, leaving the courtyard.

As the king left the group, Holan stood up and slammed his fist hard on the chair he was sitting in. "Friends … I have a terrible feeling that we need to get out of here now. We must keep moving."

Whelor grabbed a large stick of something that looked like cabbage but was sweet-tasting and stood up to walk to the edge of the room, away from the others, as the weird feeling he had gotten after seeing Methnorick earlier kept moving through his body. He didn't know why, but he agreed with Holan: He wanted to leave now, and quickly. He wanted to get away from Methnorick.

"I understand what you're saying, Holan. Believe it or not, I feel as you do," Kalion said as he glanced over at Whelor, "but the truth is that this is an opportunity to get a good night's rest, something we haven't been able to do since we left the tower." Holan grumbled but conceded that they'd benefit from the rest.

Chapter Eleven

Methnorick was growing more frustrated by the minute. So far the forest had been able to repel any orcs that had tried to enter. Each attempt to enter it had ended in screams from within the trees. Worse, none of the orcs who'd tried to enter the forest had returned.

Shouts of "Stand ready!" echoed around the field as sergeants moved through the ranks of creatures standing at the forest edge when, suddenly, a number of small objects exploded out of the treetops and flew towards the army on the field.

"Shields!" The scream echoed as the orcs lifted their shields up, only to lower them slightly as they realized the objects were the heads of their comrades that, moments earlier, had entered Fuunidor.

They could tell how each orc had died just from the facial expressions on the heads, which landed hard on the ground and rolled to stop on the grass around the army.

Quickly, the army of Methnorick erupted in screams of anger and pain and called for revenge while lifting their weapons, banners and spears high in the air above their heads.

Methnorick watched the display. The heads had been meant as a warning, but he knew better. The demonstration gave him what he needed to know about the elves and what they could do to his warriors. So he quickly screamed out new orders to his army to break into two separate groups. As the sun lowered itself behind them, the sky became filled with dark clouds and lightning started to strike within the forest.

Methnorick called for calm, knowing that the anger his army was showing was what the elves wanted, for anger leads to mistakes. He didn't want that. At that moment, a scout rode up, informing him that Kaligor's army had been seen just beyond the horizon and should be approaching within the hour.

"Good!" Methnorick said, nodding back and smiling as the scout rode off. With these numbers, including both armies, he would be able to enter the elven woods by force. He watched as, to his left, his war machines were dragged into place along the tops of the hills that overlooked the forest.

His plan was coming together almost perfectly now, better than he had thought it would, really. The creature he wanted dead would be trapped within the forest, along with his greatest foe. Those that travelled with that beast would also die under the blades of his army.

* * *

"Are you ready to take back your lands and fight for the lands of Marn?" The soft voice made Dia tilt his head up as he thought about the question. Of course he was ready, and taking back his lands was necessary, but he couldn't do it alone. The sounds of boots marching echoed in the valley, letting him know as he and the two elven warriors gently sat upon their horses, trotting along, that he had help.

Smiling, Dia looked over at the elf, who knew what the king's answer would be. "Of course I am ready. With your help and the help of the gods, our lands will soon be rid of the dark creatures that have destroyed so much and killed so many."

The elf gripped his reins tightly, for he was ready for battle, as were the 12,000 elven warriors that marched before and behind the three. They rode up the gravel road that led to the hidden opening that the elves had built many cycles ago so that nothing — not man, orc or even dwarf — could find it without the knowledge and greeting of the elven caretakers.

Soon the echoes of boots crunching and metal clashing together were heard as armor and weapons moved out of the hidden valley.

Behind this massive army of elven warriors marched over 500 ice giants. King Zakalesa, their leader, knew that if Methnorick conquered the lands around the Pilo'ach Mountains, where he ruled , his own people wouldn't be able to with stand against him, even with their size and strength.

Commanding the ice giants was the largest warrior that Zakalesa had: Gunbaater. Gunbaater wore a heavy fur cloak made from the best night wolves that roamed deep within the Pilo'ach Mountains over his armor, which had been made by the dwarves within Chai'sell many cycles ago and given to the ice giants in a trade for peace between the two beings. The armor could deflect the most powerful weapons.

Each giant held in its hands spears that were the length of two horses. Along with the spears, the massive creatures held either axes made of the best dwarven steel or swords. Each could cut through a creature with ease.

It had been many cycles since his people had fought against their cousins, the hill and plains giants, but he remembered that each time they had, they had won. *Let us hope it goes the same way in the battle to come,* he thought as his detachment finally made its way over the crest and out of the valley. They had been training now for more than two weeks, all grinning and eager for the coming fight.

They knew they wouldn't be able to get to Fuunidor in time to stop the attack of Methnorick, but they might able to circle him. Dia was hoping so as they marched out of the Pilo'ach Mountains to desolate plains, where only thick dry grass could grow under the shadow of the clouds above.

* * *

Flames were everywhere as cries of victory echoed over the fields. Burnt banners and flags flapped in the hot wind as the sounds of cracking metal echoed over the sounds of moving feet. She looked around wide-eyed, trying to understand where she was and what she looking at.

"TO VICTORY!" The scream came from just behind her, making her turn her head quickly to see what seemed like a million faces looking at her. As she raised her hands instinctively to stop them, her eyes grew large in shock at what she saw.

Instead of seeing her soft, white hands, she saw each hand covered in a leather armored glove with bright white metal. Looking down at her arms, she saw that they also were armored, as was her whole body. She stepped back in wonderment, realizing she was on a battlefield, as men and elves screamed and ran past her, not stopping.

Turning around, she saw that, beyond the dust, mist and smoke, there were hundreds — no, maybe thousands — of orcs and other creatures charging towards where she stood. She could see their mouths move like they were also screaming. Not understanding what was happening to her, she blinked hard and felt something in her right hand. She looked down to see a bright, blood-soaked sword, making her gasp. Then she saw, fluttering in the distance, a red flag being carried into battle. The emblem on it ...

"My queen ... my queen," a voice suddenly echoed loudly in her mind as she looked around the field for where it was coming from. "Shermee ... Shermee ... Wake up, Princess!" the voice echoed in her head again.

Blinking her eyes as she sat up, she realized that she had been dreaming. Shermee tried quickly to get the dark cloud out of her sight and the tired feeling out of her head when she saw where she was.

She saw Quinor lying not far away, looking back at her and nodding as he whispered to her. She looked around, blinking to get a clearer head, and saw that she wasn't on a field of battle but lying on the ground with her hands and legs bound together by a strong rope.

When a sound of music came to her ears, she looked around to see that they were both lying on the ground at the mouth of the cave.

I remember this cave ... but it didn't look like this! she thought quickly as she looked at the cave that both she and Quinor had approached, which had seemed peaceful and like a place where they could rest. Now she saw that surrounding her on the ground were bones and skulls of orcs, men and other creatures she couldn't identify. There were also furs, corpses and ripped clothing hanging along the walls, and a massive cauldron sitting over a bright, hot fire.

Standing not far away was the source of the music she heard. She saw not the quiet and timid woman that she and Quinor had approached, but rather a dirty, old, ugly creature covered in moldy green and black robes that were ripped in a few places and patched up in other places.

Quinor was looking over at the princess, glad that she was finally awake. He tried hard to get out of the bonds that held his hands tightly behind his back. Not wanting to get the old woman's attention, he moved his hands back and forth, trying to loosen the bonds, but so far it wasn't working.

Suddenly Shermee, who was trying to get out her bonds, accidentally hit a pan that was hanging just above her, making the man curse under his breath.

"Ahhhh, awake are you both? Hahaha, good!" The voice sent a chill down Quinor's back as he and the princess both looked over to see that the old woman was staring at them with a ragged smile that showed only a few teeth under the dry, dirty and bloody lips.

"I was hoping that you would be still asleep when I cut you both up, but no matter. When I put you in the bowl here, your pain will soon go away!" The woman laughed again as she walked over to stand between the two, who were now looking up at her in fear. Shermee's jaw began to shake slightly as the old woman looked down at them, putting a hand under her chin, scratching it as she thought. The princess saw broken but still sharp fingernails on the woman's right hand and was wondering who or what this woman was when she heard Quinor finally speak.

"Who are you, woman?" Quinor demanded. "We came to you in peace, and this is how you … how you treat us … by … by whatever you're going to do here?!" Quinor looked from the old woman to the table and cauldron.

The laughter that left the woman's mouth made Shermee whimper as fear took over her body upon seeing that this creature was going to kill her and eat her. Finally, the old woman leaned over and grabbed a large, rusty-looking knife that hung above her. Shermee could see that it had dark, dry blood on it as well.

"Ohhh, I am a nobody, man creature. I have lived here for so many cycles that I do not even remember my name or who I am." The old woman grabbed another knife and used each knife to sharpen the other as she looked from Shermee to Quinor, trying to decide.

"I thought you said your name was Qushe or something … Isn't that your name, my lady?" Quinor asked softly, trying to sound as nonthreatening as he could — not that the creature considered him a threat, but at this point, he was desperate to at least delay her.

The creature looked down at the warrior and laughed again as Quinor watched the two knives in her hands move like she was stabbing something. He swallowed, thinking that of all places to die … of all things to be eaten by … this creature!"

"That's the name of that creature there that I had a few days ago." Quinor looked over at the corpse that she nodded at, noticing it was a man about 20 or so cycles of age with his head lying in his lap. The woman walked over, placing one of the knives under Quinor's chin as she lifted his head slightly to look directly at her as she spoke. "It pleaded for its life like you are, warrior man!"

"No, my lady … I am not pleading, my lady. I was just trying to understand …"

"Wondering what I am. Yes, warrior man … Do not worry … Your worries will not last for long." She pulled the knife away from Quinor's throat, leaving a small cut as he blinked, watching her stand up and look over at the squirming princess.

"I think today I will have dessert first. It has not been so long since I have had a man on my dinner plate. But a girl creature … even better!" She laughed hard as she walked over, easily lifted Shermee up like she was a bag of flour, and began dragging the princess towards the table. Quinor watched, amazed that such an old, decrepit creature could do this.

"No, no … please … don't do this!" Shermee pleaded as she looked at Quinor, who was struggling even harder to get out of the ropes. The old woman just laughed even harder as the girl cried for mercy. The woman pulled her up onto the table, pushing the bones and other bits of creatures she had on it to the ground to clear it for Shermee.

"I love your strength, young one. All the better for me … It will make you taste even better!" Shermee turned her head away as the old woman leaned down, breathing heavily onto the princess's face, almost making her sick.

"Why did you drug your food then, woman?" Quinor yelled out, trying to distract the woman as she was tying the princess's arms and feet to the table. "Why not work for your food if you know your food tastes better that way!"

"I drug my food to make sure it doesn't fight me, warrior man, like I know you want to do!" The old woman grinned as Quinor pulled and pushed the ropes on his feet. She laughed, knowing that the man couldn't get loose.

"Do your drugs cause dreams, then, old woman?" Shermee asked, moaning as the ropes dug into her wrists and ankles when the woman had finally finished trying the girl on the table.

"Dreams? … My potions do not make dreams, little one. I made it so you would just sleep!"

"Your potion gave me dreams!" Shermee said through the tears that were now flowing as the old woman grabbed the blood-covered knife again and walked to stand over her, looking at the princess as if establishing where to cut in first.

"You will address her with respect, old hag," Quinor yelled. "She is not some village maid. She is a princess. From a great city in the north," he added as he continued to work on his bonds.

"And what did you dream?" she asked, not really caring as she poked a few areas on the princess.

Swallowing hard, Shermee closed her eyes for a moment and tried to recall the dream, knowing she didn't have long now.

"I was standing in a field … a field where a massive battle was occurring. Men, elves, orcs and other creatures were all fighting each other as fires burst out everywhere, making the sky red with flames and smoke and even burning the field under my feet." Shermee's voice made Quinor look up at the girl lying on the table. As he heard her dream, he wondered if she was making it up or if the potion really had made her dream what she was sharing. But then he noticed that the old woman had stopped moving and was staring wide-eyed down at her.

"Did they call you something?" she said quietly as she slowly lowered the knife down to her side.

"Call me something?" Shermee repeated, trying to remember, when the words hit her mind like a rock. "Empress … They called me their empress!" Shermee said in earnest, wondering what it meant. She looked up at the old woman, who dropped the knife and stared down at the girl with a look of shock.

"It cannot be!" the old woman said, shaking her head hard and putting her hands over her face as she walked around the table, repeating, "No … no … not her!" She stared in wonder and kept asking what it meant as Shermee looked at Quinor, who was still struggling to get free.

The woman stopped suddenly to look down at the girl, who returned the stare and gasped as the old woman then leaned down quickly and cut the ropes from her wrists and ankles, letting Shermee quickly roll off of the table. Shermee looked back at the creature, who lifted her hands up like she was surrendering.

"I am sorry, my queen … I meant no harm. I … I am sorry!"

she pleaded, looking at Shermee as her voice whimpered in sorrow. Shermee, now confused, looked at her and then at Quinor, who stopped struggling for a moment to stare up at them.

"What are you speaking about, woman?" Quinor called over from where he lay on the ground.

"The legend … the legend!" the old woman whispered as Shermee picked up one of the knives and walked over to quickly cut the ropes from Quinor's hands. As he stood up, he grabbed a rusty orcish blade that lay along the wall and pointed it at the woman, who quickly fell to her knees, putting her hands together.

"What legend, woman? What queen are you speaking about?" Quinor stood in front of the princess, who couldn't believe their luck.

"The legend … the legend that speaks of the girl who will be queen," the old woman finally said after calming down.

"Explain, woman … or, by the gods, this is the last time you shall see a sun!" Quinor pushed the blade at her as he spoke.

Swallowing hard, the woman calmed herself down enough to speak. "Centuries ago, a wise man came from the east to tell a tale of a girl from the north that would bring an empire to stand against an evil from a faraway land. She would destroy this evil, and she would rule the world in the end." The old woman's words made Shermee suddenly feel strange inside.

For some reason, the words sounded familiar to the princess. She stood, staring at the creature before her and then at the ground for a moment. As Quinor kept asking the old woman questions, Shermee suddenly remembered.

"Shermee, my dear … Long ago it was said that a girl would one day bring an empire together to fight off an evil from a faraway land, and in doing so, she would unite all the lands from sea to sea in peace". Her father's smile came to mind when she remembered him telling her the tale late at night when she couldn't sleep.

"She speaks the truth, Quinor!" Shermee finally said, putting a hand on the man's arm as he looked down at her in shock.

"What?" he gasped.

"She speaks the truth about that legend. I remember my father telling me of this legend," Shermee said quietly, looking at the woman. Her words made Quinor step back, not knowing what to say as he looked from the princess to the woman still kneeling not far away, crying for mercy now. Shermee looked at the woman again and said, "But I am not the one this legend speaks of … I cannot be!"

"But … your dream. You said that you saw the battle and the emblem of the wolf," the old woman pleaded quietly. "For the legend continues … Not all know the entire legend or where it comes from, but I do. The one that will bring unity to the lands comes from a great city in the north. She will have traveled over and under seas to get to the people she will lead and will bear the emblem of the wolf."

Shermee tightened her face as she thought back to the dream again. The scene flashed across her eyes as she saw the red banner and the emblem fluttering in the wind.

"Yes, it was a wolf of some kind," she whispered. The old woman instantly cried out, putting her hands together to bow to the ground as she pleaded for mercy.

"It is true … I have found the queen … I did not know, my queen … I didn't know it was you!" she whimpered hard through her tears as Quinor stared down at the girl he only knew as the princess.

"I am not sure I believe this, woman. Why me?"

"There is one final thing … The legend says that the queen will bear the mark of the ancients."

"And where would this be?" Shermee asked.

"On your hand!" the woman stated as she reached out and took Shermee's hand to reveal the birthmark on her hand in the shape of a wolf.

"No, my mother has the same mark."

"But she is not here in the empire like you are."

"How did you know that, woman?" Quinor asked.

"I know many things that have been and will be. And this I know: I found the queen first."

Chapter Twelve

King Mass-Lorak walked into the large room, where a fire was burning hot in the center. As he did, the few elves that stood together talking quieted down, turned and bowed upon seeing their king walk in. Motioning for them to rise, he walked to the closest councilor.

"My king ... the news from the border is not good," the first councilor said as he watched the king stare at the fire. "The orc army has stationed itself in two formations along our western border, and it seems that Methnorick is waiting for something, as he is not charging or attacking, sir." Mass-Lorak turned and walked over to the wall, where a beautifully painted map of his kingdom and the lands just around it hung. He pointed to where the councilor had just mentioned that the orcs stood.

"Do we know their standing numbers?" Mass-Lorak calmly asked.

"Together, my king, we have counted over 25,000 orcs, goblins and giantkind, along with some other creatures that we have never seen in these lands."

Mass-Lorak, turning slowly, lowered his head as he walked back over to the fire to warm his hands. As he did, he looked up and saw that the commander of his army stood, waiting for his king to give him word on when to move.

Smiling, the king said, "General Summ, my friend ... are our people ready?" Summ quickly nodded yes. "Then, my friend, the word is given," Mass-Lorak said as he slowly walked over, placing his hands on the general's shoulders. "You know what needs to be done." General Summ smiled.

"We will win the field, my king!" Summ calmly whispered as he stood firmly and then turned and left with two warriors that stood at the edge of the chamber.

Mass-Lorak turned to the rest of the elves as General Summ left. "I have foreseen this battle ... I have seen that this Lord Methnorick is the bear that will hunt our people forever unless we stop him and his armies here." At the mention of Methnorick's name, the king's face showed a hint of pain as his eyes and cheeks squirmed a bit. He didn't share the rest of the dream he had seen.

"We will give them a nightmare to remember, my king," one of the councilors said, and the others quickly agreed. Recovering from the quick pain, Mass-Lorak smiled and walked out of the room as the kingdom's call to arms rang out in the city, with bells echoing everywhere.

* * *

The group was sitting around a small fire set in the middle of the courtyard, not really warming themselves, as it was only meant to be a showpiece. Since the king had left earlier, Kalion and Kikor had sat with each other, whispering about what they each had heard from passing elves after the king had left them: The city of Blath 'Na was now haunted by creatures that none of the elves had ever seen before, and these things had moved into the eastern part of their kingdom. Somehow all communication with the small elven villages that lay within that part of the kingdom had stopped. Patrols had been sent out. None had returned.

"This means others have seen the creatures that Nicolorr told us about, but none here know what they are either," Kalion said to Kikor.

"The fact that they have gotten out of the city is not good either, and they are moving in this direction," Kikor replied. Kikor went on to say, "This is going to affect how we travel from here to Blath 'Na, for the road we were to travel on ... It is the direct route!" Kalion was nodding in agreement when they heard a roar and a clash of screams echo loudly, making everyone jump up and look around, wondering what the sound was.

"What in all the hells is that sound?" Holan called over to Kalion, who shook his head, not knowing either. Another roar thundered as a loud crash like something falling hard on the ground came down one of the hallways.

"Down there!" Niallee yelled. Quickly, Kalion looked back, seeing Niallee pointing down the hallway.

Swallowing hard, the ranger pointed to Chansor, who had leaped up on a table to get a better view of what the sound might be. "Chansor ... watch over Niallee ... We'll be back!"

Before the thief had a chance to respond, Kikor pulled out her sword from the scabbard that lay near her as Kalion did the same. They ran down the hall. Holan followed behind with Niallee next to him, leaving the druid and the thief alone. Chansor walked over to stare down at the elven maiden, slightly annoyed that he had been left to guard her.

As Kalion and Kikor ran forward, they approached each hall cautiously, looking down each way, listening to where the screams were coming from. Kikor, having the best ears, tilted her head each time they stopped to listen.

"This way ... We're close!" she called over to Kalion, who nodded as he waited for Holan and Niallee to join them. He didn't want to run into a situation without their help, he decided. Another massive roar echoed loudly, letting them know that, indeed, they were getting closer. It was something that he had never heard in his entire life, and he felt such a chill that his arms were shaking slightly now.

Kikor nodded to Niallee and Holan, who quickly stepped up to follow the elven warrior down the last hall. Niallee moved in behind them, reaching into a pouch. She had thought of something that could hopefully slow down whatever might be attacking this place. As she slowly ran down the hall, she watched the rest reach the end of the corridor and stop quickly. Thinking that they were just trying to get a plan together, she pulled out a finger-size pouch and started to think of the words to a spell that would bring out the roots from the trees that lined each square and courtyard in the city when she came to join her friends, who still stood almost frozen.

When she moved up behind them and brought her eyes up to lie on the sound that was roaring so loudly, she almost forgot the spell she needed as her mouth dropped open like the others' while they watched the commotion in the courtyard.

"Hold it, NOW!" Upon hearing the scream, the group looked over to see King Mass-Lorak, now in armor, standing with a group of heavily armed elves. They watched another twenty or so more trying to rope in a creature that stood in the middle of the courtyard before them. Niallee looked from the king over to what she saw lying on the ground before her. Whatever it was, three elves, each in a certain stage of being ripped apart and killed, had tried to take it down and failed. One elf didn't have a head, another didn't have arms and the last somehow had lost the whole lower part of his body.

"What is it?" Kikor gasped loudly as the rest watched the massive creature — about the size of small giant, maybe nine feet in height, and covered in dark fur with bursting, muscular arms and legs — bent over slightly and thrashing around, trying to get at the elves with its long, deadly looking, dagger-size claws that lay at the end of each hand. It whipped its claws back and forth, trying to catch the elves as they jumped back to get out of the way.

A few other elves that were not quick enough were thrown against a far wall as the ropes they were using were grabbed by a claw. The creature lifted the poor warriors up and over its head by the ropes and roared in triumph as the screaming elves slammed hard into the wall. Holan and Niallee, who stood beside the dwarf, shook their heads in disbelief as they both saw the face and head that roared.

Covered in fur, with long pointed ears, the creature that made the tremendous roars opened and closed its mouth, chomping its long saliva-covered fangs that were each about the size of an elven sword, trying to bite another few elves. It roared loudly again, making even Kalion step back as it turned its gaze over and looked upon him.

Kalion whispered a prayer to the gods as he stared at the creature that was trying desperately, he saw, to get away out the bonds that the elves were trying to hold him down with. When its gaze moved over to look at the elven king, the ranger blinked a few times as he suddenly recognized the creature.

Even though the eyes were the color of blood, with what could be said was gold within, Kalion tried to think of what the creature reminded him of. He suddenly lowered his blade as he looked over at Kikor, who returned the shocked look, wondering what he was doing, and then turned his head to look at the creature.

"I … I think that's Whelor," he whispered confusedly as he turned to see the massive creature lift up another elf by the neck. The poor elf screamed out as it flew up and over to land hard against the wall next to Niallee, who ran over to kneel down and help the elf out.

Kikor's head rocked back when she heard Kalion say the name. She looked over at the huge animal-like creature and then back at the ranger.

"That … that cannot be. He went to go find some food … He must be back in the room with Chansor by now!" Her words almost disappeared as she looked directly at the creature's face.

"Look at its eyes, Kikor … That's him!" Kalion interrupted her, confident that he was correct now as the creature suddenly seemed to calm down a bit for a moment, which gave the elves a quick opportunity to wrap it more with the ropes. The elven maiden looked at the reddish eyes. She squinted her eyes to look more closely and slowly saw that maybe, just maybe, the ranger was right. As she realized this, she saw movement just to her right: the king.

"You brought that thing into my kingdom … a nightmare of the gods!" Mass-Lorak almost yelled at the group as the elven king walked up, pointing to the creature now being bound up with strong ropes as it roared again. Its arms were finally bound tightly against its body, making it harder for the creature to move. The group watched it struggle slightly, roaring once in a while and finally resting its eyes on the group.

"Brought ... We didn't bring anything into your kingdom, sir. That ... that thing did not come in with us!" Holan responded quickly, not understanding the king's words.

"That ... that thing is or was one of your companions that my people caught here trying to kill my people. Luckily my guards and I were close enough that we could respond quickly." Mass-Lorak looked at the group as they continued to stare at the creature, saliva dripping out its mouth as a long tongue whipped out, quickly making a few elves back off. "But not quickly enough!" His last words brought their eyes to the elves that were slaughtered on the ground around the creature.

"Sir ... I think you are confused. That cannot ..."

"That is Whelor, is it not, sir?" Kalion said, cutting Niallee off, placing a hand on the druid's arm as he spoke. Mass-Lorak leaned his head back slightly, looking at the ranger, and then nodded yes a moment later as the group gasped, looking at the thing now staring down at them all.

"Whelor ... That can't be him. He's ... he's ... By the gods ... it can't be," Niallee gasped loudly, as did Holan, who shook his head, not believing what the elf and Kalion were talking about. That couldn't be his friend.

"That nightmare will kill every last one of us if we do not kill it now!" one of Mass-Lorak's guards said, looking over at the king, who nodded back.

"No, sir. If that is our friend ... we can find out what happened. Don't kill him, please!" Niallee pleaded as she stepped forward, lifting her hands up to stop the captain, who spoke as he lifted his bow, pointing a deadly looking arrowhead at the creature's head.

"Find out how, my lady? That thing is an animal and nothing else, and it must be stopped, NOW!" Mass-Lorak said, but he put his hand on the elf, causing him to slightly lower his bow.

"If it is our friend ... please, sir, let me try to talk to him!" she said, urgently hoping that her plea would convince the king to not kill it.

Mass-Lorak stared at Niallee and then at the rest as Kalion just stood, still looking up at the creature, amazed that it was truly their friend. *What happened to him?* he wondered as he watched. Suddenly Niallee stepped forward, putting her hands up to hopefully let the creature know she meant no harm to it.

Roaring loudly, it watched the elf step closer, making those elves trying to hold it tighten their grips on the ropes, shaking their heads that she was making a mistake. They all knew down deep that it was just playing with them at the moment. Those muscles that all could see could kill an ice giant, and their ropes were nothing to it.

Niallee stepped forward, pushing down the fear that she felt. She smiled gently at the creature, whose mouth lay open, revealing the massive fangs inside. She hoped that her instincts were correct and that the feeling that she could do something was not her imagination. This creature was their large friend.

"Whelor … is that you, my friend?" she whispered calmly as she took another step forward. "It's me … your friend Niallee. Whelor … I am here to help you out, my friend … It's all well, Whelor." She spoke calmly, slowly stepping closer. With each word, she watched its chest move up and down as it breathed hard.

Kalion looked over at the king, who he noticed was looking almost sick, like he had a fever of some sort. Kalion asked the king suddenly, "What happened here, sir? If that is, indeed, my friend, what would make him attack your people?"

Mass-Lorak looked at the ranger and then back at Niallee, who now was whispering to the creature. "This courtyard … This is a place where my people come when they need to speak to the gods within the sky, and it … he came in here, I'm told, to kill. He somehow killed three of my people that were within the sanctuary before my warriors and I arrived, barring him from killing more. We found him like this." Mass-Lorak spoke quietly, hoping, like the rest, that the creature wouldn't break out of its bonds and slaughter them all.

Kalion looked at the elves that had died and then back into the king's eyes. "I am sorry. We were not aware of Whelor's condition. We will leave right away."

Mass-Lorak listened, only nodding a few times, but he was watching Niallee as she spoke. He closed his eyes as he began to remember something else in the back of his mind just then.

"I should kill you all for this … but I will not. Instead …"

Suddenly Whelor roared, lifting his head up to look at the sky far above. As he did so, everyone in the room jumped to grab a weapon or pull the rope tighter as Kikor's arms remained open wide, showing that she meant no harm.

Niallee stepped back slowly as she watched like everyone else as the creature squirmed in the ropes, struggling — not like it was trying to escape, but like it was hurting. Only the echo in the courtyard sounded different, and everyone watched as the fur quickly began to disappear and the muscles got smaller by the moment.

The creature slowly became shorter as its head, which moments before had been filled with massive fangs and looked like it could eat any of them, was shrinking as well.

Kalion stepped forward slowly. He walked up to join Niallee, seeing that his feelings were right, as the fur-covered Whelor with the strength of ten men changed to the tall friend they knew. Whelor fell down to his knees, looking at the ground as the ropes fell away to land hard on the ground. The elves holding the ropes released them, gasping as they looked at each other in disbelief.

"Whelor?" Niallee knelt down, putting her hand on the man's back. "Are you well? What happened to you?" she calmly asked as Whelor lifted his head to look at his friend's face, tears falling down his face.

"Yes … I am ok … but I am not sure what happened!" Whelor spoke so quietly that even Kalion, who stood a few feet away, almost didn't hear. But he could see that Whelor's words trailed off when he saw the bodies lying around him.

As the big man conversed with Niallee and Kalion, Mass-Lorak, shaking his head in anger, turned and left the courtyard as his guards continued to watch a moment longer until they, too, turned and walked away, leaving only a score of warriors to watch.

"Your group must leave now … before our king changes his mind and has you all executed for this." The captain who, moments before, had wanted to release an arrow at Whelor's head spoke calmly, but his words were direct enough that Niallee nodded quickly.

The captain looked over at his sister elf and then at the ranger before leaving to follow his king as Niallee helped their friend up.

* * *

Bennak ran as fast he could as arrow after arrow flew past him, hitting the trees and the ground that he had just run past. They had run into a large group of orcs and goblins that were sitting along the mountain trail as they still made their way west.

They had rounded a corner of the trail that the two had been walking along, running directly into orcs who were resting along the trail, surprised by the sudden appearance of the two. Instantly, screams from both parties rang out along the trail as Bennak and Jebba cursed their laziness and shot back around and up the trail to get away.

They both hurried along the trail, the screams behind them making them run harder. Seeing an opening in the brush, they scrambled up the rocks and through the trees, grabbing roots and ledges as they moved up the mountainside, hearing the screams from the orcs below giving chase. Once in a while, an arrow slammed into the rocks and skirted away, causing dust to rise in its wake as they grabbed what they could to get away.

Neither said a word to the other as they panted and grunted hard to get through the trees and tight brush, eventually finding a small ledge that must have been used by mountain animals in the past to move along the mountainside. Taking a moment to catch their breath, they looked down, watching as the first orcs broke through the tree line below them, grabbing rocks and tree roots to get themselves up. When they saw the two humans, they screamed, growled and snarled up at them, baring their blackish teeth under the black cloaks. Jebba reached over and quickly threw a rock directly into the mouth of one orc, causing it to fall backwards down the mountainside.

Bennak smiled as he looked at Jebba, but the smile disappeared quickly as one, two … no, five more orcs broke through the tree line, all growling as they watched their companion fall past them.

"We need to leave now," Bennak said quickly, looking both ways on the trail for a place to escape.

Jebba, seeing that the orcs were gathering strength, agreed and also looked around for an escape. Nodding, Bennak ran ahead, hearing Jebba grunting as the human followed behind. Both breathed hard as they stepped on rocks and pushed their way past tree branches that hung over the ledge.

The screams echoed everywhere. Both knew the orcs were determined to get at them. It seemed to Bennak they were passing over the group of orcs climbing after them. When they burst out of some heavy brush on the trail, a few orcs below observed the two making their way past them above and screamed for those that could to move back.

Arrows flew up and slammed around the two, making them duck and dodge as they tried not to fall off the narrow ledge.

"Move!" Jebba grumbled through his deep breaths as he felt the wind from an arrow that just missed his head.

As they made their way into another group of trees and bushes, the arrows slowly stopped, but the screams continued, even though the distance between them was widening as they escaped. Bennak pushed hard through the branches, knowing that if they stopped to rest at that moment, it might end for them quickly — something he didn't want yet.

Looking back, he could see Jebba looking down the trail to see if their pursuers were any closer. Bennak broke through some bushes, only to find himself face-to-face with an ugly, snarling orc.

Bennak did the only thing he could do: He punched the orc in the face, causing it to fall back, giving Bennak the chance to pull out a short sword that he carried behind his back.

The orc, snarling loudly, quickly rushed Bennak, who blocked the orc's sword thrust. Bennak was able to reach out and grab the orc's throat, and in one quick movement, he picked up the snarling orc, which growled and spat at Bennak as he threw the screaming orc over the edge of the trail and down the mountainside.

"Run!" Bennak called back to Jebba, who broke out of the brush just as the orc went flying down. Jebba looked to where Bennak was also looking. He saw six orcs pulling their way up the trail towards them, the sounds of branches being broken catching up to their ears from behind.

"Bennakkkkkkkk …" Jebba cried out as Bennak moved down towards this group. "What are you doing?"

Bennak turned his head and smiled. He knew that these orcs would follow them until either they or the orcs were dead. At the moment, they had two choices: run or fight. Killing the orcs would be the easier of the two plans, and Bennak was tired of running.

"Go, Jebba!" Bennak said, gritting his teeth as the orcs saw him standing alone, waiting for them.

Jebba waited for a second more until Bennak gave him a nod and he saw that the ledge opened up to another small one just ahead. Understanding that Bennak wanted him to go, he moved past his friend and ran up quickly, only stopping when he heard metal hitting metal. Turning around, he saw Bennak, the only one in the quest he had called "friend," standing by himself now, fighting orc after orc.

For the moment, he decided that he could not run away and leave Bennak, but before he could move, Bennak looked up. Seeing Jebba's hesitation, he yelled, "Move yourself ... Do not worry about me. Just MOVE!" Bennak's words echoed as an orc fell off the ledge, screaming as it tumbled down the side of the mountain.

Making a decision, Jebba got up quickly and ran west, down the trail and away from him his friend Bennak, who was quickly killing orc after orc, each one falling off the edge and screaming as it fell down the mountainside.

Chapter Thirteen

Finfilli watched as his engineers worked hard to make the massive circular columns that stood within the chamber slowly crack under their hammers.

The final plan involved the five columns that stood near the entrance of the hall that led to where their enemy was gathering for the final push to conquer his kingdom. If these columns were to fall, the ceiling would collapse and cut the hallway off from the rest of his kingdom, where his people — women, children and the elderly, whom he had ordered to be the last stand if he and his warriors fell in battle — were gathered together tightly.

As the first columns began to crack, the engineers quickly moved to the next and then the next, continuing to inflict their damage as the echoes moved up the hallway. Not far from them, they could hear the screams and roars of their enemy, who was beginning to move.

When the final column began to crack, Finfilli smiled slightly under his helmet until he felt a massive pain within his head. His face tightened up quickly as leaned over slightly, getting the attention of the guard that stood next to him, who turned to ask if he was well.

Suddenly the dwarven king couldn't speak, as the pain took over his head, making it hard for him to see, think or even breathe. He fell over onto his knees as he finally let out a cry of pain, grabbing his head as he knocked his helmet off, sending it rolling away.

Other dwarves nearby ran over to try to help, but they couldn't find anything until they saw blood leaking out of his head. He began to squirm and shake hard under his armor, and his words came out slurred, almost like his was crying. They watched as the mighty king of Chai'sell fell to the ground, screaming like none had ever heard before. A moment later, he lay still, eyes still leaking blood down his face, mouth open from his screaming, and hands holding his head, trying to get the pain out.

The guard kneeling next to his king leaned down, trying to get his king to look at him as he listened to the king's breathing. The look on the guard's face told it all to those standing in a circle now, and they began to moan. King Finfilli was dead, and with only General Hardshield to lead them, the dwarves knew that this would be the last king to rule Chai'sell. The screams from their deadliest enemy yet roared loudly from down the hall as the first column cracked and fell to the ground, making the whole chamber shake violently. Soon the other columns followed until the last of the five columns cracked and blocked the entrance to the hall just as the dark dwarves reached its opening.

"Retreat … Make your ways to the top level!" the guard screamed out loudly as he stood up. "We must leave this place!"

A few warriors quickly picked up the king and then made their ways up the final hall to the upper chambers, where their families now waited.

It is done … Move in and end this now! The words moved quietly through the mind of the dark elf that stood looking at the creature as a smile developed on his dark face.

Your emperor wants the crown! Sunorak looked down at the dark elf, who quickly bowed slightly.

"Chai'sell is yours to take … Take it NOW!" the dark elf screamed. The others around him screamed back, all wanting the same thing. They began to rush forward as one, with bloodlust and revenge in their eyes.

My time here has ended. Sunorak crossed his arms, and making many of the dark dwarves marching by cry out in shock and run to get away, he disappeared like he had appeared, in fog and light.

***

Chansor sat on the bench as he listened to the big man he was being ordered to assassinate, but he also watched the others he pretended to be friends with as they listened carefully as Whelor began his tale of what he knew about himself.

"I know not when it began. It comes to me occasionally, like flashes of memories. Like where I am from ... I remember being bound tightly to a metal rack of some kind, with metal ropes attached to me that sent such energy through my body that ... that I never could believe the gods would punish me like that, as it hurt like nothing I have ever felt." Whelor sat on the edge of the center pool wall as the others gathered around him to listen. "I ... I do not know why ... or how this has happened to me. I do remember fishing on the seas once and being happy ... yes, happy that I was doing that," he said quietly. "I have wondered where I am from, which I am sure you have wondered as well ... but that memory does not come to me." He looked up at the faces of his friends as he swallowed, wondering how he could explain the image that kept coming to his mind of the mouth that opened as it laughed loudly at him and the eyes that were bright, almost red.

Leaning over, Kikor smiled at her friend, as she could see him struggle. The big man smiled back at her. "It is fine, my friend. Tell us who did this to you," Kikor said.

Pulling in a big breath, Whelor lowered his head to look at the ground as he spoke. "Methnorick," he said, almost like he was releasing a pain from inside his chest. *Finally,* he thought, *I have told them who I am.*

The group let out a roar of gasps, and those who were sitting down all stood up, mouths hanging open as they stared at the man who was putting his head in his hands, whispering, "I am sorry I did not say anything sooner, but I was afraid of what you would think."

Kalion's mind instantly shot back to what Meradoth's father had told him about Whelor: *"Watch him!"* The ranger's mind had been racing since then, but seeing that this man was some type of killing creature with strength he had never seen ... Nicolorr had been right to advise them to keep an eye on Whelor.

"We wouldn't have killed you, lad!" Holan said calmly, almost too calmly, he suddenly realized. Like the others, the dwarf was shocked but seemed to act like he somehow knew something had been wrong with the man for a while now.

Amlora also hadn't reacted like the world was ending, for when she heard that the Dark One had done this to her friend, she accepted what Kalion had described in stride. She felt sorry for Whelor now — it wasn't his fault.

"It is well, Whelor. We are your friends ... and we will end Methnorick and find a way to cure whatever this is that ails you." She walked up and placed her hands on Whelor's lowered head.

"Amlora ... killing that ... that thing might ... It is said that Methnorick cannot be harmed," Whelor whispered, as he didn't know what to say. Holan looked over at the commotion of elven warriors running through the courtyard, seeing that something was happening.

"I think we should take the king's advice and leave this place now!" Holan said, nodding over at Kalion, who looked at the dwarf and then at the warriors running by.

"Methnorick has a weakness, and we will find it," Amlora said, quietly thinking of Whelor and what was underneath that skin of his.

Chansor sat not far away, struggling with what to do. He also saw the elven warriors, so jumping off the bench, he grabbed his pack, and quickly tightening it on his back, he walked over to join the others. They quickly did the same as Whelor stood up and smiled at the others, glad that they were with him and not against him.

Chansor walked up and stood next to Whelor, who had recovered enough from his ordeal. Bells and calls to arms began to ring throughout the courtyard they stood in. Chansor looked up at the big man, smiling. "You want to join in with them, do you not, my big friend?" Whelor smiled back at the thief but didn't answer as he looked away.

The thief was cursing himself now, for when the group returned, whatever had happened, Chansor could see that Whelor was weak and stumbling, but his opportunity was gone.

Still hearing the raspy words in his head to kill Whelor, Chansor tried to act like he was concerned about their quest. Even as Niallee took care of Whelor enough to get him to a state at which he was at least able to travel, Chansor watched the big man for an edge. Then, as he left the room, Kalion ordered them to grab their equipment and packs as quickly as possible, for he told them that Mass-Lorak was ordering them to leave.

"What about the night's rest they promised?" Chansor piped in.

"I am sorry, my friend, but not tonight," Kikor said as she touched his shoulder.

Holan and Amlora soon were rumbling through their packs. Meradoth and Harbin earlier had gone to gather some supplies that would be needed to get to Blath 'Na City. All the others gathered their own belongings. As Niallee watched their friend, Whelor slowly did the same thing, and neither spoke about what had happened. Soon the group was gathering in the courtyard as more alarm bells sounded. The team wondered if the sound meant the city was under attack or if it was just the king announcing that they were being ordered to leave.

Kalion returned just as the third ring of the bells echoed and the voices of elven warriors moving through the courtyard sounded.

"We need to get out of here, my friend?" Holan asked Kalion, knowing the answer as he strung his pack tightly. Kalion looked at the dwarf and only smiled gently in response.

Chansor could see that the elves were arming themselves to march out of the city, and not to escort them out. The shine from their weapons and armor was a great wonder to see. "It is like water in a lake or something, Niallee!" he whispered excitedly to the one elf who would listen to him at that moment.

Holan turned and nodded to the rest the group. As they followed the dwarf out of the courtyard and down a large hallway filled with amazing sights, Chansor stopped to admire something every few seconds, so Amlora pushed him along. Chansor's giggles echoed slightly as they walked down the hall.

The group quietly walked down the hall, finally stepping out on the ground level of the palace, where they all stopped to watch the tremendous activity of elves moving before them. Armor, weapons and more were being assembled on the massive square.

The movements of warriors made the ground shake under their feet, as elf upon elf began to march past.

"So, I believe we are not staying?" Chansor piped in, making a few nod at the thief's joke.

"You need to leave this kingdom's borders now." The quiet words made each member of the group turn to see Mass-Lorak standing before them as Kikor continued to watch the elven warriors marching past them.

"My king," Niallee whispered, seeing the elven king moving out of the shadows behind them.

"I had hoped that we could have dined together before your group left … but … your friend there … and Methnorick's army has begun its attack on my border sooner than expected," Mass-Lorak quietly said as he stepped closer to the group. The elven king looked sick, his face old and weak. Mass-Lorak was showing what looked like signs of a struggle within him. His eyes were smaller and weaker, unlike what Niallee had seen when she had first met him.

"You have a quest that needs to be fulfilled. This is not your fight … so … leave now and follow the Blath 'Na Road east," mumbled Mass-Lorak as he looked over at the elven warriors marching by.

Holan grumbled something in agreement and turned to walk away towards the eastern gates, but Kalion coughed to get his and the others' attention.

"King Mass-Lorak … you should get the rest of your people ready for what is to come, just in case the Dark One is able to get within your kingdom. Move them to the eastern reaches of your kingdom,"

Kalion said gently as he also wondered why the king suddenly looked weak when before he had seemed fine to the ranger.

Just then, both Meradoth and Harbin came walking down the hallway. Each was carrying a large pouch over his shoulders, and they were smiling together. The mages had gathered what they needed and had only caught the last of the king's words as they came to find the rest of the group standing on the landing that led to the square beyond.

They did not say another word when five elven warriors stepped out of the shadows behind their king, who looked at the two mages and smiled gently when Meradoth nodded at them.

"Thank you, kind sir, but I have asked these warriors to escort you all to the gates of our city. There you will find fed horses, additional supplies and weapons." He looked at the bags the mages carried and continued. "I am sure you will need these to get to Blath 'Na … but before you go, I must inform you of something." Mass-Lorak motioned for the group to come closer, like he wanted no one else to hear what he spoke of.

Looking at their faces and then at the elven warriors, who nodded and walked to stand not far away, Mass-Lorak leaned down and took a long breath.

"Beyond this city's borders, you need to follow the road that leads to the River Scannlomore, where the Whispering Bridge brings the two halves of my kingdom together. When you cross the bridge that takes you over the Scannlomore expanse, you will enter the eastern part of my kingdom. Know that that area has become dark with evil that even I do not understand. I sense weapons from the gods … creatures … Even now my people guard the west end of the bridge from anything that tries to come from that part of the forest." The looks he was getting showed even more confusion. He drew in a long breath, feeling weaker by the moment.

"My friends, all I can say is … be careful. There are things within that forest that are worse than any nightmare!" Mass-Lorak's last warning made Holan moan, as he hated nightmarish creatures.

"You are all on your own from the bridge," Mass-Lorak stated calmly.

"Just like I want it!" Whelor's sudden words caused a few members of the group to give the big man looks of surprise. Mass-Lorak laid his eyes upon the man, looking like the elf king could reach out and kill the big man for what he had just done to his people.

"It will take you two days and a bed to get to the port city ... Do not stop for anything!" Mass-Lorak rasped, calming himself down from Whelor's words. He stood back up and motioned for the guards to return as he kept his eyes on the big man, who returned a stern look, closing his eyes slightly as he stared at the elven king.

"Mmmm ... thank you, sir, for your help ..." Kalion said, only stopping as the elven king turned and left the landing, leaving the group to stare at each other, surprised that the elf had left the way he did.

"Well ... I guess that's it then!" Chansor whispered, looking at Niallee, who watched with wide eyes as her king walked away.

"We'd best hurry then!" Kikor said, turning and putting her hand on Kalion's shoulder as she did. "If Methnorick is able to get past Mass-Lorak, this forest is lost." Kikor stepped away and followed the guards as the group skirted the marching army that was still assembling and moving to where Mass-Lorak's generals wanted them. Kalion and Meradoth stood alone on the landing, looking at the king as he finally disappeared through a doorway far down the hallway.

"What's going on, you wonder, huh! You noticed that we never got to ask any other questions," Meradoth said, slightly smiling from the corner of his mouth as Kalion looked at his friend.

"Yes, no questions means no answers either. Sometimes you wonder about other creatures. First the dwarven king kicks us out ... now the elven king ... Makes you wonder if they know something that they don't want to tell us!" Kalion said as the two moved to join their friends.

"It does, doesn't it!" Meradoth smiled as he tried to figure out an answer to Kalion question as they walked under an arch that led them out onto the grass fields that lay east of the city's buildings and soon disappeared into the heavy forest.

"Maybe I'm just ugly!" Meradoth giggled.

Chapter Fourteen

Shermee and Quinor walked quietly, not speaking to one another as they moved out of the forest where the old lady had almost killed them. Quinor remembered the old tale that he had been told as a child of a witch and how she ate people to survive. The witch had continued to whimper and cry as they gathered their belongings and moved, still on guard in case the woman tried to attack them again.

Shermee blinked as she attempted to understand this legend the woman had told her about. Somehow the woman believed she was to be empress of all these lands.

Looking at her hands and then her legs currently under the dirty clothing that she wore, the princess couldn't believe that she of all people could be an empress. Just thinking of it made her giggle and shake her head. If only her father had told her this tale the same way that woman had, she might have remembered the entire story and where it would lead her.

Stepping out onto the plains, the two moved until they reached a small dirt road that moved east to west. They walked down the road towards the west, even as rain moved in, soaking the pair instantly. Neither said a word. They had been walking most of the day, and with the rain making it dark, the sun was barely visible, so Quinor just pointed. They made their way to what was once a barn of some kind. There they searched until they found a dry spot where Quinor could build a fire for them to warm and dry themselves off by.

As Shermee sat, warming her hands from the flames that were snapping and wiggling about in front of her, she looked over at Quinor, who was staring at the fire.

"Did you know of this tale, Quinor?" she quietly asked, looking directly into the man's eyes as he looked up at her.

Tightening his lips for a moment, the man thought of what to say. "I have heard the tale, yes, Princess ... but ..." Quinor paused and looked down, and then chose not to continue. His words didn't answer her question, and she squinted her eyes for a moment, staring at him and getting slightly frustrated at his hesitation to tell her.

"If I am to be this empress that was spoken of ... this place where that old woman told us to go ... or what, Quinor?" Her voice sounded angry. Quinor suspected what she was feeling, and he didn't want to lie to her anymore.

"Methnorick knew of the tale ... He once said that the tale meant that this empress would not only control the world for the good of the people but would stop his plans. I believe he was going to marry you to control and change fate so that he would really be emperor. He probably thought that, in marrying you, he could take control of fate ..." Quinor threw a stick into the fire, making it burn a bit warmer, smiling at what he had just said.

Shermee looked down, thinking of that evil man and what Quinor had said about him as her anger grew inside. "I will not have that ... that creature, or any man, tell me what I will do or be. I will control what I am!" She stood up as she finished speaking, looking down at the warrior, who leaned back and blinked, surprised at her comment.

"What will you do then?" He realized that she was ready for what was coming next.

"This city that the old woman spoke of ... What was it called again?" she asked, crossing her arms as she thought.

"Manhattoria ... I would say it is many days' walk from here. If we could find horses, of course, that would be quicker," Quinor said, voicing what she was thinking.

"That battle we observed ... Who were they ... warriors from that city?" Shermee looked out into the darkness like she could see those men fighting again.

Quinor tilted his head as he also thought of that battle. "Well, probably from a fortress or large city nearby … Maybe they came from the capital … but probably not." Quinor was wondering where a castle might be as he stared up at the princess.

"Tomorrow … we need to find those men and have them take us to Manhattoria." Shermee's confidence was surprising to the warrior, but he was loving it as well.

"Then tomorrow, my princess … my queen!" Quinor said, smiling as he said that word. Unlike before when he said it … this time he really meant it, as the fire's glow on her face made her look like a queen, he thought, as did her beauty.

* * *

King Mass-Lorak stood at the top of the hill as he watched his warriors march below. Standing not far away were three heavily armed elven guards that protected him. He watched proudly as the 20,000-strong army, the pride of the elven people, moved its way through this, the oldest and most protected forest of these elven lands.

As he stared at his army moving among the trees, he started to get the feeling that he was being watched. He pushed the feeling away for the moment, but as he did so, the sickness he was feeling returned. He held his stomach tightly as he watched the elven cavalry ride down the road behind his warriors, the light reflecting off their spears and shining brightly back at him.

Mass-Lorak had been informed that Methnorick had moved his massive army to block any escape to the west. Methnorick didn't understand that he was blocked by the high cliffs that were part of the Pilo'ach Mountains, so he also had no escape route. Mass-Lorak was wondering what Methnorick had in mind when the feeling came back suddenly as he felt movement behind him. Lifting his chin up and slowly pulling his sword out of his belt as the feeling got stronger and stronger, he thought of using his magic.

"I was wondering if you might return," Mass-Lorak mumbled quietly.

Quickly turning around as he spoke, he pulled the sword out from its sheath and lifted his other hand to release a spell from his private stash. As he whispered, a large ball of fire shot across the hill and slammed into the figure that Mass-Lorak had sensed.

He watched as the fire enveloped the figure. Turning his attention to his guard for a moment, he saw that each of the warriors that had been there to watch and guard his back was dead. Each was now was a statue of stone.

Anger quickly rose within him when he saw the pain they had suffered on their faces. Then he looked over at the figure that was covered in flames. As he watched, the flames slowly disappeared, and the cloaked figure laughed as it stretched out its arms, hands open.

"I remember how much you enjoyed the use of fire," the haunting voice said loudly from underneath the hood as the last of the flames died away. That voice Mass-Lorak knew well, too well.

Raising his face slightly, he watched as more figures covered in similar black cloaks slowly made their way up the hill from below, each bent over slightly, one hobbling as it walked, another looking like it was dragging its foot. Looking back quickly, he saw that he was clearly alone — his people couldn't see him.

"Time has changed you!" Mass-Lorak said quietly as he watched the four cloaked figures come and stand behind the first, which he had hoped would die from the flames.

"Mass-Lorak … I want your head!" At that, it pulled out a sword and charged directly at Mass-Lorak, who easily deflected the first and second blows that slammed into him. Mass-Lorak swung around with his blade, reaching to cut the creature's head off, only to find empty space.

The elven king struck back time and time again as the two

danced around on top of the hill, each striking down and up at the other. From the corners of his eyes, Mass-Lorak saw the other four robed figures standing by and watching, letting him know that it was just the two of them ... for now.

He pushed back to give himself room when the creature slammed into him, striking down Mass-Lorak's sword. This caused an instant explosion of light and sparks, which blew the combatants back to the edge of the hill, giving each a moment's rest.

Each looked at the other angrily. Mass-Lorak's mind shot through his options, finally thinking of something good to strike with as explosions surrounded the black-robed creature.

After a long while of fighting, seeing that neither could get through the other's defenses, both jumped back to take a moment to observe the other. Mass-Lorak looked hard at the being in front of him that he had once known, long ago.

"U'Traa ... you know you cannot defeat me," Mass-Lorak said quietly as his hand twitched slightly, sending forth a tremendous barrage of arrows out of nowhere that shot across the mound and into the black-robed U'Traa, who straightened up as the arrows slammed into him.

The knight didn't move as arrow after arrow struck him in the chest and torso. Knowing that the arrows would not kill U'Traa, that the knight was too strong for such a simple attack, Mass-Lorak readied himself for another attack.

Searching his mind deeply for anything to defend himself against U'Traa's next attack, Mass-Lorak opened his mouth slightly as U'Traa fell to his knees and dropped his sword, which clanged as the metal hit the ground. A thought came to Mass-Lorak as he slowly walked towards the man, his right palm open and ready, his blade pointing directly at the hood covering U'Traa's head.

Looking over quickly at the other four robed servants, he understood they were here to keep Mass-Lorak's own warriors from helping their king. He realized that U'Traa had somehow blocked his people from seeing what was happening to him.

He stopped a few feet away from U'Traa as he observed that the knight wasn't moving now, still kneeling on the ground from the arrow attack. Mass-Lorak kept his sword at the ready as he stood and waited to see if U'Traa was still able to move and attack.

"This is the end of you, my friend. Your tricks ... everything that your master had hoped for ... It ends now!" Mass-Lorak whispered to the robed knight. Before the elven king could finish, U'Traa jumped up quickly, and the arrows that had been embedded in his body shot out, striking Mass-Lorak hard in the chest before the elf could defend himself. Mass-Lorak's eyes shot open wide at the surprise attack.

The elven king stumbled back quickly, gasping from the instant pain as he watched the knight step forward slowly. As Mass-Lorak fell back, he dropped his sword on the ground and grabbed the arrows, trying to pull them out as U'Traa reached up and grabbed the king's throat. With a quick move, the knight pushed the elf to his knees.

"Defeat me? How? I am already dead, King. Remember ... you already killed me!" U'Traa's red eyes glowed bright with anger. U'Traa laughed as he squeezed his armored hand and watched the life slowly start to leave the elf's eyes. Leaning forward so his face was almost touching Mass-Lorak's, he spoke again, his haunting voice booming on top of the hill.

"Know this, elf ... Behind me rides the horse that brings death to your people, and I am his messenger." At that, U'Traa released Mass-Lorak, who fell to his knees, breathing hard from the pain. He wondered how he had never seen this in his dreams, for, before today, he had always known what was to come. Looking up to observe the knight through his tears, he watched the creature turn to walk away, only to turn around and push his sword deep into the chest of the elven king, ending the oldest reign in the lands in one quick movement. Mass-Lorak gargled as dark blood shot out of his mouth and down the front of his chest.

Keeping his blade deep within the elf's chest, the knight spat at him, cursing him for what he had done to the knight cycles earlier. Then, in a quick movement, he pulled the sword out, causing blood to erupt from the open wound and spill out on the ground. U'Traa turned completely around, and in one sudden swing, he cut the king's head completely off and watched it tumble not far away. Throwing the elven king's decapitated body to the ground, U'Traa walked over, lifting up the head and smiling as he continued over and stood before the four others.

When he lifted up his sword covered in the king's dark blood, each of the cloaked creatures began to scream along with him. The terrifying high-pitched scream of victory wasn't heard past the hill until the spell that surrounded the elven army slowly lifted. As they heard the chilling screams of U'Traa and his servants, each and every elf instantly felt within them that the reign of Mass-Lorak, King of Fuunidor and Nakalor and all the elven kingdoms throughout the lands, was dead. This feeling shot out like a wave of light to the borders of the forest and beyond.

* * *

Kikor and Niallee walked quietly but quickly down the forest road that the elven king had told the group to follow earlier, taking them to the eastern edge of the elven city's border. Animals watched them as they quietly followed the rest of the group when the feeling that something had gone terribly wrong struck them both hard in the chest.

Stopping, each looked at the other with concern and placed their hands on their chests, wondering what it might be. Suddenly Niallee's watering eyes showed the answer: King Mass-Lorak, their high king, was dead. The two elves grabbed each other and comforted one another. Chansor walked up to stop and watch the two for a moment, wondering what they were crying about.

As the thief opened his mouth to ask a question, a terrifying scream suddenly sent a terrible chill down his back, making him grab his sword in fear of whatever it was that stood next to him. Kikor and Niallee did the same as they let each other go and pulled out their sword and staff. Looking around, Chansor wondered what the noise was, hoping the two elven warriors knew.

"Kikor?" Holan called from up the trail ahead of the three. He came running down, his armor clanking loudly. "What is that sound?" The sound of the dwarf's voice told Chansor that he wasn't the only one that felt the chills.

Kikor looked at Holan, who was holding his battle-axe at the ready. The only words that left her mouth gave Chansor chills: "Move … and move quickly, my friends." At that, she and Niallee seemed to jump upon the wind as they quickly moved down the trail and past the rest of the group, who had stopped when the scream had reached their ears again.

They moved more quickly down the road, hoping to get away from the scream. As the scream repeated again and again, it sounded like it was getting farther away until they reached a turn in the road and saw the bridge they needed to cross. A large group of elven warriors stood guard on this side of the bridge, ready to repel whatever was making the noise.

"Hello brothers … Have you heard?" Kikor asked, reaching the bridge first. As she ran up, the elves thought at first that maybe she had been making that scream and were about to defend themselves until they saw that she was one of their own.

"Are you Kikor Ru'unn?" one of the warriors asked, lowering his sword as he saw Niallee coming out of the forest up the road.

Nodding quickly, Kikor confirmed that she was and that her group was coming up soon. "You know what it is, friend?" she asked as a horse was brought up for her to ride.

Shaking his head no, the elf told her that, for a while now, those screams had been coming from everywhere, and so far, they couldn't figure out where they were coming from. As he told her this, another echo of the scream hit them.

"These mounts I have ordered are for you and your group … these weapons as well, if needed, and enough supplies of food for a week's journey, my lady. May I ask where are you all traveling to?" the elf asked as his warriors handed the reins to each member of the group as they arrived from running down the road.

"Blath 'Na … Why do you ask?" Kalion inquired as he stepped forward upon hearing the elves' whispers.

Nodding, the elf smiled at the ranger. "Then all the glory of the gods be with you and your group, as the east of this kingdom has gone dark and evil with creatures … Even our king has been unable to stop them from entering."

"Have you seen any?" Niallee asked another elf, who shook his head no.

"We have only heard their screams and movement. When we've gone out there to find and fight them off, our people have not returned, so by the king's orders, none of his people are to go past this bridge," the elf said as the group saw that the bridge, made of bright silver and gold, had a massive statue on either side representing an elven king or god none could recognize. Every few feet, a pillar stuck up like an arrow with an animal of some kind on the end, making the bridge look like it was alive in some way.

"Are you Kalion, sir?" the lead elf asked, patting the neck of the ranger's horse, which huffed, making both smile.

"I am, sir," Kalion calmly answered as he smoothed the horse's nose a little, hoping that the screams weren't scaring it.

"Then I have something for you, sir … a gift from our king to you." The elf walked over to a pile of weapons that were leaning against the statue on their side of the bridge and lifted up a cloth-covered object and handed it to Kalion, who stared at the elf, slightly confused about what the elf was giving him.

"King Mass-Lorak had in his possession some of the mightiest weapons in the lands of Marn, sir … and I'm told this might help you in your upcoming journeys," the elf said quietly as he handed the ranger the object. Kalion gently took it with both hands, not understanding what it was.

Kalion looked over at Kikor, who smiled gently and nodded for him to open it. She considered a gift from the king to be something not to worry about or fuss about. She watched Kalion unwrap the object to find within the cloth a sword, and not a regular-looking one either.

"Wow!" Kalion whispered as he completely removed the cloth from the sword. The silverish shine from the blade reflected in his eyes as he stared at it, turning it over slightly as he did so. He could see writing engraved deep in the side of the blade on both sides — a language he didn't know, but maybe elvish.

Kikor, along with the rest, walked over to look at the gift Kalion had just received. He lifted it up so she could look at the writing. "Any idea?" He looked at the elf who had just given it to him, and the warrior shrugged his shoulders, not understanding the writing either.

Kikor and Niallee leaned over and looked at the engraving. Neither could understand it, but when Kikor gasped, Kalion looked at her directly, tightening his face, hoping she knew something.

"What? You know what it says?"

She shook her head slightly. "No ... not all of it, but ... this language is one I saw a long time ago. My father once said it was what the gods spoke before there was a Marn. The only word I can understand is *Stormwind* ... It could be the name of this weapon." Kikor leaned back.

"Stormwind ... interesting name," Holan piped in as the horse behind him whinnied a bit and another scream echoed through the trees.

"Whatever that sound is, I think we need to leave, my friend," Whelor said as he tilted his head slightly.

Kikor looked directly at her friend and leaned in close so that only she and Kalion could hear. "Whelor is right ... We need to leave. Take the sword as the best gift you're probably going to get, my friend." Kikor smiled at Kalion, who nodded.

Placing the sword into the scabbard that was in the cloth binding, the ranger lifted it up and over his shoulder, letting it settle on his right shoulder as he and the others lifted themselves up onto the saddles of their horses.

As Kalion was taking in the gift, Amlora and Chansor were packing up the supplies on their horses, each taking enough to feed the group. As they all firmly settled in, the group turned around and slowly trotted over the bridge until only Kikor was left with the elven warriors guarding the bridge.

"What are your orders now?" Kikor asked, looking down at the leader of the warriors, who held onto her bridle as he looked up, smiling back at her.

"Bar anything from getting in from the east," the elf said calmly as he patted the horse's side.

"How are you going to do that?" she asked, looking at the bridge and at the group of elves who were lifting up their packs like they were going to leave as well.

Breathing in a long breath of air, the warrior looked sadly at the bridge and then up to Kikor, smiling slightly. "We are to blow it after you leave us, my lady." Hearing this, she gasped. She looked at the bridge and all its beauty and then back at the elf, whose look confirmed that he was going to do it.

"You cannot do that … What if …"

Cutting her off quickly, the elf told her that it was his orders. "And it's our people or the beauty of this bridge, my lady. I chose the lives of my people over this object." The group stepped away just as another scream echoed closer to them, making the group of elves a bit more anxious to leave.

"You need to leave NOW, my lady!" the elf said sternly. Kikor looked at the elf one more time and then kicked the hinds of the horse, calling for it to move as she galloped across the bridge. Once she was on the far side, she stopped and turned her horse around to look back.

The elf and a few others who had watched her leave lifted their hands up to wave goodbye. She answered by doing the same, and then pulling her reins, she turned and galloped away to catch the others.

It was when she had travelled at least a mile's distance that she and the others heard the massive explosion, confirming that the elves had, indeed, destroyed the bridge and their only way back to the elven city.

* * *

Bennak burst from the woods to find a grove that was open enough to let some light down onto the ground. Bennak leaned down, putting his hands on his knees as he took in a deep breath and rested for a moment.

He had been running away from the orcs now for who knew how long? The group that he had fought as Jebba had disappeared had been easily killed, but when he had run to try to catch up to his friend, he had confronted another large group of orcs that had somehow cut him off.

Not knowing if Jebba had been killed by them and thrown down the cliff, he charged into the group of orcs, his anger taking over as he screamed a battle cry he knew from a long ago, making a few orcs hesitate in their charge.

To Bennak, the fight felt like moments, but it didn't end until his large frame was covered in black blood and guts as he finally scared off a few orcs, who turned and ran away, giving the large man a chance to get away before the orcs would be able to gather and counterattack him.

He looked around at the trees, his heavy breathing echoing. *This is a peaceful place,* he quickly thought as the breeze blew through the trees. Quietly, he stood up and stretched his back, listening to hear if the orcs were still chasing him. So far … nothing.

He slowly walked across the grove towards an opening that was part of an animal trail. As he walked across the grove, a light showed up ahead and something caught his eye.

Looking behind for anything that might be watching him and seeing nothing, he kneeled down, reaching out and picking up a small object that was lying on the ground. He stood back up and looked at what turned out to be a necklace in his hand. The necklace was elven in design, but like nothing he had ever seen before. He moved his hand lightly across the item to give himself a better feel of what he held. He felt writing along the back of the item, but not knowing elven as well as some of the others, he couldn't read the writing when he turned it over.

A small red jewel sat at the top of intertwining gold and silver. He looked more closely at the necklace when his ears picked up movement coming from behind him.

Believing the orcs had finally caught up to him, Bennak turned quickly and lifted his sword, cursing himself for wasting time. Planting his feet securely on the ground, he readied himself. He watched the forest in front of him burst open, and something that he had never seen but had heard about from tales came roaring towards him. Bennak had heard from some of the elves and Meradoth earlier that Methnorick had used magic of some kind to make all kinds of creatures.

The creature, seeing Bennak, screamed a high-pitched whine, hurting Bennak's ears. As it charged towards him, it raised a huge, ugly-looking sword, dripping with what looked like blood. Bennak, not wanting to give it a chance to get the upper hand, screamed himself and charged towards the creature.

The two smashed into each other hard, metal clashing against metal and grunt echoing grunt, as each fought hard, trying to kill the other as quickly as possible.

The creature's eyes and face were almost like an elf's, but this creature's eyes glowed a bright fire-red as it moved in front of him.

Bennak took a large swing with his sword, making the other

creature duck down and back away. As it did, Bennak was able to jump back to take a moment's rest. Suddenly, catching Bennak by surprise, the elf creature laughed and, with a bright flash, disappeared from Bennak's sight.

Bennak quickly moved his head around, quickly scanning the grove. *It had to have used some type of magic*, he thought. Seeing nothing, Bennak wondered what had just happened to the creature as he turned around slowly with his sword up in defense. Still hearing and seeing nothing for a few moments more, Bennak took this chance to get away in case this was some trick of Methnorick's or the creature was playing a mind game with him.

Taking a few long strides, Bennak made it to the other side of the grove, where a trail had been made by animals. Pushing past some low-hanging branches, the big man moved with no effort down the trail, past fallen trees and a few deer that were nearby, only to see them dash deeper in the woods to get away from him.

He hoped that what had happened was not the woods playing tricks on him but something else … something he could kill. He didn't know how long he would be in these woods or where Jebba had gone, but he reached a field or clearing, he was sure he would find himself fighting elves, orcs or even humans, meaning he had to stay within the woods or he wouldn't last long.

Chapter Fifteen

Methnorick had moved his chariot to the top of a small knoll that overlooked the elven forest. Looking around, he watched his orcs moving themselves into position to charge into the forest when ordered.

Looking to his right, he watched as the large war machines moved in behind the army, getting themselves into position. A few were already releasing their massive rocks, which instantly turned into flaming balls of fire. He listened to his giants grunt and watched their muscles flex as they lifted rocks onto the cradles.

"My lord ... the armies are ready for your orders," a servant of Methnorick's said from behind as Methnorick watched his Blingo'oblin legion march into position as well. He could just make out their captain, Joocc Pama, screaming orders to be ready.

Methnorick smiled as he watched his mages hit the forest with lightning, causing fires to erupt deep within the walls of the forest. He continued to watch as a servant came running towards him. This one was wearing greyish armor and had flowing blond hair coming from his head. A manservant, he thought, as he watched the man coming up.

"My lord ... General Kaligor ordered me to inform you that he is not far behind me." The blond man, he could see, was one of the hill barbarians the cyclops general had recruited a long time ago.

Methnorick was glad to hear about Bru Edin. He slapped his side, almost laughing. He had wondered if that place would be a hitch in his plans. Now it was gone ... and soon the dwarves would be following the men with the news he had just received from Sunorak. His smile broadened.

"Inform General Kaligor that when his army enters this field, it should form up on the southern borders and attack immediately. I want to enter this forest quickly!" Methnorick's voice made the scout shake slightly as he nodded that he understood.

Methnorick's smile moved into a straight, hard line as he raised his head, looking up to see a large bird fly across the sky. He knew that this was one of the creatures he had at his command. He wondered why it was flying overhead rather than watching Whelor and his team, making sure that Chansor did as he had been commanded, as the creature had been ordered. Watching the creature another moment and then looking down at the Blingo'oblin captain who had walked up to receive his orders, his voice quickly changed into the haunting sound all knew him by.

"Let us end this!" Upon hearing the order, the Blingo'oblin smiled, showing his jagged teeth, nodded and quickly turned, running across the field to where his legion of massive warriors waited. Methnorick then looked down across the fields before him and heard the screams from the Blingo'oblin ordering his warriors forward. The rest of army repeated the same order and quickly screamed "No mercy!" as they marched forward.

Methnorick raised his arm, and the army responded with a quick and loud roar.

The forest and mountains behind echoed with the army's roar. As it grew louder and louder, it gave the army courage to begin the assault.

"TAKE YOUR REVENGE!" Methnorick shouted. The roars grew even louder at the thought of the elves' destruction.

Smiling, Methnorick clutched his hands tightly, and with a quick movement, he opened both up. An explosion of light erupted above his hands, brightening the fields and forest around him. Instantly, explosions accrued within the forest as his armies screamed their loudest and the war machines behind him began their assault, causing more explosions of fire and light as their rocks and fire landed within the elven forest, many making the ground shake. The border that protected the elven forest seemed to have disappeared with the death of their king.

***

The dwarven warriors that were left moved themselves to the upper chambers, where the families within that area of the kingdom screamed for help from the gods, all knowing that their lives were close to ending. The screams from below moved up as the dwarves assembled a last effort to stop or at least slow the dark dwarves that were close to destroying the largest of the dwarven kingdoms upon Marn.

The only dwarf left to lead the warriors was General Hardshield's second in command. The general had fallen in the last skirmish as they retreated when the columns were falling. The dwarf hadn't been killed, but the clerics caring for him told him that dying in battle would probably have been better than being killed in bed, for the screams reached the area where the clerics were doing their best to care for the wounded, not giving much hope to those they cared for.

Prince Cu Legbasher Finfilli, son of the late king, who had also been Hardshield's second in command, was thrust to the forefront of the situation to command the last of the dwarves. The young dwarf did his best, but even with all that, he knew this was the final stand.

Finally, the dark dwarves burst out of the stone and rock that their cousins had hoped would stop them. As they begin to file out and move quickly up the last hallway, Finfilli ordered the last of his archers to wait at the entrance of the hallway to release what was left of their arsenal at the dark dwarves as they came out one by one from the rock wall. At first it seemed to work, but the archers found that it wouldn't last long, as their supplies grew low.

"Get everything — beds, cabinets, tables, everything — that we can use to block their advancement into the city. Our families won't last long. Think of them as you fight … This is our last chance!" Finfilli screamed out as he watched the dwarves quickly pull whatever they could to block the hallway entrance.

Knowing it wouldn't last long, the prince assembled a last group of warriors, which he hoped might cause at least some confusion, when the dark dwarves burst through this wooden wall they were building up.

Shaking his head slightly, he couldn't believe that he would be the last of a long line of generals and kings in this place. He began to hear the archers who had volunteered to fight a rear guard to give his warriors time to put up the wall scream out in pain as the first of the dark dwarves reached them.

"Here they come!" he screamed, making those dwarves that were holding furniture drop what they had and grab their weapons to assemble not far from the wall. They all waited, knowing that this was it.

He looked at each warrior around him and saw that they gripped their axes, spears and whatever they had tightly. Many old dwarven warriors and women, knowing that this was it, had also left the city to come and defend this last entrance.

"My lord … how could this have happened?" an old dwarf asked. The prince noticed that the old warrior could hardly hold onto the heavy axe he gripped.

Swallowing as he tried not to show the fear he held deep inside, he smiled gently at the old dwarf and then blinked and got out the only answer he could. "I know not, my friend … but we did our best to defend this fortress. All we can do is fight to the last and let the Qlorfana know that their cousins are not weak … We will die with honor here!"

The old dwarf nodded back as they looked at the wood wall beginning to collapse back towards them. The first signs of the dark dwarves' weapons could be seen pushing through, and their screams could be heard.

Finfilli and many others around him closed their eyes and said last-minute prayers to the gods, hoping that if they died, they would enter the afterlife kingdom in glory. When he opened his eyes, the wall had completely fallen back, and he watched his own warriors scream and charge forward.

"CHAI'SELL!" was heard above in the halls, where the families all held each other tightly as the battle continued. All could feel the rumble through the stone walls.

* * *

Within the forest, elven warriors released everything they had towards the orcish armies charging into their homeland. Elven captains screamed orders to the archers to release what they had as warriors assembled not far from the edge of the forest, waiting for orders to counter the orcs now moving into the shadows of their homeland.

So far no elven mages had been able to join in the battle, making it harder for the regular army, but they knew that this was their fight … Many had voiced this truth earlier, and every elf knew it would end up only one way if they didn't fight their best. The loss of their king discouraged them at first, but Methnorick had made a mistake, as the whispers moved like the wind. His charge gave them the courage to take a stand and fight. Kings come and go … Fuunidor didn't.

Far behind, lines of thousands of elven warriors stood waiting quietly for the order to charge out and wipe out the orc army that was moving into the forest. Even though scores had fallen to arrows from the elven archers, the orcs weren't stopping. The screams from the battlefield made many in the rank and file of the elven army angry. A few became nervous that they might fail their people, but luckily, many sergeants and captains saw this and tried to calm them down by repeating tales of their people from before many of them were born, telling them that, in the end, their people always made it through.

"Marn will always be elven!" they called out, bringing smiles and cheers from the Fuunidor elves. Hearing the tales of famous warriors and how their people had always lived made many feel better and gave them strength to fight for what was right.

***

Far away on the eastern edge of the forest of Fuunidor, Kikor led the way along the road as the group made its way towards the eastern border. No one spoke about what had happened with Whelor or the king's warning, or about the fight that the elves faced against Methnorick's approaching armies. No one spoke of the screams or the feelings that were creeping into the minds of everyone, but all knew something was terribly wrong around them in this forest.

Even Kalion, who had wanted to stay, knew that leaving was for the best now. He remembered what Meradoth's father had told him back in the tower. Nicolorr's warnings made him quicken his step. Methnorick had woken up the use of magic to assemble creatures never seen on the lands of Marn, but as they heard the screams that kept them on edge, Kalion wondered how these creatures had made it inside this peaceful kingdom.

The forest seemed normal to all that walked within it. Chansor, still not caring about anything, whistled as he sat on his horse, moving down the trail. The thief was bored and had wanted to stay with the elves and find out what he could, but he also wanted to see the great city of Blath 'Na, and the group wanted to get there quickly. Besides, his mission was with the group. If he had stayed with the elves and his master had caught up with him … Well, he didn't want to think about what would happen to him.

Once in a while, he was sure he could see movement in the trees, and he knew that his eyes were telling him the truth. The creature that had followed them this far kept calling to him, wanting him to kill. The creature hadn't spoken to him in a while, but looking ahead at the back of Whelor, Chansor knew his mission to kill the man was even more urgent after what he was told Whelor had done within the city.

While Chansor whistled, both Amlora and Holan, who sat together on one saddle, chatted quietly to each other. Holan spoke of how much he missed his people and wanting to get underground soon, as he was tired of being under the trees this long. He remembered the feeling of sitting in front of a raging fire within the mighty halls of his people.

Amlora giggled as she listened to the dwarf and then spoke about her time with her brothers, running in the fields, playing and being with the animals of the forests, and how it had changed her view of life upon Marn.

Both knew that this Methnorick was out to take these things from them and this journey might be the only thing that could stop him. Finding the princess might stop the evil creature somehow.

Meradoth sat mumbling quietly to himself as he read a scroll, learning new spells given to him by some elves. He would learn them quickly enough to play his part in this mission. Harbin, who was doing the same nearby, thought of ways to make skirmishes end more quickly.

Whelor sat quietly, not wanting to engage in any talk with the others, for it might bring up conversation about what had happened to him again. Niallee, who rode just behind him, held her staff in front of her on her saddle, keeping an eye on him like she was waiting for him to change again.

Upon entering the elven forest, the man had shown a side that she couldn't quite put into words. Whatever was within him, she only hoped it was something that was fighting on her side and not something that Methnorick had control over. She had asked him once, but he had turned his head and didn't answer, so now she watched him from the corner of her eye. She saw sweat run down his face like he was fighting whatever was within him.

At the end of the long line of the group rode Kalion and Kikor, each whispering to the other about the sounds that the elf was hearing. Every once in a while, she turned and watched the road behind her and the group. She whispered to the ranger about having a feeling since leaving the elven city that someone or something was watching them. Kalion watched as she quietly turned and observed the road and forest around them, listening to the sounds.

As they made their way down the road covered in leaves, a massive echo of screams burst forth. It almost sounded like they were surrounded, so they trotted into a dark grove with old trees bending low, making it too dark for the group to see.

As Kikor entered the grove, she caught sight of something moving to her left within the tree branches. Leaning over slightly, she whispered quietly to Kalion, trying to let the ranger know that something was wrong.

"We're being followed, my friend." Kalion nodded and pulled his reins to slow his mount down as Kikor did the same.

"I'll stay here in the rear and let you move forward to find a spot to watch. Then I will see if my feelings are true, and if they are ... then I will grab it," she said as her eyes found Kalion's. "Get yourself ready and be careful." Looking around at the others silently moving ahead, Kalion smiled back at the elf. Kalion suddenly felt something for the elf that he hadn't felt before ... He was worried about her.

Nodding, Kikor moved herself down like she was checking on her horse as the rest moved through the grove to the far side and disappeared down the road quickly, but not too quickly, as Kalion had told Holan to hold onto his horse as he jumped off. Kalion hid behind a large tree, waiting to see if the elf was right, and pulled out his smaller blade, not wanting to get stuck in the heavy brush.

As he did so, the ranger wondered who in their right mind would be tracking them. Could it be a scout for Methnorick or something worse, he wondered, as he breathed slowly and waited, watching his friends move on to his left.

He knew that Kikor was, in her own right, the best warrior he had ever met in battle, so he believed her warning. But since seeing Whelor's sudden change, he hesitated to believe anyone now.

And what of these feelings he was sensing for her now? He missed and loved the princess, and that was why he was here, but ... Kikor now?

"Gods above … why do you do this to me … now of all times?" he whispered quietly.

He blinked to make his vision sharp when he heard a yell and clap of something to his right. He knew that it was Kikor doing something, but he couldn't tell what until he heard the rush and snapping of branches like something was moving hard through the trees to get away from her.

Whatever it was, it sounded like it was close. He jumped out from where he hid, thinking it was probably a squirrel. As he jumped out, however, he pulled out both of his blades, bringing them up in defense, only to jump back at what he saw.

"Holy gods!" he called out just loud enough that whatever he was looking at screamed back in response. The ranger stepped back once again, not knowing what to do, as Kikor came riding up behind it, screaming for him to kill it.

Chapter Sixteen

When the first ranks of his army got within axe range of the elves, Methnorick ordered his orcs to charge hard. Soon roars from the elven forest reached his ears. He watched many orcs and goblins fall with arrows in their chests as they moved hard through the thick brush and trees, trying to get to the archers and the elven warriors that were waiting deeper within the forest. Not caring about their losses, Methnorick raised his hand and ordered another heavy barrage from his machines.

Quickly, fireballs flew up and into the forest, causing fires to explode and smoke to rise throughout the forest. With the lightning strikes, he knew it wouldn't be long before the elves would have to retreat. When he got news that his second lines were ready, he quickly ordered his goblin archers to release another deadly cloud of arrows. A smile formed at the corner of his mouth as he watched his orders being quickly carried out. A huge wave of arrows launched up into the air and over the battlefield to slam into the elven forest.

As the arrows landed, roars from within quickly turned into screams, and Methnorick's smile widened, knowing many elves were dying at that moment. Raising his arm, he gave the order for the third line to advance. This time, however, instead of just charging forward, they marched across an open area at a marching pace, holding their long pikes and spears in attack position. The third line of his army was larger than the first two lines, and this one also held within its ranks some of his most experienced warriors from the many orc tribes.

Elven archers that were lucky enough to survive both the barrage from the machines and the goblins' arrows launched another assault of their own, sending arrows slamming hard into Methnorick's advancing warriors. Methnorick watched orc after orc fall over as arrows killed one after another.

In retaliation, Methnorick gave his archers and war machines orders to return fire. Quickly, the elven arrows were overpowered by his own weapons, and the elven archers retreated to the safety of their forest. As Methnorick watched from the safety of his chariot, he observed his forces advance through the trees to enter the forest, followed soon after by the sound of elven screams.

Methnorick looked across the field and began to laugh loudly as he watched the ancient forest erupt in flames. Fiery rocks flew high into the air, lightning slammed hard into the trees, and arrows flew everywhere as his army moved.

"YESSSSS … I LOVE IT!!!!" he yelled, laughing loudly. "I LOVE IT!"

* * *

Kalion stood, still not believing his eyes as he took in the small flying creature screaming at him. It flapped its wings hard to stay in the air with the elf riding it.

Kalion jumped back quickly as Kikor succeeded in pulling the creature to the ground before it could escape and fly away. As they tumbled to the ground, the creature screamed loudly, trying to use its small claws to dig at Kikor and its fangs to grab and bite at her.

"Kalion, help me!" Kikor screamed as she tightened her grip on the unfamiliar creature, having never seen anything like it before in her life. It had to be one of Methnorick's, she thought, as her grip slipped slightly.

SMACK! Kalion's sword pommel hit the head of the creature hard enough that it stopped struggling long enough for Kikor to roll over and hold it down with her weight. Kalion pointed his sword at its throat as it moaned from being hit in the temple.

"What in all the gods is this … this thing?" Kalion asked. Kikor shook her head as they both stared at the creature.

Along with two leathery skin wings that ended in claws, it had a body like a dog but with a long tail that ended in a large, deadly looking dagger point. Its two rear legs were larger and longer than the front ones, yet all four limbs held claws that could rip skin apart with ease. But it was the head that intrigued Kikor. It reminded her of something from the legends of the gods. Its head was long, like those of the fanged crocs from the swamps that she lived near many cycles ago. Its skin was at least as leathery and muscular as that of a croc; in fact, Kikor wondered if a sword could puncture the skin. However, this creature's fangs were long enough to be elven daggers. And its eyes, she saw, were red like fire.

"You think that this was the creature making that scream?" Kalion asked. "It almost sounded like it."

"Maybe … but I believe that I heard more than one out there. This creature might not be alone, so we need to be careful." Kikor looked around the forest as she spoke. Kalion did the same.

"We should kill it before it wakes up. Its screams might have already told …"

A scream erupted from the forest, cutting Kikor off as she and Kalion looked around for the sound that was getting closer by the moment now.

"Youuuu haveeee nooo ideaaa, elffffff!" The voice sent a chill down Kikor's back as she slowly looked back down at the creature. "Release meeeee nowwww, elffff … and myyyy brotherrrr willl leaveeee youuuu!" Its tongue flapped out slightly as it talked. Its voice made Kikor swallow slowly.

What is this thing? she wondered as she stared deep into its eyes. Suddenly words began to form in her mind: release … release … release. She also felt as if the creature in her grasp was growing and changing.

Kikor lost her grip and fell back as the creature suddenly flapped its powerful wings. Kalion, whose eyes were trained on the forest in search of the creature's "brother," turned back to help Kikor just as one of the creature's wings struck his face hard enough that it knocked him back onto the ground. Free of its captors, the creature quickly flew into the air before looking down at Kikor as she watched it hover overhead.

"Youuuu are gooddd, elfffff ... I will haveeee neeeddd offff youuuu soonnn!" At that, the creature flapped its wings and quickly disappeared into the thick forest. Kikor watched it go for a moment longer, and then she blinked and turned to Kalion.

"What ... what happened, Kikor?" Kalion moaned as he got himself up slowly, holding a hand to his face as blood seeped out of the gash on his cheek. Kikor turned around to look at the ranger staring at her in confusion.

"It ... it took me by surprise and used its tail, I think, to knock me off!" Kikor lied, not knowing what to say as she walked up, pulling out a strip of cloth to wrap around his face to get the bleeding to stop.

"Are you well?" he asked quietly as she finished. Kalion eyed her closely, but she simply nodded.

"Listen ... we need to get out of here now and catch up with the rest, my friend. Whatever that thing was, it has companions out there," Kikor said as she turned away from the intensity of Kalion's stare to walk down the trail, where her horse was eating some of the tall grass. It looked up as the warrior grabbed its reins, and in a quick move, she was on top of the saddle, looking back at the ranger.

"Hurry, Kalion!" she repeated. Kalion looked at her and then back towards the dark grove, wondering what had really happened. However, as another scream pierced the air, he knew his questions would have to wait. Kalion jumped on the horse behind her, and both rode down the trail hard as more screams echoed around them.

***

Shermee and Quinor stood at the top of a hill, looking out across the fields before them, taking in the scene of the battle that had recently been waged.

"Who knows?" Quinor whispered to the princess when she asked how long they had been asleep from the witch's potion.

Below, they saw the corpses of dead orcs scattered everywhere.

Arrows had taken down a number of them, but Quinor could see that most had been killed by blades. Here and there, both could see the bodies of warriors of the empire, still adorned in their once-bright uniforms, lying dead amongst their enemies.

"I do not know how many men were in that column of warriors, but I see at least two score on the field," Quinor said, mostly to himself, but Shermee looked at him and then back down as she felt both anger and sadness at the loss of so many.

"You think the men won the day, Quinor?" Shermee asked quietly.

Quinor shrugged as he also wondered. *Orcs leave their dead where they fall, but men and elves normally try to collect their dead, if possible ... and so far I have seen no sign of any men.*

"Let us go beyond that crest, where can see more. Maybe the men are that way, my lady." He smiled slightly as he stepped forward. Both walked down the hill and made their way slowly through the field covered in dead. Half an hour later, Quinor stepped to the edge of the crest to look down onto another field, this time smiling at what he saw as Shermee made her way to his side.

"The men are just beyond that group of trees over there. I bet they are resting and caring for their wounded." Shermee looked towards where Quinor pointed. She saw a large number of cavalry and warriors gathered under the cover of trees.

"Well, let's go!" Shermee stepped forward but was stopped as Quinor grabbed her shoulder, shaking his head no.

"I think it would be better if I approached them first. You stay here, out of sight, and watch. I will go ahead and try to get their attention!" Quinor said, smiling.

Before Shermee could argue with him, Quinor stepped away, leaving his swords with her as he walked down the hill and across the field with his hands open to his sides, hoping that the men could see that he was not armed.

It didn't take them long to see him, as five heavily armed warriors moved quickly towards him, swords out behind shields. He raised his hands above his head.

"I am unarmed ... I come in peace, sir!" he called out as they screamed at him to halt.

"I'm known as Quinor ... I come from the north." He lowered his voice as the men rushed up, pointing their swords directly at his chest and throat.

"What are you doing here?" a dirt-covered man asked. The way he was dressed, Quinor took him to be in charge.

"I am traveling across the empire, sir, and saw this ... this scene and then your men here ..."

"Who are you aligned with, sir? Who do you serve?" another man demanded.

"I am myself, sir ... I serve only me," Quinor lied, not wanting to reveal the princess just yet.

"Are you alone?" the first man asked, looking past Quinor to the hill and trees beyond the warrior.

"Yes ... yes, I am alone." Quinor swallowed, looking at the men cautiously.

"Liar. You two take him to the camp ... You three go to those trees and find his companions!" Quickly, Quinor was grabbed and pushed towards the camp, which, he could see now, was full of activity.

He looked back quickly, seeing the three warriors move up to where he knew Shermee was hiding. He hoped they wouldn't kill her ... Hopefully her beauty would stop them.

***

As Kalion and Kikor caught up with the rest of the group, they were immediately pummeled with questions about what had happened and where they had been. Kalion got down off the back of the horse he had been sharing with Kikor and took his horse back from Holan as he shared the details of their encounter with the unusual creature. As he spoke, no one noticed the look of concern on Chansor's face as he looked from one point in the sky to another, watching for his friend.

The road rose slightly out of a small wooded glen and opened onto another small grassy field, where the group stopped suddenly as they observed the first real signs of something being terribly wrong in this forest.

In the middle of the field lay three dead deer. But it wasn't the animals that made the group pull their reins hard — it was the sight of what had apparently killed them.

Kneeling around the deer were ten or more beings digging into the bodies of the fallen animals as if they hadn't eaten for cycles.

Every one of them was covered in blood as they mindlessly chewed on the raw flesh. The sight of some pulling out the insides of the animals made Amlora groan slightly and look away, feeling slightly sick.

"Any ideas?" Kalion whispered just loud enough for the group to hear. All shook their heads, not knowing what to make of the sight, as Kikor looked for a way to get around them. Unfortunately, the opening where the road continued through the forest was on the other side of the creatures.

"Kalion … there is the opening. If we're quiet enough, maybe we can get close enough to make a dash for it before those things can get to us," Kikor pointed out.

Kalion nodded to her and turned in the saddle to look at the others. "I'll go first. Take it slowly, but be ready to move quickly … Understand?" Kalion stared at each of them until they nodded.

Kalion gently kicked his horse forward and slowly moved along the edge of the field to get around. Once he had made it past the creatures, he waited as each member followed until only Whelor remained.

As Whelor watched Kikor go, he gripped his reins tightly as the sight and smell of the blood and animal carcasses being eaten not far from him began to overwhelm his senses. Unfortunately, he couldn't help but groan over the effort, which caught the attention of one of the creatures.

Kalion saw the same thing that Whelor did as the creature stood up and began to stumble towards him. This attracted the attention of his companions as one creature after another stood up and began to move towards the big man.

Cursing, Kalion pulled out his blade and signaled to Whelor to hurry when, suddenly, the creatures let out a chilling scream, confirming to Kalion and the others that these were the screams they kept hearing in the forest.

"WHELOR ... MOVE!!!!!" Kalion yelled. However, Whelor needed no further urging. He kicked his horse hard, just as the first creature got within a few feet of him and the mount.

Kalion now noticed that a few wore the uniforms of the elven warriors from his kingdom. He cursed again under his breath as he got a better look at them. Their ripped and bloodstained clothing had been evident from the start, but now he could see their faces. They all looked ... dead. Blood leaked from their mouths slightly, their skin appeared to be decaying, and the smell ... was undeniable.

He had seen enough. As he turned to catch up with the others, he only hoped that he wouldn't have to fight them off. Somehow he got the feeling that if they hurt him ... he might become one of them.

* * *

The scouts he saw came riding hard back across the open field, keeping themselves close to their horses to cut the wind better. *They must be bringing terrible news,* Dia thought as he watched them approach.

So far the journey from the elven glen to this point had been uneventful. They had seen no signs of orcs on the field, but there were many signs that they had traveled this way. How many, he couldn't tell, but he heard a few elves guessing aloud that the number must be in the thousands. Here and there they saw a weapon that had been dropped, and early in the morning, they passed a dead hill barbarian. The lack of action gave Dia plenty of time to talk to the warriors around him. He couldn't help but think of his son Frei as he listened to their excitement and hopes for getting revenge for the villages, brothers and sisters that had fallen to Methnorick so far. They all hoped to meet the Dark One on the field of battle, and soon. Dia could see that many of them were new to battle, even though, as elves, most were probably many cycles older than Dia. He only hoped for the strength to last throughout the long battle he knew was coming.

As he turned his attention back to the scouts speaking to the elven leaders, a rumble began to spread down the lines of warriors. They were close. Dia smiled as broadly as the warriors by his side as one of the elven generals began to address the restless group.

"Over that rise, our enemy engages with our cousins. There we will stop him … There we will mark his grave with our sword. Today we begin the end of Methnorick!" the warrior yelled. Nodding at Dia, he continued, "Today we will have our revenge for what Methnorick did to Brigin'i and Levenori!" Dia thrust his fist high in the air and yelled out the name of his homeland as others around him did the same.

As Dia readied himself for the battle ahead, he saw the forward lines move away from the main part of the army, riding their horses hard until they were only points on the horizon.

"Where do you think they are going?" he asked the warrior who had been assigned to be his guard during the march, an elf over 200 cycles of age. The warrior smiled at Dia as he responded.

"Those warriors are going to attack Methnorick's army. Either way … he will know we are coming!"

"The Dark One made a terrible choice — he separated his armies too much!" another of the elves behind him called out. "This means victory for us, for he stands no chance." Everyone around Dia cheered as he nodded in approval.

The night before, Dia had made sure his sword was the sharpest it had ever been. Each weapon he could get his hands on now lay on the side of his horse: a small bow, a clutch of arrows, three smaller swords and a long dagger. He had no plans to meet Methnorick empty-handed, he had told the swordsmith, who had just nodded back.

Dia thought of his wife, Shermeena. Her face floated before him, as did those of his sons. They were all dead now, all killed by Methnorick. Finally, the image of his daughter came to him. He wondered if the group he'd asked to find his daughter was still alive. Had they found his daughter? Dia gripped his reins tightly and shook his head to clear his thoughts as the army began to pick up speed. The time for vengeance was upon him.

* * *

The dark dwarf warriors were cheering and yelling over the success of their victory so loudly that the dark elves walking between them had to cover their ears. They understood why the smaller creatures were so happy. It had taken these dirty creatures many cycles to realize their dreams of seeing the mighty Chai'sell fall. Now that victory was theirs, the dark dwarves ran everywhere, trying to find jewels and weapons and celebrating their victory in other ways.

Banners were ripped down from the "Kings Hall," and armor that lay on the walls was pulled down.

After all, none of the king's family still lived after the prince had been killed trying to defend a family against a score of dark dwarves in one of the upper halls.

"No matter if any of them survive … This is the Qlorfana's now," the dark elf in command said as he and the other elven warriors watched the dark dwarves celebrate. "How many of these Qlorfana live? Do you have numbers?" he asked, grunting as another one of the excited dwarves pushed by, not caring that he almost knocked the elf commander over as he struggled to carry a large chest full of coin. As he set it down, he and the chest were surrounded by what looked like hundreds of their kin.

"I believe there are about one thousand, but probably less ... That last skirmish in which the enemy was able to collapse the ceiling killed many," one of the smaller elves replied.

Nodding, the commander turned and walked out of crowded area, ordering, "Find me the leader of these Qlorfana and bring him to me in the guards' chamber at the very top of Chai'sell.

Pushing himself past happy dark dwarves heavily weighed down with the trophies, the commander found himself standing before the giant gate that led to the outside, opening south onto the Edin Plains. On the other side were orcs that had been ordered to make sure no one escaped.

As he stood there, wondering how to open the gate, a loud grunt from behind made him turn his head as a dirty, bloody dwarf covered in gold chains and jewels approached. Unlike their cousins, the dark dwarves didn't have kings, so this disgusting creature was the closest thing they had to a chief to lead them.

"You called, elf?"

"This kingdom is yours now ... but outside this gate are thousands of orcs, and they want in!"

"Ahhhh, let them rot out there in the rain. This is ours ... not theirs!" the dwarf yelled back, cutting the elf off. "My people — not those things out there — fought and died here ... This is ours!" He repeated this again and again as he stared up at the elven warrior, who could only smile back.

"I understand, dwarf ... so my people are leaving. Run this place how you want. Just know ... the orc creature will want it as well!" With that, the dark elf walked past the dwarf and returned to where his own were gathering in an antechamber, leaving the dark dwarves' chief to stare at his back and look up at the massive gate, cursing it as he did.

"You will not open ever!" he yelled at the gate. With his attention on the gate, the dark dwarf chief didn't notice the dark elf locate the lever that unlocked the massive stone doors. Chai'sell might have been in the dark dwarves' hands for the moment, but not for long.

Chapter Seventeen

Methnorick watched as his orcs charged into the forest line, screaming cries of victory as they made their way in. Suspecting that the elves would have a trap awaiting his warriors, he turned and nodded to a servant, who ran off to relay his orders.

Soon he heard the war machines stop their assault as they were slowly moved forward by the hill giants. As they took their new positions, the orc archers followed suit, stopping their assault and moving forward until they stood just before the forest's edge.

As he watched his forces move into their new positions, Methnorick heard cries of pain coming from the orcs engaged in the forest fight with the elves.

Methnorick was just about to begin the next advance of his army when he saw movement to the south as something was slowly making its way north towards where his army was.

"Kaligor!" he said quickly. "Finally!"

Not wanting to wait for Kaligor's arrival, he quickly sent a scout to intercept the group, with orders for the cyclops to begin his attack. Turning his attention back to the army he was leading, Methnorick gave the signal for the next assault to begin as well as orders for his reserves to stay ready in case the elves somehow were able to launch a counterattack.

Inside the thick forest, his orcs were gaining ground deep in the elven kingdom despite sustaining massive losses. For every elf killed, five orcs met their end.

Meanwhile, the elves were struggling in their battle to hold back the Blingo'oblins, which had succeeded in pushing past the shield walls. Despite knowing the forest floor by memory, the elves began to sustain heavy losses as they tried to counter the huge creatures, only to be pushed back time and time again.

When the orc archers entered the forest with the next wave, the elves finally pulled back to a point where a large cliff looked over the main road that wound itself through the forest. From here, two elven mages set up traps, hoping that the Blingo'oblins would fall into them, giving the elves more time.

Finally, the reserves that Methnorick had placed at the back of the army were ordered forward. Methnorick smiled as they entered the fray, knowing that this group would achieve its objective of making a hole within the elven lines.

Soon battle cries echoed everywhere on both sides, and arrows flew wildly, knocking down warriors on both sides. Pleas for help came from seemingly everywhere as clerics moved through the ranks and did their best to help the wounded, risking death themselves as the orcs attacked areas where the wounded had been assembled.

Having been informed of Kaligor's arrival, General Summ ordered the lines to move back and form at the Polanii Gorges, an area where three gorges came together to form a deep expanse that would not be easily crossed. Here, the elven general knew, his warriors could hold off the orcs.

As they moved near the cliff, the mages went to work. Some used their elven magic to collapse the floor of the forest, trapping the approaching orcs, while others forced large boulders down into the gorge, crushing several more scores of the dark-cloaked creatures.

"It is done, my lord …" Methnorick turned to find his favorite servant kneeling as he delivered the news.

"Speak." Methnorick stepped forward as Lord U'Traa stood up, pulling back the hood of the black cloak he wore to reveal the face of a once-powerful elven warrior. Now, in its place was a decayed face with fury burning in the reddish eyes.

"The king is dead … Your quest is complete, my lord!" the raspy voice echoed out of the skull as the eyes looked at the Dark One, who just nodded.

"King Mass-Lorak … King Dia … and King Finfilli … They are all out of my way!" Methnorick smiled as he turned to look at the battle below, feeling confident that victory was in his grasp, when suddenly he got a burning sensation in his head that only he could feel.

Not wanting his servants to see his discomfort, Methnorick walked towards a nearby grove of trees, as if seeking privacy. Once there, surrounded by darkness, he knelt down quickly on the ground as the burning pain began to overwhelm him. *My lords … I obey and wait for your message,* he thought hard as his eyes began to water.

Methnorickkkk … you have done well … but we await word that is it done! the voice echoed as tears started to fall down his face from the pain.

I finish this today, my lords … My word is given to you! he thought, almost crying as he formed the words in his mind.

We will hold you to that promise. Suddenly the pain disappeared. As he opened his eyes and shook his head, he realized that someone was yelling his name. When he stood up and walked out of the grove, he was met by U'Traa, who was standing there, looking at him with an intensity he hadn't thought the dead elf capable of.

* * *

Kalion and the others had finally reached the eastern edge of Fuunidor Forest, fighting hard to get there since leaving the Whispering Bridge. To them, it seemed a cycle since they had been standing within the elven capital city.

No one could remember just how many skirmishes they had fought against the screaming creatures to get to this point. All they knew was that the creatures had kept moving, regardless of which weapons had been used against them. As a result, the only thing the group could do was ride hard to get out of the area whenever they had encountered them.

Luckily, no one had gotten hurt in any of the fights, but they were now exhausted from lack of sleep. Each time they tried to rest, another group of creatures came out of the darkness of the forest. One particularly close call resulted in the loss of two horses, so Holan, Chansor and Amlora had to ride with others. Now, as they looked across the massive expanse that lay before them, they could finally see their destination: Blath 'Na City.

"I have a bad feeling about this, Kikor ... but too late now!" Meradoth said calmly as he squinted his eyes. All could see the city's wall in the far distance. "And naturally there is yet another group of those despicable creatures moving this way." The mage sighed as he pointed to a group of thirty or more creatures slowly approaching their position.

"Well, Kalion ... the city is there. How about we get moving before those things get to us?" Kikor said, almost smiling at the ranger, who nodded back at her.

"Whatever it is that burns within that place ... hopefully we can find shelter for the night and finally learn where the princess is!" No one was inclined to argue. Kalion hit his horse's hind with the reins and was quickly followed by the rest of the tired group as they rode hard along the road towards the City of Ports.

✻ ✻ ✻

Quinor cringed as he watched the soldiers drag Shermee into the tent, knowing instinctively that he'd failed her again. He could see that she had fought them as hard as she could, and noticed that one of the soldiers was missing. Had she actually managed to kill one of the men with the sword he'd left with her? As he listened to the soldier give his report to General Vana, a smile crept to his lips as he heard how Shermee had made the man pay for touching her by kicking him so hard in the crotch that they had had to leave him there for a while as he cried out like a child.

Ordering the soldiers to send a cleric to the wounded man and to wait outside the tent, General Vana stood up from his chair to look at her and then back at Quinor.

After what seemed like an hour, the stone-faced general uncrossed his arms and pointed to Quinor as he addressed Shermee. "This man lies. So are you going to tell me what you two are really doing here, or should I have the both of you executed right now?"

If his life hadn't been on the line, Quinor might have laughed at the speed with which Shermee told her tale, from the moment of her kidnapping to her last encounter with the old witch.

Quinor held his breath the entire time, praying that she wouldn't reveal his role in her troubles. Not that he'd really blame her at this point. Thus far, he'd hardly been what one would expect of a queen's champion. In fact, she had saved his life far more often than he'd returned the favor. Just as she was saving his life right now … yet again. As she neared the end of the story, Quinor vowed to himself that he'd never fail her again. That is, if they lived through this interview. "Sea elves … I heard they were only a myth of some type," Vana whispered.

"They are real, sir!" Shermee said, smiling as she thought back to their underwater journey.

"My orders are to guard the Father Gate … Somehow advancing orcs were able to get by us somehow," Vana responded as he stared at Shermee, arms crossed, trying to decide if he believed her. Finally, he appeared to come to a decision. Nodding, he uncrossed his arms and sat back down at his desk. "I believe that we should get you to the capital before you head any farther north at this point."

"Have you heard any news from the north, sir?" Shermee asked.

Vana shook his head. "Not for weeks now."

"Can you help us, General?" Shermee asked, hoping that they could at least get a horse to help them get to the city more quickly, but the general had turned his attention back to Quinor, who looked decidedly uncomfortable yet also determined as he met the general's gaze.

"What is it now? I suggest you refrain from lying to me."

"Sir, I'd lie to the gods themselves if it meant keeping the princess safe from harm."

General Vana peered at the young man bravely holding his gaze and nodded in approval. "Speak."

"Sir, there's a bit more you should know."

Quinor then explained what the witch woman had told them about who Shermee really was: the queen from the legend.

"I have heard of this legend … What makes you think that this girl here is the empress of this legend and not just some lost princess?" Vana asked. "No offense, ma'am."

Shermee just waved her hand at the general, eager to hear what Quinor would say next. After all, she too wanted to know how he could be so sure.

Quinor explained, "I have a vivid vision — not a dream, but something I can't get out of my mind — and I am not sure where it comes from, but I have had it since we awoke on that beach. I can see her standing on a balcony with all types of humans, elves, dwarves and other creatures hanging on her every word."

"If the legend is true … and you are to be the queen of the empire … we must help set you in the right direction. But know this: The one that runs the empire currently will not be easily swayed and will not give up power. According to the legend Quinor recounted, you still have two more trials to overcome. I believe Minister Halashii may be one of those, but be warned … Do not trust him." Suddenly Vana stood up and walked around the desk. He motioned to the still seated pair. "Come with me."

Glancing at each other, Quinor and Shermee jumped up to do as ordered. Stepping outside the tent, they found the general already giving orders for ten of his men to accompany the pair to Manhattoria. As the men prepped for the journey, the general took

Shermee off to the side to speak to her privately.

An hour later, Quinor, Shermee and ten men were on the road towards Manhattoria, comfortably riding horses provided by Vana as Shermee thought back to the conversation she had had with the general.

"Just keep your ears open ... There will be people you can count on within the city ... but be careful who you choose to trust with the whole story." Shermee thought about those words again.

"The outcome will determine what happens next, but I will send everything I can to assist the empire to its rightful end!" Shermee was not sure what that assistance would look like, but she prayed to the gods that she would be prepared for whatever would come next.

Chapter Eighteen

The elven scouts moved quietly along a road that wound through the small canyon that separated the Pilo'ach Mountains from another, smaller range of mountains.

As the scouts trotted through, they could see the heavy black smoke rising high into the sky south of where they were, and slowly, as they moved closer and closer, they could hear the familiar sounds of battle: the screams, explosions and more that were quietly echoing against the walls of the canyon.

Catching sight of the orcish army below after jumping off their horses to make their silhouettes smaller, they quickly took in the positions of everything. Then, jumping back on their saddles, they rode hard back north, meeting the elven army marching just north of the canyon's northern entrance.

When the leaders of the army were informed of how close they were, they sent out word for everyone to be ready to move like an arrow. Dia and a few giants that were walking near him could be heard grumbling that it was about time.

Pulling out his sword and holding it tightly in his grip, Dia waited for the words "Charge hard, charge fast and take no prisoners."

As banners were unfolded and held high around him, Dia tilted his head slightly down, eyeing the canyon as he caught sight of the smoke now. He didn't have the same sight as the elves, but the smoke told him they were close.

"FOR MARN!" The scream echoed loudly across the lines of elven and frost giant warriors as they quickly began to move forward and pour through the canyon as though it were an opening in a wall to burst out at the southern end, screaming for blood.

* * *

Methnorick seethed as he raced towards Kaligor's position. U'Traa had pointed out to him that the elves were not only counterattacking but had suddenly been joined by another unknown army of elves that had surprisingly appeared from behind the war machines, destroying them so quickly that the giants and orc engineers working the machines never had a chance to escape. So great was Methnorick's fury that he had killed no less than two dozen of his own orc soldiers by running his chariot over them

Spying Kaligor, he rode up to the cyclops, sparing no time for even a greeting. "Head south. Now!" The black-robed man then turned his horse and began to gallop hard along the road as orcs, seeing their leader ride off, began to follow.

Kaligor watched Methnorick's retreat with a sense of disgust, even as he ordered his forces to push hard into the forest directly in front of him to let Methnorick safely pass to his position. The cyclops knew that something had gone terribly wrong as soon as his Blingo'oblins burst out of the forest and left the cover of the woods.

Hearing screams and sounds that shouldn't have been coming from his left side, he lifted himself off his saddle, gasping at what he saw. Cursing the Dark One's stupidity, he immediately ordered the bulk of his forces to retreat, leaving only those protecting Methnorick. Close on the heels of the Blingo'oblins, moving in between the elven warriors, were the armor-covered ice giants, creatures he thought had been killed many cycles ago.

Now, as he sat there, watching a victory being snatched from his grasp, his eye caught sight of the elves raising their spears and swords into the air in triumph, having protected their lands from the Dark One. *For the time being*, Kaligor angrily thought. Suddenly the voice of his orc servant reached his ears.

"My lord ... what do we do, sir?" the orc pleaded.

"We follow Methnorick!" Kaligor said, cursing himself. Never in his life had he retreated from a battle. If it was the last thing he ever did, he would see those elves on their knees, pleading for mercy.

Kaligor cursed through his clenched teeth as he kicked his horse hard, and they headed across the fields south. Hundreds of thousands of orcs turned south and ran for their lives, many dropping their weapons as they did so, leaving the field littered with metal.

*　*　*

Dia, who rode hard to catch up with the advance warriors, was amazed at how quickly the elves had won the field. He had thought Methnorick's forces were unbeatable, especially when he had heard the news that the same army that had destroyed his beloved city had destroyed Bru Edin recently. Now all he saw was their backs as they ran away.

Lines were put together quickly along the southwestern edge of the rock formation that rose from the Pilo'ach Mountains in the west. Here the elven warriors watched for a potential counterattack, but the only beings they observed were a pair of black-cloaked riders that suddenly appeared on the field.

*　*　*

Dia brought his horse to a stop alongside those of the elven leaders, all of whom had stopped to now calmly regard the pair, as if awaiting their next move. Neither had moved a muscle yet as they sat atop a pair of massive black steeds, staring into the faces of the thousands of elves.

"They are servants of Methnorick's, I believe … knights of some kind," Dia murmured, breathing the words out as he tried to hold in the slight fear he was feeling.

"You have seen them before, sir?" one of the elven leaders asked as he soothed his horse.

"Once … I saw one once … long ago in my city. It almost killed me and my …" Dia's voice trailed off as the robed riders suddenly turned and rode off in the same direction Methnorick's forces had run, leaving the field as quickly as they had appeared.

As the riders disappeared over the horizon, the elves began to cheer once again that they had won the field and the day, jumping up and down and dancing everywhere.

Soon a massive celebration began on the field as elves from Fuunidor, joined by their cousins from the north and their allies the ice giants, cheered and danced under the stars as the sun finally set.

Dia watched the same group of young elves he had ridden with earlier now drinking from a horn, dancing and smiling. He wondered what Methnorick's next move would be. His army had been ripped apart, but it was still massive. As long as Methnorick was out there, he would remain a threat. Still, he couldn't help but smile. After all, the elves had stopped Methnorick's continuous victories. Tonight was theirs.

* * *

"What do you think?" Niallee whispered as the group stood at the main gate of the City of Ports. Although smoke still rose from behind the massive walls, all was quiet outside, giving the city a sense of peace in what everyone could feel to be a place of death and dread.

From the scattered horse carcasses and orcs littering the ground around them, it was obvious that a battle had taken place here recently and that the battle had been quick. Half of one of the gates lay in pieces.

Chansor had been studying the damage to the gate when he heard a gasp from Amlora. As he followed her eyes and saw the ground just inside the gate, he instinctively pulled his sword and slowed his step as he moved forward.

The ground was literally covered in bodies. And not just those of warriors of Blath 'Na, but also those of women and a few children, as well as those of many of the creatures that the group had fought and escaped from in the forest, their heads cut off in some cases.

"Those decayed creatures are getting closer," Meradoth said, gasping through the smell as the group slowly got past the gates.

"There have to be people still alive in this city … It's a massive place. It wouldn't just collapse without a fight. There must be survivors. We just have to find them," Kikor said, her voice echoing through the area as they cautiously moved around.

Kalion nodded. "We have to move quickly … Like Meradoth said, those things from the forest are still pursuing us. And there's something else out there as well," he added, not missing the pointed look Meradoth shot him. *Ah, so he has sensed it as well*, Kalion thought as he came to a decision. Turning to Kikor, he said, "Meradoth and I will stay back and guard the gate for now. The rest of you can search for survivors." Kalion held his new sword in a defensive position as he looked outside.

Nodding, Kikor hurried the rest of the group down the main road, leaving Meradoth and Kalion alone in the courtyard.

"This reminds you of Dagonor?" Kalion whispered to Meradoth. He couldn't help but think back to that place, barely able to believe that they had stood in that castle only a few weeks ago.

Meradoth didn't answer, but he held his staff tightly as he watched the dead creatures moving closer and closer. They, however, weren't his main worry. He could easily stop them, if needed. It was the other presence, the one that had allowed Kalion to see it, that concerned him at this point. Something else was afoot here.

Both men stiffened slightly as a black-cloaked figure appeared over the hill, apparently invisible to the flesh-eaters that had been pursuing them, as it moved past them unmolested.

Taking a quick, deep breath, Kalion tightened his grip on his blade, but Meradoth grabbed the ranger's shoulder and shook his head. "No, my friend. There is something else going on. It does not seek to attack us … For now I can hide us from sight with a cloaking spell, but you will have to stay quiet."

As Meradoth finished whispering his incantation, the sound of laughter echoed quietly towards them. The pair stared across the field, seeing that the figure had stopped, its hood slowly moving left and right like it was searching for something.

"Kalion … Kalion!"

The ranger turned to look at Meradoth with a look of shock and confusion as he heard his name echo throughout the now-abandoned streets.

"Kalion … give up now, Kalion …"

The ranger's mouth began to shake as the voice dug into his mind, and fear began to rise slowly throughout his body. Meradoth felt his friend shaking and instinctively knew that Kalion wouldn't be able to hold on much longer. Luckily, the voice of the creature was loud enough that Meradoth was able to whisper another spell to transport himself and Kalion far enough down the road to sever the hold the creature had been able to establish on Kalion. As Kalion shook his head to clear it, they could still hear the voice in the distance.

"KALION!!!!!" the voice echoed throughout the city as they turned a corner a few blocks down. "I WILL FIND YOU!" the voice rang loudly as they escaped deeper into the City of Ports.

Chapter Nineteen

Five miles south of the Fuunidor forest, Kaligor alternated between feelings of rage and boredom as he stood before the ranting and raving man. Rage at being five miles south of the Fuunidor forest instead of inside it. And boredom over having spent the past hour watching the Dark One pace back and forth, screaming at everything and everyone as his other commanders, both orc and Blingo'oblin alike, stood nearby, quivering as he walked by them. Granted, more than a few bodies now lay on the ground where Methnorick had taken out his anger on those who'd annoyed him. Kaligor had remained as still as a statue throughout the killings. He would never quiver before Methnorick again.

Joocc Pama, the commander of Methnorick's Blingo'oblin guards, tried to reason with his lord. "My lord ... the attack from the north was a complete surprise to all of us. We had no scouts there. We all believed the elves were trapped in the forest. I never thought they would come from behind."

Methnorick shot a look that made the massive creature step back, knowing that Methnorick could destroy him with a thought if he chose to.

"It was within my grasp!" Methnorick kept repeating as he walked back and forth. "Within my grasp!" Kaligor wanted the same thing. He kept himself quiet, looking at the man as he thought back to what had happened as well.

"How could Fuunidor collect and move its army around behind me? I did not believe that Mass-Lorak had the tools or the warriors to mount such an attack!" Methnorick slammed his fist against a tree that stood nearby when Kaligor felt a presence move up next to him and heard the voice of Lord U'Traa ring out.

"It was not Mass-Lorak that mounted the counterattack, my

lord. I killed the king. No, it was elves not from Fuunidor but from somewhere else that seem to have been hidden from your view." The dead elf pulled back his hood, revealing the decayed skull that made Kaligor squint slightly, wondering what U'Traa could be speaking about.

"What other elven people are there out there?" Methnorick snapped his eyes at the undead knight. "Kaligor here destroyed and killed all within Levenori." Methnorick looked at Kaligor. "Did you not?"

"Yes, sir. Without a doubt," Kaligor answered.

"The few small elven tribes that live among the Pilo'ach Mountains are of no measure and could not mount such an attack with the numbers I saw ... So who are they?!" Methnorick approached U'Traa angrily, making even the knight step back.

Shaking his head, U'Traa merely stared back at his lord. Methnorick turned and yelled, "I have killed every last elf out there. No man or elf could form a defense and do what just happened."

"My lord ... I did recognize one face in that army that attacked from the north," U'Traa replied calmly, almost too calmly for Kaligor's keen ears. Intrigued, he moved for the first time in more than an hour, crossing his arms to listen closely.

Methnorick turned and looked at the knight, shaking his head in disbelief when the elf didn't continue speaking. "Who?" he rasped loudly.

"Dia, my lord ... I saw that human, King Dia!" U'Traa let the words slip out slowly, as if he were purposely trying to taunt Methnorick. Fascinated and knowing that in a moment the whole area would be burning, Kaligor turned towards U'Traa to find the knight's red eyes trained on him. Methnorick exploded in such anger that he let out a massive wall of hot flames that quickly killed all orcs and goblins that were in the area, making those marching by at a quick pace move their feet even faster.

Methnorick's hands glowed red as he clenched his teeth tightly, until he slowed his breathing down enough that he could talk.

"Dia is alive and is fighting with the elves?" He watched U'Traa nod yes. "Bring me that fat man … NOW!" he screamed at Joocc Pama, who bowed quickly and ran off to find Baron Parnland, the man who was supposed to have brought the king to Methnorick earlier.

Methnorick leaned his head back slightly as he thought about his situation. "What numbers do we have left, my friend?" He stared at Kaligor, who let his arms down.

"At last count, my lord, about 70 percent of the troops you had before you assaulted the elven forest … although that number might be down to 50 percent by now. In any case, not enough, I believe, to counterattack Fuunidor now." Kaligor's eye caught the red eyes of U'Traa, who turned to look up at the giant cyclops.

Methnorick turned, stating, "We have the same number we had before the attack and more waiting within the Sernga Mountains."

"Send messengers ahead … They are to join us immediately!" Methnorick shouted.

He watched his orders being carried out until the unmistakable sound of the baron whimpering and begging for mercy reached his ears. He smiled as he saw that Joocc Pama himself pulled the fat man by his armored collar across the ground and threw him down hard in front of his master.

Methnorick shook his head slightly as Parnland groveled at his feet, begging not to be harmed, even as he realized that he was surrounded by creatures with stern looks on their faces.

"Parnland … you have failed me. Do you understand? You have failed me!" Methnorick rasped through his teeth as he watched the man clasp his hands together.

"My lord, I did what you ordered me to do. I was …"

"ENOUGH! Dia is alive, you fool … He was marching with that elven army that kept me from my victory!" Methnorick stepped closer.

"He can't be, my lord. He … he disappeared. Your orc warriors should have killed him in the forest, my lord!" Parnland continued to plead for mercy until finally Methnorick lifted a hand to quiet the man down.

"I have had enough of you, Parnland. I have a plan for you … From now on, you will be a messenger between me and Dia. Do you understand me, Baron?" Methnorick spat out the last words, not believing he had taken this man in to help him destroy the old king.

Swallowing, Parnland quickly nodded yes. "My lord … I know Dia. He will kill me the first time he sees me!" Parnland's whimpers made Methnorick turn a bit and laugh hard.

"No, Baron, he won't be able to kill you … because you're already going to be dead!" With that, Methnorick nodded to Joocc Pama, who leaned over and grabbed Parnland's collar again. No one spoke as Parnland screamed out for mercy, begging and pleading for the gods to save him as the massive Blingo'oblin pulled him along the ground.

* * *

General Summ walked the halls that once had only been used by the king. He and three guards who trailed behind him silently entered the small chamber once used as a planning room for all matters that the king had worked on for many cycles to keep the kingdom running.

As he entered, he saw four elven warriors and the king that had once ruled Brigin'i.

"My friends, thank you for coming to the city … I will get right to the point. We need to take advantage of Methnorick's retreat. Any thoughts?" He looked at each of the elves, who looked back at him. Only Dia sat looking at the table. Summ could tell he was tired. He had been told earlier that the king had lost much and traveled far to get to this point.

"Well, all signs point to Methnorick's forces being drastically cut as a result of our attack. However, he still possesses a large army that could turn at any moment and counterattack us," said Kelic Lor, the youngest prince seated at the table.

"I say we fight!" yelled a silverish-haired elf with one eye. He had lost his eye fighting one of the Blingo'oblins as he entered the battlefield earlier. The wound made half of his face black and red … but his anger for revenge drove him to keep going.

"My lord … Soosu is it?" Summ saw the elf nod and smile back at him. "Where exactly do you suggest we engage in this battle?" he asked, knowing that a full charge might be a foolish thing to do at this moment.

"The road that rolls south … anywhere along there that we can catch them?" Soosu asked. When no one responded, Summ motioned for a map to be brought over and rolled out on the table. Everyone except Dia stood up and leaned over to study the map.

"Forward scouts inform me that this is where Methnorick's rear guard is … just south of where the Warsaa Glen opens up fully to fields and hills just beyond," Summ said, pointing. The others nodded and began discussing ways to move their army down the same road. Kelic advised having a separate column of warriors just east of the main forces so they could counter an attack in case Methnorick was able to spring a trap.

Everyone agreed to the idea, giving Kelic the command of that column, which would consist of about 3,000 warriors in total. Soosu would be given command of the rear guard, Summ, the forward guard, and the others would lead within.

"My lord, Dia … have you anything to add here?" Summ politely asked the king, who, to his surprise, slowly lifted his head to stare at each of the elves in the room as a smile slowly formed on his lips.

"Your plans sound like they will work, General … but what of the battle itself? I do not believe that your question as to where you want that to happen was ever answered." Dia's statement made the rest nod slowly as they turned back to the map to pore over it further.

"The road here looks like it continues on to the ..." Soosu squinted closely and then suddenly broke out into a grin. "What say you of the idea of sending a messenger to the empire to see if they can help?" The elven lord's question triggered an old memory in Dia. He stood and walked over to look at the map as well, as everyone discussed ideas on where to stop the Dark One.

"What is that there, sir?" Dia asked, seeing a point that looked like it might be a city represented on the map. The others followed the king's finger to see that, indeed, in the far south, on the coast just north of the Sernga Mountains, lay a small, almost circular mountain range with a tiny black spot lying within.

Summ squinted as he tried to think back. "I do not know that place, sir. This was the personal map of our king, so he might be the only one that knew." He looked over at the captain that had accompanied him to the chamber. "Caed ... find that seer of ours. I am sure he is in that grove he uses as a temple. Bring him here quickly!"

Caed nodded and ran out of the room. The rest heard him calling out for help in the search.

While Summ had been talking to the warrior, Dia continued looking at the map, leaning closer when he saw something that caught his eye. When Summ finished and looked back, Dia waved for him to look down at the map again. "Here ... the road winds through this wide ravine, but these forests on either side of it in the south ... It almost looks like an enclosed field with only two ways out: the ravine or this glen here. Am I seeing it wrong, sir?" Dia's idea made the rest smile, as they also saw what the man was pointing out.

"You're suggesting that we trap Methnorick there. Good idea, but we would need to get ahead of him as well, sir. I do not think Kelic could get his warriors ahead without being seen by Methnorick ... Surely you're not that fast?" Soosu smiled at Kelic, who shook his head.

"You ... get me a messenger, quickly!" Summ ordered another

of the guards, who left instantly. His order caught the others by surprise as he smiled.

"We might not be able to get the empire to fully help us in this endeavor … but look at this my friends: The Father Gate is just beyond the Sernga Mountains. They have a large contingent of warriors guarding it, I believe!" Summ looked at each of the elves, who nodded in understanding.

Quickly, Summ gave the messenger the order to gather five others and make their way south, taking different routes to get to the Father Gate with his message: "Help us trap Methnorick."

As the other captain left the room to carry out Summ's orders, Caed returned with another elf. Unlike the warriors gathered in the room, this elf wore ragged brown robes. In addition, his hair was very long and covered in leaves and small bones, and he used a long staff to hold up his body.

"Sir … this is Abu Pumic. I believe he is the one you asked for." Caed wiggled his nose as he spoke, as the smell of the seer made him wince slightly.

Summ and the others looked at the old elf seer with wide eyes. Those familiar with the old elf knew that he could foresee many things; however, not all came true. Summ stepped forward, coughing slightly as the smell hit his nose. "Sir … Abu … I … we need your help. There is a mark on this map that I believe could be something from ages ago … but before we do any more planning, I need you to confirm my thoughts." Summ swallowed again as the elf looked up from under his long hair, peering at him with his wrinkled face.

"Ahhhh … I was waiting to hear from you, young one. Ever since our beloved king passed on, I knew I was going to be called soon to explain many things," Abu quietly said as he stepped closer to the table. Dia stepped back and nodded at the elf as he walked up.

Abu looked at the king, and smiling slightly, he lifted his other hand up, closing his eyes as he pointed his palm at Dia. "Your daughter is alive, King … I can feel her presence." The words shocked Dia, who had been thinking of Shermee just moments earlier.

"You can … you can see her?" Dia asked excitedly. Abu nodded slightly as he opened his eyes, looking up at the man's face, which showed that he wanted more information.

"She is alive … and is at this moment … in command of her life!" Abu's words were confusing to Dia, but he was glad to hear that she was alive, and well, it seemed. Before he could think to ask anything further, Summ interrupted them by clearing his throat as he pointed his finger to the mark on the map.

Abu looked where the general was pointing and then back to the warriors with a wide smile on his face. "You asked me here to tell you what that mark is, Summ? Seriously … you took me away from my temple for this?"

"What is this place?" Summ quietly asked, almost smiling at the old elf.

"That, my friend, is God's Haven. Only a few of us knew it really existed … but, of course, it is hard to keep a secret like that hidden. But that is what you, I am sure, thought it was. It is real … so may I go now?" Abu asked, almost bored now. He had hoped that the reason for his being there was something more urgent than this. He was a bit angry now.

"Of course, sir … Thank you for your help!" Summ motioned for Caed to take the seer back to his grove temple. As they left, Dia crossed his arms, wondering what was so special about this place that its name got the others whispering excitedly. Even Summ looked at the king and smiled widely.

"The trap is about to be set, King!"

Chapter Twenty

Shermee and Quinor rode towards Manhattoria, protected by the warriors that General Vana had provided. They had been traveling for several hours, so when they could finally see the spires of Manhattoria in the distance, everyone gave out a tiny cheer. While Quinor had been content to converse with the other warriors, Shermee had spent the past hour buried in her own thoughts. But now that she was about to face her latest dangerous rival, she needed to know more. Turning to the warrior next to her, she said, "Tell me more about this high minister."

"Well ..." the warrior began, considering. "He is ambitious and will attempt to stay in power at any cost."

"Do you think I face any danger from him?"

"Quite possibly. He has been acting very strangely lately, and I believe he is a bit unstable. I think it would be wise for you to have outside allies before you meet with him. You may be a princess from a distant kingdom, but I wouldn't trust him."

"What do you suggest, then?" Quinor piped in as he rode up beside the man.

"I think you should find his major opponent: Jacoob. He has been attempting to defeat Halashii's government in various ways for the last five cycles. But take heed. Finding him may not be easy. He is currently in hiding, and so far I haven't heard of where he might be."

"How do I find him then?" Shermee asked.

"Well ... we will take you to a region of the city that might have people that can point you in the right direction."

"Might have people?" Shermee asked skeptically.

"Honestly, General Vana has an idea of where Jacoob hides, but chooses to ignore this information. He is a military man to the end and will follow orders. He has not been given direct orders to root him out. I really don't think he agrees with the high minister, but he is our leader, so Vana will not challenge him."

Turning his head, the warrior smiled as the gates of Manhattoria loomed before them. As they crossed a massive but beautiful bridge, Shermee could tell that the city was still currently enjoying peace.

Holding her reins with both hands, Shermee was amazed at the sights of this city. Her father and brothers had spoken of this place as the mightiest and the biggest city upon Marn. Its spires and towers rose high into the clouds. Waterfalls seemed to be everywhere she looked, and the colors of everything were just amazing to her. She saw men, elves, dwarves and even a few gnomes walking about. Quinor smiled at her when she looked at him with wide eyes.

Quinor had never been here before, so even he was caught by surprise to see the capital of the empire as beautiful and magnificent as it was. Everywhere he looked, he saw food, clothing and weapons, the likes of which he had never seen, being bought and sold along the road they moved down. The smell of food being cooked hit his nose, making his stomach rumble loudly, but he knew they had to continue on. Their presence here was important, and he knew it, so he told his stomach to quiet down.

They finally came upon an inn and stopped outside. The warrior looked around for a moment and then looked at Quinor and Shermee. "Go inside and talk to the barkeep; tell him that you are looking for Jacoob. He will ask you a few questions to be sure you do not work for the high minister, so just be honest and you should be fine."

Jumping off their horses and tying them to a pole, Quinor and Shermee thanked the men. After the men rode off, Quinor and Shermee opened the door of the inn and walked inside. The first thing that hit Shermee was the smell of stale ale and some kind of food. The food smelled wonderful, and she wondered if they had time to eat. She looked over at Quinor, who inhaled deeply but shook his head, letting her know that their hunger would have to wait. He then spotted the keeper behind the bar and started to walk that way, with Shermee following.

"Excuse me, sir, we were told you might be able to help us," Quinor stated. When the barkeep turned and looked at him, Quinor lowered his voice and leaned in. "We are looking for someone called Jacoob."

The barkeep looked from Quinor to Shermee and back to Quinor before he asked, "And who are you?"

Quinor opened his mouth to explain when Shermee jumped in. "Sir, I really need to find this Jacoob. I have been told he is the only one who can help me."

"Help you with what?" the barkeep asked.

Shermee regarded the barkeep's intense gaze and was sorely tempted to lie until she recalled the warrior's instruction to be honest. Taking a deep breath, she told the barkeep her story, all of her story. This took some time, and the barkeep looked at her suspiciously until he heard the name Vana, at which point he nodded slowly.

"Can you be the one?" The barkeep stared at Shermee for another long moment before nodding as if he had made a decision. "Jacoob … I believe lives along the shores of the River Vete that runs through the middle of our city. Once you leave the inn, follow the road to the right all the way to the end. There you will come to a high wall. Just to the right of that, you will find a path that is somewhat hidden. Take that path along the river, and he will find you," the barkeep whispered, looking around, hoping he hadn't been heard.

Shermee thanked the man and turned to leave, when she turned back. "How will I know him?"

"You won't. He will find you." As the two left the inn and got back on their horses, they found that the warrior who had been with them since entering the city had returned to make sure they had found what they needed. "Did you find out where you need to go from here?"

"Yes," Shermee answered as she turned her horse and continued down the road to the right. Quinor again thanked the man and pulled his reins to follow the princess.

It took them about an hour to get through the city and its crowds to where the barkeep had directed them, at which point they dismounted. Quinor tied up his horse, as did Shermee, when a man stepped up to them, looking suspiciously at them.

The warrior turned to them and said, "I know not how long you both plan to speak to him … but over there is a tavern, sir. I will be waiting for you to come back up. If you are done by night's shadow, I will be there." As he spoke, the warrior moved himself off to stand near a small water fountain when some guards marched by in order along the road.

Quinor walked up and shook the man's hand as they nodded to each other. "I never caught your name, sir … I am Quinor."

"Hiro … I'm called Hiro!" The man smiled as he peered at the girl that he had just escorted many miles to get her here safely. "I heard some of your conversation with the general earlier. Is she really going to be our queen?" he whispered to Quinor, who smiled, looking over at Shermee and then back at Hiro.

"I believe it … but we are, of course, here to find proof," Quinor answered as Hiro nodded.

Quinor then walked over to stand next to Shermee, who wrapped her arms around her body like she was cold. But he saw that she was looking over at the river below and the city beyond.

"What troubles you, Princess?" he asked, almost whispering.

She looked over at the man, smiling slightly. "Nothing. This place is so … so peaceful. I hope that Methnorick does not get to destroy this place," she replied quietly.

"Let us hope that does not happen, Princess … but right now we need to find this man to discover what lies in your future." Quinor offered his hand to her, which she took as they walked over to a small opening in the wall, where they both saw dirty, moss-covered steps going down.

"Looks like no one goes down this way much ... so mind your step, Princess!" Quinor said as they both slowly descended, only slipping here and there, until the roar of the river made it hard for them to speak to each other without yelling as they came to the bottom.

The spray of the river dampened both of them slightly as they stepped onto a ledge that had once served as a walkway. From this position, they could see a small cottage nestled just under one of the massive bridges that extended over the river.

"I do believe that is where we need to go, my princess!" Quinor yelled over the roar of the water as he pointed towards the structure.

Shermee felt a sudden chill down her back and wondered if it was from the cold water or what was before them. "Only time will tell," Shermee whispered to herself.

* * *

Meradoth and Kalion moved down the street, being vigilant about their surroundings. Many of the buildings and houses were vacant, their doors left open and their belongings strewn on the ground.

Soon they came upon another courtyard. This one had a fountain in the middle of it, showing off some horse at the top of the statue as the water continued to flow out. This area normally would have been filled with people talking and laughing. Now, without the people, it sounded like a roaring river.

"Where is everyone?" Kalion asked. He shut his mouth quickly, as his voice echoed across the courtyard. Then he whispered, "Where do you think they've gone?"

Meradoth shrugged his shoulders as he stepped over to the fountain, watching the water within the pool move around calmly.

He turned and sat down on the edge as he placed his staff on his lap. He pulled in a long breath and blew it out as Kalion walked up, still looking around.

"Where are our people? They weren't that far ahead of us when we closed that gate. And, by the way, my friend ... what was that thing? And how did it know your name?" Meradoth whispered, giving the ranger a look of suspicion.

Kalion tilted his head slightly as he thought back to what had happened back at the gate, seeing the image of that black figure in his mind.

"Kikor and I discovered and caught, for just a moment, some creature she could feel had been following us. It was something I had never seen before, but it was ... The feeling I felt while fighting it was the same I felt at the gate just now." Kalion looked directly at Meradoth as he finished.

"What happened when you captured it? Where and when was that, by the way?" Meradoth leaned back as he asked the question, confusion in his voice.

"Back within the forest. After you took the group through that grove area, she was able to catch it ... for just a moment, though, before it got away," Kalion whispered, looking around as he got the feeling he was being watched.

Meradoth followed the ranger's eyes for a moment and then looked back at his friend. "What did it look like?" Meradoth asked, interested in hearing that part now.

Kalion leaned back, looking at the ground as he tried to remember those few moments he had held the creature before it escaped their grips.

"Well ... it was small, about half the size of Chansor. And it had wings, a really long tail, claws that looked like they could cut through anything, and a mouth almost like a wolf's ... but stronger and sharper. But the most amazing thing about it was its eyes. Those eyes told me a lot. It was evil in all ways you could believe." Kalion felt a chill run down his back as he described the creature. He had hoped never to come across it again … but that thing at the gate had given him the same feeling.

"We had better move … if they kept moving to the inner circle of the city and to the port itself, it could take a while to get there ourselves." Kalion started to pull himself up from the fountain edge, only to be stopped as Meradoth grabbed his arm, pulling him back down.

"I am here for another reason, Kalion. My father told me that my mother was within this city when it went silent. If she is still alive, she will know what happened here, and she could, I believe, help us find the princess and maybe tell us what the creature was that attacked you two as well. She has an ability to see people wherever they might be."

"Well then … Where would she be?" Kalion knelt down to check out a box, believing it had food in it.

"She would have been within the black tower at the center of the city. That is where my people gather to pray and practice our art!" Meradoth nodded towards the tower.

As Kalion followed the mage's gaze, he caught sight of movement at the far side of the courtyard, making him pull his sword and staff closer to himself as he mumbled words to get himself ready to destroy the threat, if attacked.

"Curse the gods … It's one of those dead creatures!" Kalion whispered through his teeth as he cursed again.

Kalion tapped his sword on the fountain edge, making a loud bang, which echoed, getting the creature's attention. The creature stood up, looking over at the two now standing together.

Instantly, it screamed and jumped over a box that lay between it and the two, knocking the box over and spilling out the food inside. Suddenly, an arrow appeared and burst through its head. The creature fell into the fountain, splashing Kalion and Merdoth with the cold water.

As the two looked down at the creature and then at each other, they heard a familiar voice, which made them both relax.

"You two should be more careful … This is not a place to sit and watch a fountain now."

Kalion followed the voice and saw Kikor jump from an open window of a building not far away. After she landed, she walked over, smiling at the two. Meradoth almost laughed at the situation. She was right: They had been lazy for a moment.

"Are you well, my friends?" Kikor asked calmly as she approached them. Both nodded at her as she stopped to look at the creature lying now in a pool of red water.

"The rest are down the road, hiding in a building with some survivors of the city. You will not believe what happened here, Kalion … This place disintegrated within a few days. These creatures … They are running rampant everywhere." Kikor looked at the two as she gripped her bow tightly beside her hip.

"We had better get ourselves together, then, and find a way out. Do they know if the port is still open?" Kalion asked the elf as they moved to follow her to where she had left the group earlier.

"I believe one said they thought it might be, but you'd better speak to them." They moved around the corner of the building she had been hiding in. She told them she had gone there to wait for them, knowing that sooner or later they would come this way. As they had done before, they cautiously moved down the street as Kikor told them that if they were bitten, scratched or hurt by one of those creatures, they would turn into one sooner or later.

Finally they got to where the group was hidden. Kikor pulled away the large wood plank that had been placed over the door to protect those inside. Soon Kalion and Meradoth were smiling and nodding as they saw the group.

Kalion sat down in a corner, taking some water from a young girl as he met the survivors and listened as they told them what had happened.

"It was like waves from the seas … The city was eating itself alive!" an old man whispered to Kalion.

"Have you seen the soldiers that guard this city? Have they come through this way?" Meradoth asked.

"We haven't heard or seen any of our people for three days, sir. When we saw your group, we thought that maybe you were survivors as well. But now … well …" The old man trailed off.

"You know how to get to the port, then, do you not, sir?" Kalion asked the man directly.

"I do, sir. But as I said before to your friends here … that is where the council ordered the city's populace to move to when the gates fell. We couldn't get there quickly enough, so I know not if it still is working." Kalion turned to Kikor and Harbin, who were standing not far away now.

"Your thoughts, my friends?" he asked.

"I don't know how the princess could have survived this, Kalion. If she is hidden here or somehow escaped … it's going to be even harder now to track her," Kikor said.

"Like I mentioned, Kalion," Meradoth whispered, "my mother might still be breathing, and she could help."

Kikor frowned at Meradoth. "Mother?"

Kalion turned to Meradoth and folded his arms. "Tell them," he ordered.

When Meradoth finished, he looked at Kikor, who touched his shoulder lightly to get his attention. As he looked at her, she nodded towards the man in the corner. "I believe he knows something," she whispered.

Kalion walked over to stand next to the man. "And you, my friend … What do they call you?" Kalion asked calmly, trying not to alarm the man.

"I am no one, my lord. I am just a worker who got stuck trying to get out of the city," the man whispered to Kalion, who raised an eyebrow as he nodded towards the sword on the man's hip.

The man sighed and dropped his head. "That princess you speak of … Is she blond … maybe 15 to 20 cycles of age … about this high?" The man's hand came up to his chest as Kalion looked from him to the group, who moved closer as the man's words revealed that he knew the princess.

"Where is she?" Meradoth's words made the man look at the mage.

"She … I took her to a ship that was going to sail to the Black Isle … along with a few warriors that I was told had taken her from Brigin'i in the west. They sailed just as the city began to fall apart, sir. That is all I know, sir. Please … I meant no harm to her." The man held up his hands, hoping to give them the sense that he was, indeed, the victim in the whole matter.

"The ship that took her … and those warriors … Did they work for Methnorick?" Harbin asked, leaning on his staff now.

"I know not of a Methnorick, sir. But the warrior that held her … He was called Quinor, I think. She wasn't harmed … No bonds held her, sir."

"The Black Isle is a few days' travel upon the water, Kalion." Meradoth's words made the ranger nod.

"I am sure, though, that my mother will have even more information for us." Meradoth's words made Kalion look directly at his friend.

"Let us get there, then. I have had my fill of this place." Meradoth nodded at his friend.

Chapter Twenty One

The elven armies combined, forming the largest army ever assembled in the known history of Marn. Ice giants and those men that had been hiding in the high hills that lay just south of Fuunidor also joined ranks with the elves as they marched south to meet Methnorick.

Dia was told that the place on that map — a city of ancient power and strength known as God's Haven — was where the elves believed the gods had once ruled from. It was the last place that the gods had lived before leaving for the stars and was still home to the most religious city in the lands.

Dia was told that the warriors that guarded God's Haven were cleric warriors, some of the most formidable of their people. General Summ guessed that the city had a standing army of about 8,000.

That should be more than enough to trap Methnorick, thought Dia as he sat upon his saddle. His thoughts were soon interrupted by what sounded like gasps of pure horror.

"Gods help us!" he heard someone whisper next to him, bringing his attention back to the road, which had been blocked by hundreds of bodies impaled on poles.

Dia gently kicked his horse forward as the others began to move through the almost forest-like scene before them until he came to a pole that lay in the middle of the road. He stopped and looked up, his mouth opening up as he saw the face of Baron Parnland looking back at him.

With dead eyes, red from the blood that had pooled up inside them, and hands hanging down, he was bent over the pole that had been pushed through his stomach. The man's guts had leaked out and drained down the pole to gather at the bottom. Dia leaned his head back slightly as he thought about the baron for a moment. Then shaking his head, he spat at the ground and walked away.

* * *

The Black Tower, so named for the black stone used in its construction, had been standing within the city of Blath 'Na since its beginning. The fact that it still stood when the group came into the center of Blath 'Na gave Meradoth a moment of happiness until he saw the destroyed gate that now hung from its hinges. As the group moved through the grounds around the tower, they found more signs of attack. The stables and barn had been burnt to the ground, with two horses lying on the ground. Their bodies hadn't been eaten yet, according to Whelor.

Harbin approached a long stairwell that circled the outside of the stone tower, leading to the entrance, only to hit an invisible wall. It was Chansor who caught the mage as he tumbled backwards, mumbling about stones that had been painted to look like stairs.

Meradoth walked over to where Chansor was moving his hands slowly across what looked like empty space. As he reached forward he felt the stone wall as well. Harbin, who had recovered, shook his head, whispering he should have known that there would be defenses up.

Kalion and Kikor stood just inside the gate wall, peeking out as they watched a group of the creatures they had encountered in the forest moving by on the far side of the square. With the creatures was the one that had spoken Kalion's name at the gate. Kalion was sure that he was the same type of creature as the others, only now transformed to look like a man.

As they stood guard, waiting for the others to sort out their next steps, Meradoth climbed the stairs as far as he was able and then stood with his hands and arms open wide.

Meradoth hadn't said anything out loud, but his presence was getting the attention of those things anyway. He almost groaned aloud at the sight of so many turning their decayed heads towards where the group was hidden.

"Mother ... please. It is I ... your son. Please open the door and let us in ... We need your help!" Meradoth communicated to his mother without words. He was so desperate to find her that he was oblivious to the creatures that were walking towards the tower grounds.

"Are you sure she is here?" Chansor whispered as he also looked at the dead things moving towards him. "Meradoth ... did you hear me?" he asked, looking over at the mage and stepping back quickly when he saw that his friend's eyes had turned totally white.

"Harbin ... look!" he rasped. Harbin stepped around, putting his hand on the thief to calm him down, when he saw what was happening.

"All is well, my friend. He is talking to someone within this place!" Harbin calmly answered. Just then, both heard what sounded like a swoosh of air moving through a tunnel.

Chansor put his hand out and found that the wall had disappeared. He smiled as he looked up at Harbin, who nodded down at the little man.

"Hurry ... She will not hold it for long, my friends!" Meradoth's voice made both jump in their boots as they saw that Meradoth's eyes had returned to normal. The mage whispered loudly to the rest to grab their mounts and bring them up the stairs quickly as Chansor and Harbin stepped forward to see a large door open wide, with a bright but warm light shining out of it.

As they peeked in, a woman dressed in familiar clothing, much like Harbin's and Meradoth's, stepped into the light, motioning for them to hurry in. They soon found themselves in a room that was getting rather crowded as the others ran in, pulling their horses up the stairs, leaving just Meradoth standing there with a wide smile.

"Mother ... I knew you would be here!" he said excitedly.

"My son ... hurry inside. There are dark forces that want to get in

… Hurry!" she said, pulling her son in. The dead creatures, seeing their victims escaping, all screamed that sound that had become all too familiar over the past few days now. They stumbled through the broken gate and towards the stairs. Meradoth's mother turned and walked in. She whispered something, and the door's edges shined brightly for a moment.

"Well … not really the best way to say hello and welcome … but welcome to the Black Tower!" The woman smiled as she looked at the dirty and tired faces staring back at her.

"My name is Tiffanori, and I keep this place … Be welcome at its darkest hour!"

※ ※ ※

Vana rode into the gated tower of the Father Gate with the men moving behind him as he listened to his men standing guard explain that, so far, everything had been pretty quiet since his leaving. Only a few groups of trolggs had tried to get across the bridge, but so far they had not been successful.

Vana informed those gathered about his victory against the orcs. The cheers within the Father Gate could be heard down the ravine, causing a few animals to perk up.

The general then got off his horse and moved into the tower, with his second, Commander Tevanic, following close behind. As he moved into the room that served as his office, he turned, stating, "I met someone else along the road … a princess from the north, who traveled with a warrior. I think our empire is moving into a new age. Do you remember the tales of the one who would be queen of the empire?" He did not wait for a response before he continued. "I think I met her! Only time will tell." Hearing his second snort, the general turned.

"What are our orders, sir?" his second asked from the shadows as Vana crossed his arms, thinking about it for a moment.

"We carry out our current orders: Guard this gate and bridge …

until we are told not to."

Vana frowned at his second in command. He knew their orders. Something else was obviously on the man's mind. "So are you going to spit it out, or will I have to beat it out of you?"

Tevanic blinked, grinned for a second, and then grimaced again as he replied, "Sir … not much did happen while you were gone, but there were many refugees that were moving away from the north, and they reported that Bru Edin had been totally destroyed and that the 'Dark One,' as he is being called, was moving towards the elves at Fuunidor. Do you think we should still sit and do nothing?"

Putting a hand up and smiling at the man, Vana sucked in a nice long breath of cold air. "My friend … we do not have the men that could change the course of any battle in the north. Unless the capital sends us relief, we are all that stands in the way of this Methnorick getting into the empire … so make sure our men are ready for whatever might come. I'm off to recover, my friend!" Turning, Vana left Tevanic standing alone in the hall, confused slightly by the general's reluctance to discuss options.

* * *

Sunorak walked calmly down the streets of Blath 'Na, followed by large groups of the reanimated dead as he searched for that new group of adventurers he had seen earlier: Kalion and the others.

Suddenly he had to stop as a winged creature flew over him, casting a shadow as it did, and landed hard on the road.

Sunorak let his hands move to his sides as he stared at the winged creature, with its red eyes staring back at him. He winced slightly as a loud, booming voice began to echo deeply in his mind.

WHERE ARE THEY, SLAYER? The voice repeated the question as he blinked through the pain.

Who are you? he thought back. *Who are you looking for?*

He watched the wings flap a few more times and then stepped

back as the creature landed on the road. He struggled to free the hold on his mind enough to make a defensive move when suddenly the creature began to transform.

Soon he stood before a dark-cloaked woman, whose reddish-black hair flew into the wind as she turned her head.

"The group of travelers that came into this city from the west … I have been tracking them for a very long time now. Where are they, slayer?" She spoke calmly, and he could hear her confidence in her voice.

I have only seen what you see behind me. They now rule this city. If they have come within it … it now belongs to them!

"Why are you here, slayer?" she asked, her voice calm as she probed further into Sunorak's mind.

I came here to observe what these things have done. Soon I will be joining our master, who is in battle with the elvenkind in the west. They are under my hand, and my hand alone … and they will be in the battle there soon! he thought proudly, which, he saw, made the woman smile.

"I can feel the lie in your mind, slayer. Tell me where they are … or join your creatures in the death they want to give you!" Suddenly Sunorak fell to his knees with a scream to rival that of the dead creatures.

Realizing that this woman meant to kill him if he resisted her, Sunorak wept and held his hands out. "Please. I don't know where they are. I can no longer sense them, but," he screamed again as another wave of pain raced through his head, "I believe those that you are searching for are now in the center of this city … They …" He stepped back as she smiled and quickly transformed herself back into the winged creature. As she flew high in the air, she turned back towards Sunorak with one final message. *Your master has failed in his quest to destroy the elven creatures … At this moment, he retreats to the south!*

Sunorak didn't dare doubt the creature as he thought about her words. Methnorick had failed. Failed … how?

Chapter Twenty Two

"What do you mean her ship sank?" Kalion's face lost all of its color as he heard Meradoth's mother speak. "What happened?"

"Do you know if she is alive, Mother?" Meradoth asked, lifting a hand to calm the ranger down.

Closing her eyes for a moment, she smiled and slowly nodded to her son. "Not only is she alive, my son ... she travels within the empire at this very moment!" Kalion breathed a sigh of relief.

"She was taken to the empire by one of the sea warriors, along with another warrior ... I believe he was the one taking her to the Black Isle, but now he protects her." Kalion frowned when he heard that her kidnapper had turned around. "She travels with her kidnapper?"

Tiffanori nodded her head. "Yes, who now serves as her protector."

"What is she doing down there?" Holan grunted as he poured a drink for himself from the food and drink the mage had offered.

Chansor, who sat at the other end of the table, was chewing on a piece of chicken, keeping his thoughts to himself as he stared at the big man. He still had no idea as to how he was to kill the man.

"She walks within the capital," Tiffanori continued. "She had started traveling towards Brigin'i when something changed her path and led her to Manhattoria."

"Well, at least there she is safe, my friends," Amlora said quietly. "If the princess learned that Brigin'i fell, why would she go back?"

Tiffanori laughed gently. "Isn't it obvious, child?" she asked, looking towards her son with love filling her eyes. "Family." Several of the others nodded their heads in agreement.

"So, if the princess is now safe and secure, where do we go from here?" Whelor broke in.

Tiffanori looked at the big man long and hard but said nothing as a loud roar drifted in from the outside, catching their attention.

She continued as if Whelor had not said a word. "The creatures that you encountered outside have overrun the city. However, there is another creature now present. One that seeks all of you. So it is time for you to go now. She paused and looked over at her son before she continued. "I must stay, however, to keep the power and knowledge that resides within these walls out of the hands of those that are dark and evil." Seeing the look of determination on his mother's face brought sadness to Meradoth, but pride as well. His mother had always been the strong one in his family, he quickly realized. She, not his father, had been the one who had fought off evil for many cycles.

Another roar and scream from the outside brought everyone to their feet as the ceilings and walls began to shake.

"What is it?" Whelor asked as he turned his head from the sound to the mage.

"I am not sure I know the answer to that, but we must find a way to get you out of the city," Tiffanori said, thinking of a hundred different places to escape through. "There is not much time, and you must get out, but heed my words. Our gods even today still use us!" Tiffanori said, sucking her lip in. "Their machines gave me and my kind power, but those same machines have changed others over time."

"Changed? What do you mean?" Kikor asked. Meradoth knew what she was about to say, and his mother stared back at him with a look of urgency that said he needed to explain to them what they needed to know.

"No time to explain now. Just know that the gods belong to you as well." Tiffanori smiled when her mind came up with an escape route that she could get them through. "Now we must make our way down to the tunnel at the base of this tower. It will take you outside the walls of the city and into the forest."

Quickly holding up a hand, she directed the group to move

through the corridors of the tower and slowly descend into the dark and damp of the thick rock and stone tower until all they heard besides their feet stepping on wet stones was the drip, drip, drip coming from moisture seeping through the rocks.

Chapter Twenty Three

Methnorick pulled his cloak tighter around himself as he sat quietly upon his horse. He stared out from under his hood, watching the army he led move south. The scouts were reporting that the elves were amassing an even larger army.

So far those scouts, who had been tasked with carrying his message to the tribes of orcs that lived within the massive mountain ranges, had not returned. This war had turned in a direction he didn't like, and he was going to strike the elves hard for the trouble they had caused him, but only when he was ready.

The rain slammed hard onto the ground, making the trek even more miserable for those moving the carts and wagons down the road, so much so that a few giants chose to lift some of the carts onto their backs to get them through.

Kaligor sat upon his mount with his cloak wound tightly around himself as well, but his eye stayed trained on the back of the man who called himself Methnorick, the Emperor of the North, the Dark One, who, for the first time in their acquaintance, dared to turn his back on the enemy. This angered the cyclops more than Methnorick could even imagine.

He gripped his reins tightly as he considered his options. The thought of killing Methnorick even shot through his mind, but he didn't want to anger those that led Methnorick by inadvertently changing their plans. For all he knew, this retreat could be part of their plan, so for the time being, he kept his mouth tightly closed.

* * *

At the very bottom of the tower, the group led their horses through an opening large enough for them to get through and down into the dark, dank chambers covered in spider webs from decades of disuse. "Ever thought of cleaning this place?" Chansor quipped, but Tiffanori's sudden intense stare made the thief quiet down as torches along the walls sparked and lit the passageway.

Soon they reached a large entryway with a barred gate that creaked as

Tiffanori whispered a spell to open the structure. The sound echoed loudly, making many wince from the sound of the metal cracking.

"This will take you under the city to an area far to the south. From here on out, you must all look after each other, and protect your friend," she said, nodding towards Whelor. "He is the key to stopping Methnorick, or fulfilling his plans. Don't let it be the latter." With that, Tiffanori stood to the side as the group peered into the darkness, only hearing the echoes of dripping water from within it.

Tiffanori suddenly felt a pain in her stomach, one that she hadn't felt for many cycles. She looked up at the ceiling for a moment as the group slowly made their way past her until finally Meradoth and Kikor were standing in front of her.

"Come with us, Mother. You've done your job here ... Please!" Meradoth pleaded with his mother as Kikor stood off to the side, watching the group disappear into the darkness beyond even her vision.

"May I ask you, my lady ... Do you know how this ends ... with Methnorick, I mean?" she asked, cutting Meradoth off, as she felt that the woman wasn't going to leave. The elf could see that something was distracting her now.

Tiffanori looked from her son's sad face over to the elven warrior, who, she could see, was a leader amongst leaders, and shook her head. "Make your way to the empire. That is the next step on your journey." Turning towards her son, she said her goodbyes.

"My son ... my Meradoth ... I have missed your face for many cycles. You have become what I hoped. Protect your friends ... Fight for what you know is right. And take yourself south and follow your destiny." Meradoth opened his mouth to argue, making the woman smile at him. She hushed him quietly, putting a finger on his lips. "You know I have to stay here, Son … This tower must not fall to Methnorick or any of his disciples that march with him, and I know he is not the only creature out there hoping to get inside this tower. Go now, Son, so that I can protect our legacy." Turning slightly, looking at the ceiling quickly and then back at her son, she added, "Know that I will always be with you, my son!"

Meradoth tried to say something, but he couldn't think of the right words. He saw her smile back at him. "Hurry … You must leave now!" she said as the ceiling rumbled, causing dust to fall down.

Meradoth nodded and hugged his mother tightly. As he turned to leave, she called out once more.

"When you find the princess, she will no longer be the same girl that Kalion sought. You might have to prepare the ranger. He will find not a princess but a queen of all the lands!" With that, Tiffanori closed the gate and backed into the darkness.

Despite Meradoth's anguish, he couldn't help but smile at the thought of Kalion's upcoming surprise as he turned to catch up with the others. Their journey had taken another turn … This one, though, was taking them to the empire of a great queen.

* * *

Chansor was in a state of panic. He knew that the creature outside the tower was the very same creature that had been trailing the group for a while now.

He had to do something, he thought quickly as he and the others walked down the tunnel that seemed to not have been used since the beginning of time. Rats and mice ran away as they approached. Harbin and Meradoth used their magic to ignite the torches that lined the walls, revealing the fact that the tunnel was quite large, at least four bodies wide and eight feet in height.

The thief held his dagger with a fidgety hand as he continued to watch the back of Whelor's head a few feet ahead.

"Whelor, Chansor, can the two of you run ahead and see where this goes?" Kalion's command almost brought the thief to tears, as he couldn't believe his luck. Chansor turned and grinned at the ranger and ran by the big man, who merely grunted and handed his reins to Meradoth before following the thief up the tunnel.

When they were both out of sight, Kalion whispered for them to all stop. Guessing what the ranger was going to say, Amlora was the first to pipe in.

"Kalion … if you are thinking of killing the man … I, for one, will not let you do that." Amlora stood, patting her horse's head softly as she looked at Kalion, who shook his head no back at her.

Kalion held his horse's reins as he also patted his horse's nose softly. The rest stared at the ranger as the man thought about how to answer their questions about what to do with Whelor now.

Meanwhile, Whelor and Chansor made their way through the tunnel, walking past stones that had fallen over time from the ceiling. Neither spoke to the other. Whelor worried that Chansor didn't want him around, or that Chansor might even fear the man for what he was, so he kept quiet.

Chansor, though, was considering his options, trying to find a way he could kill the man without it being suspicious to the others when they caught up. But he was also considering how he would get the man back to his master … He must wait until they were out in the open.

It felt to Chansor like they had lived in the tunnel for ages when they stopped for a moment to take a break from their quick pace. Both pulled out water, and Whelor looked down past his pouch to see Chansor staring back up at him.

"You worry about me, do you not, my little friend?" Whelor asked quietly as he lowered his water pouch. He waited for a moment for the thief to finish his drinking and then continued his observation. "I can promise you, Chansor, that I mean you no harm!" He watched as Chansor lowered his pouch and swallowed his water, using an arm to wipe the water from his face.

"You seem ... different to me, Chansor. But you do not need to worry!" Whelor repeated when a cool breeze suddenly rushed down the corridor, hitting them both.

"You felt that?" Chansor whispered, breaking the silence.

"I did, yes ... We must be close!" Whelor stepped forward first and moved quickly down the tunnel as Chansor pulled out his dagger and followed.

As they approached the end of the tunnel, Whelor stopped and smiled at the sight of the blue sky. "We found it!" he whispered as he looked towards a green field with heavy forests beyond.

"We made it, my friend ... We're safe!" he said when suddenly he felt a massive pain like being stung hard by large bees many times on his right side. His face became a mask of pain and confusion as the thief plunged the dagger again into Whelor's side, making the big man gasp loudly as he staggered back.

"Chansor ... why?" he gasped as he hit the ground. Chansor walked around and stood over him, holding a dagger covered in his blood.

"You should have kept yourself hidden, beast," Chansor sneered. "I was tasked with finding and killing you, my friend, by Lord Methnorick long ago ... You shouldn't have come in from the cold!" The thief almost laughed proudly, as he knew he was close to finally finishing his journey now.

Cursing loudly as he heard his name being called out by Kalion and the others, Chansor looked down at Whelor, whose eyes were almost closed, and smiled.

"Say hello to your gods! At last my task is done, and I have killed you," Chansor whispered, dropping the dagger on the ground. Whelor watched in shock as wings burst out from Chansor's back and a large cloud of dust circled around the thief as he flew away.

    For many moments, as he felt the life draining away, he lay on the ground, thinking about his life, his journey from so far away to this moment. *Methnorick has won. I am ready*! Whelor whispered to himself as he heard the rest getting closer by the moment.

Chapter Twenty Four

Jebba had been running away from various bands of orcs for what seemed like hours when he stopped to lean against a tree. Exhausted, he uncorked his water pouch and greedily swallowed half of its contents as he scanned the clearing. Seeing nothing but a few birds, he closed his eyes to rest for a moment.

A snap made him open his eyes quickly as he pulled out his sword. As he looked around, he realized that it was darker than before. And colder, Jebba realized, as he began to shiver.

Cursing himself for having fallen asleep out in the open, Jebba began scanning the forest floor for kindling to start a fire when he heard another unmistakable snap. Grasping his sword tightly, Jebba whipped around in one quick motion.

Nothing. Still, he knew that he was no longer alone as he inched his way back towards the deer trail he'd seen earlier. He also knew that his pursuer wasn't any of orcs that had been chasing him earlier, as they lacked the patience to stalk anyone.

The closer he got to the trail, the more on edge he began to feel. Reaching the edge of the path, he closed his eyes and took a deep breath, willing himself to calm down ... and failing miserably, he realized, as he opened his eyes and felt a rush of fear course through his veins. Overwhelmed by the unfamiliar feeling, Jebba failed to immediately notice the figure now blocking his path.

Lifting his sword up to defend himself as the shape moved forward, he noticed a hand moving up and felt a sharp pain, making him grab his chest tightly as he began to wince from the pain.

As he stared up at the shadow that still hadn't moved into the light, he sucked in a loud breath and tried to speak. Unable to do more than gurgle blood, he dropped his head to discover why, and saw a sword buried in his chest. Shock loosened the grip he'd had on his own sword. Jebba could do nothing but watch it clatter to the ground as he fell to his knees.

He looked up slowly as he heard footsteps getting closer. Pain began to move through his body. He was dying.

He blinked a few times through the tears that were forming. He seemed to recognize the shape as it moved out of the trailhead shadows to stop before him. As Jebba looked up, not being able to say a word, the being leaned down and pushed the sword deeper into Jebba's chest, making the warrior gasp.

"Shhhhh, man creature ... Dream of your gods, as you will be meeting them soon ... Shhhhh," the shape whispered as it raised a finger to its mouth.

The shape moved closer, revealing the form of a dark elf. He reached up and grabbed Jebba's shoulder, quietly whispering, "Man creature ... a mouse could have tracked you."

More blood poured out of his mouth as Jebba's vision began to darken. The elf slowly helped Jebba lie down on the ground and leaned over him with a smile that made Jebba angry as the last moments of his life crept away. Cleaning his blade on Jebba's clothing, the elf placed it back in his scabbard before going through the man's pockets and pulling out what he thought would be good to take. When he was done, the elf stood back up and turned to disappear into the forest.

Moving through the brush, he moved east off the mountain towards where he was told his people were gathering, near the once-powerful human castle of Bru Edin.

* * *

Amlora worked faster than she thought was possible as she tried to take care of Whelor's wound. Truth be told, once the bleeding was stopped, she saw that the wound wasn't as bad as she had feared. As she placed thick patches of moss and a few other druidic spices on the wound, she realized that she had certainly seen worse in the course of their journey. Whelor groaned each time she tightened the bandage. Amlora ignored him. He would live. She suggested that he use the pain as a reminder.

"I'm not groaning from the pain!" he whispered to her. Her mouth tightened as she nodded at her friend. She understood what he meant. Their companion for this whole trip, Chansor, someone they'd considered a friend, had tried to kill the big man for reasons that no one, including Whelor, understood. Whelor told them that the only thing Chansor had said was that he was finally done with his mission.

"Kill the bastard is all I can say. He betrayed us and almost killed Whelor here … He needs to pay for it all!" Harbin said, still seething over how Chansor had fooled them all.

"We need to keep moving. The dead creatures could attack in the middle of the night out here!" Meradoth stated, sounding urgent.

Kalion looked over at the cleric tightening up the cloth around Whelor. "Amlora, is he ready to travel?" Amlora nodded as she began to help the big man up. "Kikor …" Kalion was about to ask her to take the lead when he noticed that she was staring at something with almost a look of wonder on her beautiful face. "Kikor," Kalion said quietly as he turned fully to face her, "what is it? Do you know this place?"

The elf nodded and pointed south and east of where they were. "We stand upon a place of reverence. This is the Orkani'feln, where cycles ago my people destroyed what they thought was the largest orcish army upon the lands." Kikor turned back to the others, smiling proudly as she shared the legend.

"When the battle was finished, my people, hoping to send the orcs a message never to rise again, placed the dead in a huge pile and lit them on fire, making the skies for miles turn black as the bodies burned. Since then, the gods have covered the bones of the orcs, making that large hill there." Kikor pointed to a hill that rose up just to their west.

Suddenly the horses began to get restless, and the group began hearing what sounded like air rushing down a small alleyway when Kalion's horse reared back. The others grabbed their reins tightly as everyone looked around, wondering what was going on, when Harbin cried out.

"LOOK!" he screamed as he pointed north.

Before their eyes, from one part of the city of Blath 'Na, which stood far enough away that it was only a long wall with a few buildings sticking out above it, a large cloud was rising up.

Black and red in color, it slowly rose high above the city. They could see fire sparking up from the city's buildings around the bottom of the cloud that slowly was turning into a massive mushroom.

"Mother!" Meradoth moaned. The group looked back and forth, all realizing that Tiffanori must have fought off whatever had been pursuing Whelor. Kalion, thinking of the journey ahead, wondered if the creature that was doing this was the same one that had known his name.

"I am sure she survived, Meradoth. One thing I can say about your family … You are all survivors!" Niallee said calmly, placing her hand on his shoulder.

"We'd best keep moving … We don't know if any of those creatures might have survived. We could all still be in danger!" Kalion said as he looked directly at his friend with sympathy.

※ ※ ※

Methnorick finished killing the last orc and goblin that had annoyed him, the blood splashing out in a large arc and landing on a few standing around him.

Methnorick then turned towards a quivering man who once had been a great leader of his own people in the principality of Sawla'mor but was now shaking under his clothing.

He quickly looked down as Methnorick walked over to stand in front of him and pushed the point of his now-bloody sword into the general's chest.

"You are to take your troops and make your way to the Sernga Mountains, where you will give the orc bands gathering within this message!" Methnorick pulled a rolled parchment out from under his cloak and pushed it at the man's chest.

"My emperor!"

Methnorick was still standing amidst a pile of dead bodies, watching his messenger ride away, when a captain of orc archers approached and kneeled in front of Methnorick, holding a parchment out.

Methnorick unrolled the parchment after breaking the seal, knowing right away who it had come from. As he read the message, his face went from shock to urgency. Elves had been spotted marching south, very close.

"Quickly … send the word out. The army is to form into marching order … NOW!" Methnorick called as the orc archer captain ran towards the forest, disappearing within it.

Within the hour, Methnorick and his army had gathered back on the road that led south as Methnorick himself sat on top of his horse, reading the new report he had been given: *Elven army a half day's march from camp!* Methnorick had known that they were following, but he hadn't realized they were that close. He cursed himself for being so lazy. "Of course they would be!" he whispered, lifting his head to watch the thousands of warriors beginning the retreat south.

Kaligor, who rode beside Methnorick along with Lord U'Traa and a mage who hadn't spoken a word to his lord since the retreat had begun, merely looked at Methnorick, trying to hide the contempt he felt for the man.

"Half a day's march, Kaligor … half a day. How could they have formed themselves up and marched so quickly? Those high and mighty creatures shall pay for my loss at Fuunidor. When I gather the orc bands from the Sernga Mountains, I shall erupt from the south and destroy everything in my path!"

Bowing his head slightly, Kaligor stared at Methnorick's back as he spoke. "We will mark the lands with elven blood … None shall live when we are done with them, my lord!" Kaligor felt his words were true, but he wanted to do the same to Methnorick, for their retreat was an embarrassment for him, and he couldn't blame anyone except Methnorick.

Chapter Twenty Five

Quvan heard the loud horns echoing through the area as he made his way through the woods. Racing towards the first signs of people he'd heard in days, he rounded a large boulder to find himself staring at a pair of massive towers that seemed to have appeared out of thin air; each tower was taller than any that the elf had ever seen in his two hundred cycles of life.

The sudden appearance of armed warriors on the tower wall stopped Quvan in his tracks. He sure hoped that he was in the right place as he called up to them, keeping his hands up to show he came in peace.

"I carry a message from Fuunidor!" he said quickly, hoping they could hear the urgency in his voice. "We need your help."

None of the warriors assembled on the wall responded to his call. Nor, in fact, did they move at all as Quvan waited, growing increasingly annoyed as he thought about how he had traveled so far without being caught by orc patrols only to arrive at a place where no help was to be found. Disgusted, he lowered his arms and turned to leave, only to stop in shock as he found himself face-to-face with another elven warrior a full head taller than he was, who somehow had snuck up behind him without a sound.

"I take it that you are the one in charge?" Quvan drawled calmly, determined not to show this elf his nervousness.

The elf looked him over for a moment longer as Quvan took in the clothing of the warrior before him. Long green robes that opened in the front, showing his black trousers underneath, were bound tightly with a leather belt that made his chest look larger as the robe gathered loosely around it.

His hair was pulled back and held by a gold-looking disk, as were his ears. Quvan had never seen elves dressed like this. He was about to ask about his clan when the elf spoke.

"Why would you think that?" the elf asked, narrowing his eyes at Quvan. "I am the one you are seeking, my brother … I speak for the one that rules within." The elf smiled as he spoke calmly. "What are you called by your own, my brother?"

Swallowing, the messenger licked his lips before he spoke. "Quvan … my name is Quvan. And who are you?" the messenger asked.

"My name is Huanic, my brother … I am the mouth of God's Haven, brother!" He smiled at the last words as Quvan's mouth fell open in relief upon hearing where he was. He realized that he hadn't believed the stories, even as he'd set out to follow the orders given to him by General Summ. Now all he could do was stare in awe as he watched what was happening between the two towers.

* * *

Shermee and Quinor walked through the dark entryway and continued down a hallway that looked like it hadn't been used for many cycles, as cobwebs hung across the openings and along the walls, until they turned a corner to find a man sitting in front of a fire that roared in a small fireplace along the stone wall.

"I have been waiting for you for many cycles, my queen." The whisper made Quinor pull out his sword slowly as Shermee stood just behind the warrior, wondering if this was some trap.

"You have no need of that, my friend … Nothing here will harm you unless you fear knowledge. Welcome, Shermee Vaagini, former princess of Brigin'i, future queen of the empire. You too, Quinor of the Northern Reaches, welcome!" The man slowly rose from the chair, which creaked as he stood up.

"You're … you're a mage, sir?" Quinor asked as he took in the markings on the front of the robes the man wore.

Smiling, the man looked down at his front. His hands came out of the sleeves to clasp tightly in front of his body. "I am Johnna Smyac ... I am what you might call the librarian of this city!"

"Shouldn't you be in the library and not in this ... this place?" Quinor looked around as he spoke, taking in the piles of books, rolls of parchments and tables covered in maps and more.

"I am where I need to be. Now sit, for I have much to tell you."

Shermee swallowed as she caught his stare burning into her eyes. "We were told that you know of the legend. You called me your queen. Please, sir, tell us. What is so special about me?" Shermee asked, impatient to learn more about her fate.

✳ ✳ ✳

Huanic smiled as Quvan tried but failed to contain his awe at the sights he had been seeing since being led through the force field that shielded the place from the outside world.

"God's Haven!" Quvan whispered as he walked down the main road beside Huanic. The city was massive. Everywhere he looked, he saw buildings polished so brightly that the wood shined almost as much as the gold trim edging many of the structures. As for the citizens he saw walking around, while they were all elven like himself, like Huanic, they were all taller than Quvan, and all wore bright, colorful robes.

Quvan turned to Huanic, unable to contain his curiosity any longer. "Who are you people? What is this place?"

Huanic's smile widened as he led Quvan into an antechamber, where three more elves stood talking to each other. "Why, brother, you are in the birthplace of the gods!"

Quvan could only blink at Huanic, who chuckled as he turned to address the other elves.

"Brothers, it would appear that the prophecy has come to pass. This man brings a message from Fuunidor."

"Fuunidor?" the elf on the right whispered quietly. Quvan could see that this elf wore his robes tightly around his body. Around his waist, he had a gold belt pulling the robe, which fell to just below his knees, where Quvan could see a pair of purple boots lined with jewels and gold trim. His hair had been pulled back just like Huanic's, revealing his long ears, which had a few chains hanging from them.

At Huanic's nod, Quvan pulled out the parchment from under his robes and handed it to the elf, who slowly broke the seal and unrolled the parchment so the other two could read it.

"So … the rumors are true then. This Methnorick is marching south, hoping to gather the orcish tribes who live in the Sernga Mountains to join him," the second elf remarked.

"What are Summ's numbers? Do you know? How many spears does he have marching behind him?" the third elf asked.

"I left at least 15,000 marching with my general, sir!" Quvan answered as he watched the three elves turn and whisper to each other before finally turning back to him.

"God's Haven will assemble to help our brothers in Fuunidor! We know of Methnorick … and know what he is capable of doing!" The elf snapped his fingers, and a maiden appeared from behind a column, carrying a tray of food and water. She stepped up to Quvan, who looked at her and then at the other three.

"Feel free to refresh yourself with food and liquid before returning to General Summ with our message. Let him know that we will be in place when the time comes."

* * *

A sentry ran into the chamber where General Vana sat, going over maps, to report that a lone elf wearing light armor was crossing the bridge to the Father Gate and being pursued by a contingent of orcs just moments behind him. Vana stood and moved to the door in one swift motion. As he walked, the sentry continued his report by saying that the guards had already been targeting the orcs when he had left to report to the general.

The pair got to the gate just as it closed behind the elf. Vana walked up to the messenger, who was bent over, catching his breath, and handed him a jug of water. Nodding, the messenger swallowed a gulp of water as he looked at the faces of those that had gathered around him.

The messenger looked up. "My name is Hapif of the Green Tree People, sir. I carry a message for General Vana."

Vana lifted an eyebrow, genuinely surprised. And curious. Why would elves be so eager to get his attention? Nodding to the elf, who slowly pulled out the message and handed it the general, he opened the message and quickly read the words before handing the scroll to his second.

"What do you think, Tevanic? Can we assist our young friend here?" Vana looked at the messenger, who raised an eyebrow at his comment, sure that he was at least a half century older than the general before him.

"I do not know if we have the men to help you in this trap!" Tevanic cut in as he took in the elf before him.

Hapif nodded. "So is no your answer, sir? I certainly understand wanting to maintain a strong force here, after all." Hapif paused and then turned back to Vana. "Methnorick almost made it into my homeland, but we were able to fight him off — just barely — and chase him south from Fuunidor ... this way, sir!" the elf stated.

"He's marching to us?" Tevanic gasped loudly and then groaned, leaning back as the elf nodded yes in return.

"More reason for us to stay put here, sir, and fight behind the walls, rather than on a field with no protection." The commander's voice almost sounded like a plea to the general, who listened to both for a moment.

"How many spears does your general have behind him, friend?" Vana leaned back, as he wanted to know this before he answered anything else.

The elf's forehead rose slightly as he thought. "I believe 15,000 march with General Summ, sir ... However, that was before more of my brothers came out of the Pilo'ach Mountains to help us rout Methnorick and make him retreat south."

Vana sucked in his lips as he thought. Tevanic recognized the look and groaned.

"Sir ... you can't believe that the men here can make a difference on a field. What if this Methnorick wins the field and finds nothing here to stop him from entering the empire? They would all be slaughtered before the army could assemble!" Tevanic stated, still hoping that Vana would refuse to commit any men to help the elves.

"Tevanic ... the orcs have already crossed into the empire once before. This gate is nothing but a symbol of the empire's power ... That's it. If Methnorick does win the field that General Summ hopes to bury him on, this gate won't be able stop him." Vana put up his hand to stop Tevanic from arguing further as he turned to Hapif.

"I will leave enough men to guard the gate itself, but I believe your people will need each and every sword to defeat Methnorick in the end ... So I will commit the men of the Father Gate to help in that defeat. If we die trying, then we die defending the empire!"

Vana stood up then, as did the elven scout, who bowed his head in thanks for the help.

"Tell General Summ that the men of the Father Gate will help in your battle!" Vana smiled back at the elven scout.

"I thank you, sir ... I thank you both!" Hapif smiled widely as he spoke.

"Come along, young elf. I will find you some food. Commander Tevanic, call the Father Gate to arms and get the men ready to march!" Vana ordered his second, who nodded and bowed slightly and left the room, yelling out commands as both elf and man smiled at each other.

"Now, tell me more about this Methnorick," Vana requested as they left the small chamber and walked down the dank hallway, quietly speaking to each other as around them the men of the Father Gate quickly assembled for war.

Chapter Twenty Six

Kikor brushed her horse gently as she kept a watchful eye out for any of those creatures that they had encountered in the city. It was true that the group had ridden all day and hadn't even encountered an orc, but she couldn't shake the feeling that they hadn't seen the last of those creatures.

As she scanned the area, her gaze soon fell upon Kalion as the ranger walked along the perimeter not far ahead of her. She had caught him looking at her with more than a passing interest several times throughout their journey, despite what he claimed to feel for the princess. Were his feelings beginning to change? She knew that hers had.

"Stop your probing, please … I am fine!" Whelor's roar snapped Kikor out of her reverie. She turned to see Amlora holding her hands up.

Kikor smiled at the big man as Amlora winked at her. Meanwhile, Kalion, who had come running when Whelor yelled, walked over to Meradoth, who was joking to Whelor that he could burn Amlora away if the man wanted. Whelor's frustration showed on his face as he stared over at the mage, who smiled back.

"Amlora … if he's fine, let him be." Kalion tried not to laugh at the scene before him.

"He's more than fine, Kalion … He's recovered from the wound like it didn't even happen!" the cleric declared as she walked past Kalion, who turned to look over at the big man leaning on his horse's saddle. He turned slightly to stare down at the ranger as Kalion approached.

"I am fine, Kalion. My anger is not towards Amlora. I will apologize to her. It is just that every time I feel her touch the wound, I want to kill that thief … the traitor that tried to kill me!" Kalion nodded and leaned up against the horse as the two warriors quietly spoke.

"I am sure you will have the chance, my friend. Our journey is not over. We still have a long way to go. In fact, keep that anger … I have a feeling we will need it very, very soon!" Kalion placed a hand gently on Whelor's forearm as he spoke. "Meradoth's father told me you were dangerous … but I do not believe you to be a danger to me or the others here!" Whelor just nodded at Kalion's reassurance.

* * *

Methnorick tightened his grip on the reins of his mount as the rain finally let up enough so that the army could march without slipping and falling in the mud. Still, he kept his eyes on the mountains ahead; it was a race and he knew it.

Deep within those mountains were thousands of orcs and other creatures that had fled there over the cycles to get away from the elves and men trying to kill them. Methnorick was sure they would gladly follow his banner when they heard his plans.

Riding close behind, Kaligor was making plans of his own. He still hadn't decided if he wanted to fight or kill the man riding before him. Fortunately for Methnorick, Kaligor's thoughts were interrupted by a scream from high above.

Kaligor glanced up and kicked his mount gently to continue on as the creature swooped past and flew around in a few circles before landing directly in front of Methnorick as orcs scattered to give the creature room.

As Kaligor slowly trotted up, he watched the massive black-skinned creature transform and in a flash shrink to the size of a small man as he walked out of a cloud of dust and slowly knelt down in front of Methnorick.

"It is done, master … The creature is dead!" Kaligor looked from the creature over to Methnorick, wondering what he meant.

Whatever it was, the news pleased Methnorick.

"Good!" Methnorick replied joyfully. "And your sister … Where does she roam?" Methnorick asked, leaning slightly in his saddle as he looked down at the man.

Swallowing hard, he replied, "The last time I saw her, she was preparing Blath 'Na for you by ending the reign of the last one that could resist you!"

"Good … You have done well, Chansor. With the creature gone and now the capital ready … when Sernga rises, all of Marn will bow to me!" Methnorick raised a fist up as he spoke the last word. Orcs marching by looked over and saw their leader's excitement, which, in turn, made them roar loudly, knowing that they might be retreating … but to a better position.

"We march to Sernga, Chansor … Join us now!" Methnorick said as he kicked his mount into motion.

As Chansor watched the army file past him, his thoughts went back to when he left Whelor lying on the ground, bleeding to death from the knife wounds he had given him. He swallowed as a sudden feeling of doubt crept into his mind.

The mission is over, Chansor, he thought to himself, shaking his head slightly. *You're with Methnorick now.* The thought made him smile as he turned and began to follow the army.

* * *

General Summ, when they got to a crossroads, ordered one of his captains, who had been marching on his eastern perimeter, to attack Stych Castle and try to recover it. Methnorick, Summ believed, might be using the port of Stych Castle to resupply his armies.

As Summ came over a rise, a messenger approached and handed him a parchment. As he read the numbers and direction of Methnorick's army, he looked over the map laid on top of his saddle.

His advisors that rode around him held wide smiles, all thinking that events could be going their way finally as the general repeated what he had read.

So far Methnorick's army had been marching so quickly that he knew by day's end the Dark One would reach the hills that lay just before the mountains where he hoped to catch him in his trap.

He kicked his horse and rode hard to where the forward patrols were slowly riding ahead of the elven army. He was amazed that Methnorick wasn't offering any resistance. There was no rear guard trying to slow them down. He found that fascinating, but he couldn't worry about it. He had to hurry his army along.

※ ※ ※

The elven captain that had been sent to deal with Stych Castle sat on his saddle, scanning the land for any sign of orcish movement. So far the night had brought only a few skirmishes as orcs hidden within the ruins of Stych Castle and the destroyed village tried to make a break for the forests that lay across the large fields that surrounded the port castle to the west. In each skirmish, though, the orcs were slaughtered easily.

So far the attack had almost gone perfectly; so perfectly that none of his warriors had been even injured. Earlier his regiment had come to the last point where they could hide before they would be seen by anything within Stych Castle. The scouts he had sent out earlier had observed that no orc sentries had been placed, and he could hear singing coming from the village, where he counted many dead bodies lying on the ground and clouds of birds circling them. Methnorick must have thought Stych would always be his, the captain thought, smiling under his helmet.

Thinking about how perfectly the attack had gone, he was proud of his cavalry. They had done it like they had been trained. His warriors had spread out in a long line and slowly trotted down the hill, trying not to make much noise so they could close the distance before they were seen. What had surprised the captain was that his warriors had been able to make an almost easy approach to within just a few lengths of the village gates before an orc leaning on a wall, drinking, just happened to look up from his drinking horn.

The attack was swift and hard, as his elves rode in hard, screaming their battle cries and riding over many orcs that had run out to find out what the noise was. A few tried to fight them off, only to die as quickly as they had come out of the buildings.

A small number of orcs that had tried to make a break to get away were killed easily, so now his warriors did the only thing that was left for them to do. They waited for the runner that they had sent to General Summ to ask him what to do now after securing the castle. In the meantime, the captain told his warriors to make it look to any observer or spy of Methnorick's moving past like the village was being defended — by orcs, of course. So his warriors, all complaining about the smells, put on orcish helmets and held shields up as they walked around slowly.

His ears caught the sound of movement coming from the hill that his cavalry had ridden over earlier in its attack. The captain called out for his warriors to ready their arms. A few not near their mounts quickly made for the walls that they had been building and made their bows ready, scanning the dark, waiting.

When the horse and its rider were confirmed to be the runner he had sent, he yelled out for his warriors to stand down and to finish their work, as he knew that they would be leaving soon. The elf runner rushed up and jumped off his horse before it even stopped, with the biggest smile the captain had ever seen. He ran up to give the captain a rolled parchment.

Opening it up, he read the parchment that held General Summ's signature. He told his second to get ready to ride out, as their new orders were to make it to the shoreline and to quickly make their way south to where he was to meet with General Summ and the army at an old dwarven fortress that stood just north of the border with God's Haven.

He watched his warriors quickly finish their walls and defenses, making sure each fire was built up enough to stay lit for a while. He gave final orders to set traps since they had to leave this place. He hoped the illusion would work. When they finished, each elf jumped on their mount, and they slowly made their way to the port and shoreline of Stych. There they turned south, picking up their pace as they left the ruined human village to meet with their people moving to corner the Dark One.

Chapter Twenty Seven

Summ was looking over the map when a scout from the south rode up to inform him that God's Haven was on the march. Cheers erupted from the elves walking nearby that overheard.

"This is great news this day, my lord!" one of his commanders said as the scout rode off. Summ turned to him with a large smile.

"We need to make sure that this day keeps bringing joyful news," Summ replied, looking down at the map.

As the news that God's Haven was joining them spread through the ranks of the army, the excitement became unmistakable.

The sound of singing as their people walked by made Summ smile. His people would survive this battle, if not the war.

* * *

Shermee sat in front of the fire, trying to process all that Johnna had told them.

According to Johnna, the high minister of Manhattoria was in league with Methnorick and could only be defeated by being killed. Shermee was not sure that she wanted to start her legacy this way.

Quinor, on the other hand, knew he would have to do something in order to make her queen, for he was determined that this would happen. She was the one, so if the high minister had to die because he was in her way … He would take whatever action was needed to ensure she became queen.

Shermee looked down at her hands, squeezing them slightly, wondering if she had the strength in them to do what she had been told by Johnna as she lifted her head to look over at the man.

Swallowing slowly, she stood up and looked down at Johnna, who smiled slightly as he looked back at her. Shermee stated, "All right, then, our next step is to sort out these trials."

"Might I suggest, Your Highness, that your next step should be to get some sleep? You have much to think about. And do. You will need your rest," Johnna stated.

Shermee smiled and nodded slightly as she followed Johnna into a room, where she found both a bed and soft-looking chair in the corner. She fell fast asleep before the old man finished lighting a fire.

* * *

Captain Bataoli marched at the head of the army as they left God's Haven and made their way up the road north towards the field where General Summ believed they could trap Methnorick's army. His advance scout had reported the presence of a ruined building at the top of a small hill that looked over the main road in a field around the dwarves' forest of Ribbwa'nor. This was the location where General Summ was coordinating the trap and attack on Methnorick.

Bataoli considered what the Fuunidor general was planning. General Summ believed that their armies could trap this Methnorick on those fields, with the glen, guarded by sharp rocks like a pair of gates, lying to the north of the fields and no escape possible to the west or east. The opening to the south was the only means of escape. Bataoli agreed with Summ's strategy. His army would block the south entry while General Summ blocked the northern entry, keeping Methnorick bottled up there. Timing was also critical in order to keep Methnorick from being able to deploy his full strength of warriors, war machines and cavalry.

"You know that we could fly north and plan our positions on the field, my friend … Best to be prepared!" Lugtrix said calmly to Bataoli, making him smile at the mount. The massive Pegasus he was riding was such a powerful beast, and so knowledgeable, that taking his advice might be warranted.

"Just us, my friend?" Bataoli asked, trying to hide the humor in the question, already knowing the answer.

"Of course ... Surprise is on our side, do you not think?" Lugtrix responded as he flapped his wings, sensing the humor coming from Bataoli.

Nodding as he sucked in his lips, trying not to laugh, Bataoli motioned over to one of his sergeants to take over the lead of the army.

"Now or never, my friend ... Let us go and see what is ahead, shall we?" Bataoli whispered as he gripped the reins tightly.

As soon as he said the words, the creature took a few steps forward and began to ascend, flapping its wings as the pair rose high above the army. As Bataoli turned back to marvel at the army marching beneath them, a flicker of light farther south caught his eye.

"Lugtrix ... turn south ... I see something," Bataoli called out to his friend.

"South? I thought you wanted to go north ... Did you forget something back home?" Lugtrix's humor almost made the elf smile.

"No ... I see torches farther south of Haven ... Someone is marching behind us!"

Lugtrix turned south as Bataoli focused on the torches.

Soon it became apparent that another army marched on the road — not from God's Haven, of course, but farther south. In fact, the entrance remained hidden. Bataoli was confident that whoever marched below had no idea that they were passing the birthplace of the gods.

"Your eyes are better than mine, my friend ... What do you see below?" Bataoli called out as they moved through a cloud. He was curious about who was holding those torches.

"They are not moving like orcish or goblin creatures, my friend. They move more fluidly ... like your people or ... or men!" Lugtrix answered a few moments later as they flew out of the cloud and swept over the road.

"Men? What men would be to the south of us … unless?" Bataoli shook his head.

"The empire … They have to be men from the empire!" Bataoli called out with excitement as they descended lower, careful not to spook the men below. Still, Bataoli needed to know for sure. Flying even lower, Bataoli raised his fist high as they got close. "EMPIRE!" he screamed out as they rushed over the men below.

To their delight, cheers erupted from the darkness, and both saw the torches move around in circles as the men, whom they could just make out, also raised their hands up to cheer to him in return.

"We might survive this!" Bataoli called out to Lugtrix, who huffed again as they turned back north.

Chapter Twenty Eight

Methnorick's scouts rode ahead into the ravine in search of any signs of resistance or a trap. But nothing came out and attacked the orcs and goblins as they rode their beasts through until they found themselves turning the long corner and entering the wide field that lay beyond.

Taking in the sights of the field and where the road snaked around to move through a forest opening on the far southern side, the orc riders pulled their reins to move their beasts around, and in one quick snap, the group roared off back north to inform their master that the way ahead was open.

As the orcs disappeared from view, a group of elven scouts moved out of the forest to meet in the center of the road.

"Here they come!" the sergeant whispered as they disappeared.

Methnorick, meanwhile, was pleased to hear that the last open area they had to cross before reaching the foothills of the Sernga Mountains was clear. He ordered his heavy troops — those orcs that were carrying any equipment — to move to the side and let the light troops — those warriors that could run quickly — push their way through the ravine.

He wanted to get through this small enclosed area in case there were elven archers or a mage near the area. U'Traa's warning that elven scouts had been seen worried him more than he let on, but now he was almost there.

It didn't take that long for the army to get through the opening of the ravine.

* * *

Bataoli's army had gathered before dawn at the mouth of the vale where the Boralki ruins stood. Bataoli had circled the field of battle and found no sign yet of Methnorick, but he could tell that they were close. Earlier he had ordered the rest of the Pegasi cavalry to fly forward to secure the fields around the tower and make it ready for the army, knowing that they should get there by daybreak. Now they were in position to block Methnorick from getting out of the vale and heading farther south.

Breathing in slightly, he looked over and observed some of the proud faces of his warriors marching in their columns. He knew that, in the end, skill would win this battle.

* * *

"You recognize them, Kikor?" Holan whispered.

Nodding but not saying a word, Kikor looked at the elves in the shadows as two horses came out of the dark.

"Well then, girl, don't keep it a secret," Holan hissed. "Who are they?" he asked again.

"Sorry, Holan … Fuunidor elves!"

"Are you sure?" Kalion whispered. "How can you tell?"

"Ohhh, I am sure, my friend. They are, indeed, Fuunidor elves. Fuunidor elves wear armor laced with green … It's to give the enemy the illusion that the forest is moving!" Kikor explained without looking at Kalion, who tried his best to use what light there was from the moon above to take in the armor and clothing of the elves looking back at them.

"What is going on?" Amlora asked Whelor, only to find that he had moved himself a few steps away.

Whelor argued a bit with her but stopped when she placed her hand on the man's arm. "If you want to kill Chansor, I understand, my friend … I really do. But right now we need to determine our next steps here."

"Isn't anybody going to answer the lady?" another voice called out from the darkness as it finally dawned on the others that they were completely surrounded. One by one, elven warriors stepped out of the darkness until the group found themselves staring at over twenty elven archers, all pointing their arrows at them.

"You are to come with us ... There are those who wish to speak to your group." The elf leader raised his hand and then lowered it, indicating to the rest of his warriors to lower their bows.

Kikor tilted her head, as if listening for something, and then nodded and slowly lowered her weapon, prompting the others to follow suit. Kalion hoped that Kikor knew what she was doing as the elven warriors led them down the small trail that circled its way down to the road not far below.

As they stepped onto the road, Kalion heard Amlora gasp as the reason for Kikor's surrender suddenly became clear: They were in the midst of the largest army of elves any of them had ever seen. No one spoke as their captors directed them to a small grove, where five elves stood looking over a map.

They turned to see the group walk up to the edge of the grove. The group was made to wait while the leader of their captors addressed an older elf in the group, who waved them over when finished.

"I'm told you were in Fuunidor recently," the elf remarked as he slowly looked at each member of the group until his eyes landed on Kikor, who bowed her head slowly to him.

"Sir, my group and I were recently in your kingdom before traveling on our way east to Blath 'Na ... but we had been under the impression that Methnorick was attacking your borders. Were we wrong, sir?"

Smiling, the elf laughed slightly, as did a few of the other elves.

"He was there ... until we routed his armies and sent them running south!" the elf declared confidently as he walked forward to stand before Kalion. "And who might you be?"

"My name is Kalion Sa'un Ukka of Brigin'i."

The mention of Brigin'i caused murmurs to start among some of the nearby elves. Summ looked at the group again, this time more intently. "Kalion … I remember hearing of you and your group." He looked over at Whelor. "We are at this moment chasing Methnorick and what is left of his armies south in hopes of cornering and wiping his kind off the lands before he can get reinforcements that are within the Sernga Mountains."

"If you mean to make war with Methnorick, we will join you!" Whelor said excitedly as he stepped forward. Kalion looked at the big man, feeling the sense of power in his voice.

He looked at the rest of his friends, who slowly smiled and nodded back at him.

Turning and looking at Summ, Kalion stepped forward. "We will all gladly join you if it means destroying and killing the creature that has caused us all misery."

Clapping his hands together, Summ ignored Kalion, his gaze now trained on Whelor. "You are most welcome to be where you want in this fight. I believe it would be good to have you on our side." Again he looked over at Whelor pointedly before beckoning his squire. "I must ride forward now … Methnorick's army, I'm told, has entered the last phase of our trap for him!"

The group watched the general turn and jump up on his horse with his elven guards. They quickly rode off south, leaving Kalion and the others with the elven archers.

"Here is your chance, my friend!" Kikor said, looking at Whelor, who looked down at the elven maiden and almost snarled at her as he stepped forward to join the marching elves, followed by the others, who also joined in the march south.

※ ※ ※

When Shermee awoke, she found a fresh pitcher of water with cleaning supplies. She took the opportunity to refresh herself as best she could, even using some of the water to rinse her hair, before donning the clothes that Johnna had obviously left for her. She took the rags that she had been wearing since almost the beginning of this adventure and threw them into the fire as she left the room to find Quinor sitting in a chair, also looking refreshed. Quinor took one look at her clothing and blinked twice at what he saw.

A long black dress with yellowish writing that represented the ancient name of the elvish and human kind flowed over a pair of black leather boots polished to the highest possible shine. Around her waist, she wore a gold belt with the emblem of the imperial queen, and around her torso and chest, the robe was pulled together tightly over a pair of shoulder pieces that protected her upper body and shoulders.

Her hair was pulled back tightly, and she wore a simple band of gold that covered her forehead with the small emblem of the queen.

She looked at Johnna and asked, "Where did you get these clothes?"

"There were stored … Do not ask me where they are from or how they came to be in my possession, but I knew one day our future queen would come to me, for that is the first trial: She will seek out the rebel of the empire to learn her fate."

She walked over to stand in front of a mirror. As she gazed at it, she admired herself, not believing that these clothes had been kept hidden for many cycles until now. Swallowing deeply, she turned slowly around to stare at the two men, who waited for her to speak. As she did, both men could see that she had changed.

"Let us begin this!" Shermee said with confidence.

✳ ✳ ✳

The movement through the ravine and glen had been undisturbed, which both relieved and worried Methnorick. He ordered sergeants to whip their warriors to move more quickly.

The echoes of the whips rang out like thunder. Impatient to get a clear view of the mountains, Methnorick rode forward, leaving his army behind.

As he moved around the last corner of the ravine, he pulled his horse to a stop. Pushing back his hood, he closed his eyes and breathed in the cold air of the morning as he gathered his thoughts. All that was needed to turn the tide of this war back against the elves and men still fighting him was to join his army with those of the tribes of orcs within the mountains.

He opened his eyes as his ears began picking up the screams of his army moving forward and the snaps of whips that continued to echo out of the glen.

Looking across the field, he saw the ruins to his left and high cliffs to his right, but these weren't what caught his main attention. It was the movement at the southern edge of the field that made him stand up in his saddle.

"Noooo!" he rasped loudly as his eyes fell upon a familiar sight marching out of the forest.

"ELVES ... HERE!" he screamed out as the sounds of his army got closer and closer.

Pulling the reins hard and kicking his horse, he returned to where Kaligor and U'Traa were slowly riding with the rest of his army, in the middle of the columns making their way forward.

As Methnorick rushed over a hill along the side of the road, both could see that something was wrong before they heard him screaming about the elves.

We have a problem! Kaligor thought to himself as he looked at the Dark One and the field before him.

Chapter Twenty Nine

They call it the calm before the battle, when two armies stand and wait, looking at each other, watching, checking out their strengths and hopefully finding their weaknesses. For two hours Methnorick's orcs had moved out onto the field, which U'Traa mentioned was called Ribbwa'nor, and positioned themselves along the southern cliff face that was part of the ravine and glen behind them.

Methnorick ordered Kaligor to position himself on Methnorick's left flank, facing the elves, and U'Traa to take the right flank as Methnorick, along with his prized guard, prepared to lead the army from the middle, where he could command the entire field of battle.

Orcs, goblins, giantkind and other creatures that where within the army broke up into the planned battle groups and, after lowering their shields, stood quietly and waited. Those orcs that had been in battle with Kaligor grew impatient after a while and started to stomp around, grumbling about wanting to charge their enemy, who, the rumor was spreading, numbered only a few hundred, but the cyclops had a few whipped to calm them down.

Methnorick sat on his saddle and considered his options. The Fuunidor army still pursued him. Now his route was blocked by another. *From where did they come?* he wondered. *There is no elven kingdom or forest that they rule in the south ... unless they are from the empire!* Methnorick cursed the high minister. *He lied to me!*

Looking at his Blingo'oblin commander, Methnorick said, "Pama ... give the order to advance all ranks!" Methnorick ground his teeth tightly as he spoke. His hands glowed red from the anger he was feeling as he looked down at the captain of his guards and then back at the helmets and banners flapping in the wind far away among the elven ranks.

"Yes, master!" Pama smiled from the corner of his mouth as he bowed and ran to carry out Methnorick's order to advance.

※ ※ ※

Shermee strode down the main avenue of Manhattoria, flanked by Quinor and Johnna. While no one paid any attention to her, despite the clothes, it didn't take long for a sergeant of the guards to recognize Johnna and call for him to halt, making the old man stop quickly in his tracks.

"What goes on here, Johnna? Why are you out here … with this woman?" the man asked, giving Shermee a confused glance as he looked her up and down quickly and then looked back to the old man, who smiled gently.

"Have you not heard? I guard our queen." Johnna motioned to Shermee, who smiled. The guard raised his eyebrow and laughed as he looked at the young girl before him.

Johnna smiled at the man and then nodded to Shermee, who nodded and smiled back as she turned fully around and stepped up to the guard.

"What is your name, sir?" Shermee asked calmly. The sergeant's laughter suddenly died as he heard her voice, which was like something out of a dream. Something about it made him feel … warm.

"My … my name is Grith, my … my lady!" the sergeant whispered as he noticed that his men, who had also been laughing, suddenly went quiet as well.

"Grith, I am Shermee … your queen. Do you agree that I am who I say I am, Grith?" Shermee asked, almost smiling at him as she spoke.

Nodding yes slowly, Grith knelt down, leaving Shermee surrounded by the group of guards. Scores of citizens now also observed her as she turned slowly around.

"Hear me, citizens of the Empire of Pendore'em and Edlaii … My name is Shermee. I am here to lead the empire over the dark evil that will soon come to your lands. I am your queen … Hear me, all, and spread the word!" Upon hearing this, those around the guards started to kneel down around her as well.

Johnna turned and whispered to Quinor, "The second trial: They will bow down before her."

* * *

Shermee quickly found herself surrounded by scores of people all cheering for her. She touched as many hands and faces as she possibly could as word spread that the legend was true and the queen from the north had come to the empire.

High above in the tower, Halashii was being informed that there was a young woman on the main road calling herself the queen of the empire.

Halashii stood on the balcony and watched from high above the large crowds of citizens gathering in the streets. He could just make out a blond-haired woman in the middle of all of the people.

Cursing the woman, the high minister vowed that she would never stand where he was as he turned around and quickly bent over his desk to scribble out a message on a small piece of parchment. Calling out a messenger, he gave the parchment to the man, who left quickly, leaving the high minister alone for a moment longer. Soon, however, the cheers echoed into his chamber, making him close the door.

* * *

Since marching onto the field of Ribbwa'nor, the army from God's Haven hadn't been able to believe the size of the army they were facing. Not that any of them were worried; they would face them like their people had always faced their enemies: with honor and strength. In the end, God's Haven would win the day.

Bataoli had ordered the Pegasi to keep out of sight. Very few creatures even knew of their existence — including Methnorick, Bataoli surmised — which made Bataoli smile as he observed the slowly advancing forces. As for the men of the Father Gate ... he reminded himself as he glanced back at the contingent of men who had joined them at the southern exit at daybreak that their cavalry would be needed very soon.

So far the monks of God's Haven had watched the proceedings with almost an air of boredom as they stood behind their shields. General Vana could be heard calling for calm as his men caught sight of the advancing orcs. Their horses whined and jumped around until their riders could hold them down enough to turn their attention towards the enemy.

"Remember ... you are not just fighting for your homes and family ... You are fighting to end the reign of terror that these creatures have spread across the land. Let's end this today!"

Cheers came from his men as the elves stayed silent. Not that Vana had expected them to say a thing to him or his men; they were trained not to say anything in the heat of battle, he had been told a while earlier by one of their council members.

Now, as the screams of the enemy signaled their approach, Vana pulled out his sword and stood back, looking left and right as his men followed suit.

"PREPARE YOURSELVES ... HERE THEY COME!"

Chapter Thirty

The orcs drew themselves into their battle lines not far from the elves, breathing hard, showing their anger and distaste for their enemy that stood not far ahead. They held weapons that ranged from swords, spears and axes to a few others never seen before. Many were holding shields, but most held a weapon in each of their large hands, grinding their teeth together and staring at their enemy, which at the moment was staring back, standing behind a line of heavy elven shields. The orcs knew they would have to get over or through these shields that had been brought together to form a temporary wall in order to get at the flesh of the elf creatures hiding behind them.

Kaligor rode back and forth behind his battle formation, trying to keep his orcs from charging forward, having already seen a few try, only to get cut down by well-aimed elven arrows from the south.

Each time one fell, his orcs screamed their anger at not being able to charge forward, but he yelled for them to hold back until the time came.

As he waited for the signal from the Dark One, he kept his lone eye on the elven heads peeking around the shields and looking north at Methnorick's massive army, which was returning the menacing look.

They look nervous, he thought, making his giant mouth smile widely.

On the far side of the field, U'Traa himself was waiting upon his mount on Methnorick's right end. His subordinates that were nearby were trying to keep the horses still, which was a hard task for the orc captains, who had to whip a few riders who moaned about wanting to charge forward. They all wanted to charge and run the elves over as hard as they could.

As a heavy wind flew past U'Traa and his horse reared, his hood fell back so that many orcs standing nearby observed the creature's decaying head. A few backed away and a small number tried to hide under their helmets, all feeling their skin burning from the presence of Methnorick's servant.

The fear coming from his own warriors would have made U'Traa smile, but since he didn't have lips or working skin to cover his face, his jaw just dropped slightly as he held onto the reins of his horse and turned around a few times, waiting for the signal.

On Methnorick's far left perimeter, along the edge of the thick forest, the dark elves sat quietly on their furry beasts, waiting for the Dark One's signal. Luckily their mounts were calm and trained not to move until told to. They licked their jowls and snarled once in a while, as they could just make out their prey, but altogether, their small continent was largely silent.

In the middle of the main contingent of orcs and other dark creatures, spears were waving back and forth and horn calls were blaring as the Dark One, Methnorick, sat among the banners flying his emblem. He sat silently upon his horse, holding the reins tightly with his gloved hands, the only movement coming from his long cloak that whipped slightly when some wind came. He kept his head under his hood, thinking of what was before him.

An unknown number of elven warriors were hiding behind what looked like a well-planted wall of shields. To his right, he could just make out a battalion of horse cavalry, which looked to be men carrying a banner he didn't recognize. But no matter. U'Traa would finish them soon.

The first charge, which was only meant to scare the elves, didn't work, he noticed, so he kept his orcs back to see what the elves did. But they did nothing — no counter, nothing. Discipline, he saw, was working well for them at the moment.

Everything is ready, then, he thought. Everything, that is, except his reinforcements, the Sernga Mountain orcs. But no matter ... He would push hard to get through.

None shall survive this day ... Their children will be mine from this day forward. The thought made him smile under the hood he had pulled over his face, only letting the shadow of his smile be seen.

Looking left and then right, the dark emperor was about to raise his hand to call for the elimination of the enemy when he heard a commotion behind him. Pulling the reins right, he quickly turned around to look back north.

NOOOO! he thought instantly.

Each and every creature within earshot heard their emperor curse the gods as they looked upon what he had seen.

Pouring out of the glen mouth that he himself and his army had come out of only an hour or so earlier, the Dark One and those of his subjects that could see watched elf warrior after elf warrior run out and form quickly into battle lines, each holding their weapons tightly, ready for anything.

He cursed again when he caught sight of the massive forms of the ice giants lumbering through the opening. Methnorick knew he would have a real fight upon his hands now. His eyes fell upon many banners and flags held proudly by the elven warriors. He recognized many as being from Fuunidor, but many he had never seen before. But it was a blue banner with a ship upon a lake that made the Dark One's hands begin to glow in anger and surprise.

"DIA!" he roared to himself. The old king's banner would only be flying if the man was still alive and able to ride.

"I should have slaughtered that fat baron's whole family!" Methnorick snarled through his clenched teeth as he saw a rider with long whitish hair and not clearing an elf in size coming out.

Many of his orcs, realizing that they were surrounded, began to drop their weapons in the hopes of finding an escape through the forests or the cliffs in the west. They turned to move, but their sergeants and those in charge quickly snapped their whips to get them back in line.

"My lord ... Your orders, sir. What do we do?" a voice echoed in

Methnorick's mind as he stared at the elven warriors pouring out and filling the field to his north. He even caught sight of what had to be their leaders — elven generals riding on their horses — galloping out to catch their warriors and shouting orders to get the lines in order.

"MY LORD!" The voice finally got his attention as he looked left and noticed his Blingo'oblin commander, Joocc Pama, standing not far away. The commander was holding his massive sword in one hand and a whip in the other, staring back at him with a look of confusion.

Before he had a chance to mumble a word, loud cheers erupted from the elves and men who had been able to stop the Dark One's forces from marching south. Elf and man alike lifted their weapons into the air as they watched General Summ's Fuunidor elves march hard to catch up to Methnorick and trap the Dark One by filling up the northern part of the Ribbwa'nor Fields.

The roar from the southern elven contingent made many more orcs whimper, not knowing what to do now that their advantage, both in numbers and in the ability to maneuver the field, was lost.

"Your orders, my lord?" Pama repeated, speaking loudly to be heard over the sounds of elven armor echoing as their enemy rode onto the field before them. Everywhere along Methnorick's lines, whips were snapping hard to keep the orcs and others in line. Many more, Methnorick could see, were struggling to hold their warriors together.

"Damn orcs ... such weak creatures!" he mumbled under his breath.

I'm trapped! he thought.

* * *

Moments earlier, General Vana had been upon his horse, trying to see how many were under Methnorick's banner, but he was having a hard time of it, as many orcs were moving back and forth, trying to get themselves in order.

"I count at least a few thousand, sir," one of his men called over. The general nodded as he lost count and gave up.

"Well, it just means more for us to cut down, men!" Vana smiled as he heard his men laugh back to him and saw their horses move around excitedly.

Looking to his right, the general could see the elven monk warriors readying themselves behind the shields that had been planted hard into the ground to be used as a wall. Holding their long, club-like spears tightly, many, he could see, were young and inexperienced in warfare, but that would change, he thought. Hundreds of elven archers stood behind the monks, pushing arrows into the ground for easy access as well as pulling and testing their bows, making sure everything was tight and ready.

As he stared down the back side of their lines, he got the attention of a few who lifted their hands up, acknowledging him. He smiled and returned the wave when he noticed the movement of many elves who had been hiding behind the shields now jumping up and lifting their weapons into the air.

Maneuvering his horse around, he looked north, wondering what in all the lands could make them happy at this moment, when he caught sight of the movement that was making his men cheer.

"Fuunidor … Fuunidor is here, General!" a voice echoed through the cheers as Vana smiled widely, nodding that he saw them.

"We did it!" he whispered to himself. "We stopped the Dark One, and now it's only a matter of time before we can finish this."

As he and the elves from God's Haven watched what looked like hundreds of thousands of their brothers from the north pour out of the glen and get themselves formed upon the field, he quickly called for his own men to keep themselves calm and be ready for the signal to ride forward.

* * *

In the north, General Summ and those of his war council, along with King Dia and the group of warriors that his elves had found along the way south, finally made their way out of the ravine to get themselves on the field, just as the clouds snapped a few flashes of lightning, making the orcs and the other dark creatures south of their position on the field look more threatening.

Screaming for order, Summ made sure that each battle line was formed and ready as he looked south, not understanding why Methnorick hadn't attacked his warriors when they were easy prey and small in number. *Interesting*! he thought as he held his reins and called out for each and every warrior to ready themselves.

Standing just ahead of the elven general and his contingent stood the group from Brigin'i, waiting for the word to be given.

"I think we caught the Dark One by surprise!" Kalion mumbled to his group, who were taking up their positions at the rear of the elven army. They all nodded in agreement.

Kikor herself could easily make out the dark form of the thing that was calling himself emperor, the Dark One, and many other things, sitting upon his black horse in the middle of his army — just sitting there and looking at Summ's army forming before him.

It would be so easy for me to finish this right now! she thought.

Gripping her bow tightly along her side, she prepared to throw herself hard into the battle that she knew was about to start as she caught sight of Meradoth and Harbin running to her left to also get themselves ready. She smiled from the corner of her mouth and shook her head slightly, noticing they were almost acting like children the way they were running.

Amlora and Niallee were gone, getting ready for the wounded and preparing their remedies, leaving only Holan, Kalion, Whelor and herself to stand there, silently waiting. Around them, the only things moving were the horses, whose breath puffed out of their enlarged nostrils as they breathed hard from the ride south.

Summ himself sat upon his own horse and looked at the Dark

One facing him, knowing that Methnorick must be staring at him at that very moment. *Who knows?* he thought.

Pulling in a deep breath, the elf leaned down slightly and, in a quick snap, pulled out his sword from the saddle scabbard and prepared himself inside for what he needed to do to lead and survive this battle to come. At that moment, his elven eyes caught the sight of dots in the sky far to the south, moving towards him.

At first he didn't know what to make of them, but then, when a few of his own warriors also noticed the dots floating in the sky, whispers flew by about what they were. A huge smile formed on Summ's face, as he knew that at the very least, his people had a chance.

"PREPARE YOURSELVES!" he called out, looking over at three elves standing not far from him, who nodded back as they lifted the large horns to their lips that would deliver the call for each and every being of light to charge forward. Just then, the ground began to shake under their feet, causing many horses to cry out, jump and circle around nervously as rocks from the mountains behind them began to roll down onto the ground.

Summ, holding his now-frightened horse, began to almost feel the very air around him being pushed to the ground as his ears rang from a loud, sudden scream that echoed high above the field. Those that could covered their ears as a dark shadow moved across Summ's warriors, causing them to go from a stance of pride to one of fear as his formations quivered, wondering what was happening.

Lifting a hand up to protect his face, Summ looked to the ground as it got dark for a moment and then lightened up as something flew over him. He could hear the sound of something huge flapping its wings as it passed him. Looking back up, he heard whimpers and gasps as he gasped himself at what he saw.

"Of all the gods!" he whispered.

Flying up into the air was a creature he had never seen in his many cycles of life — but one he had read about as a creature from history. The massive beast flew slowly up and circled the field above

Methnorick's army, which Summ could hear now cheering and roaring at the presence of the creature flying over them.

Gazing back up at the flying beast, he looked it over as quickly as he could as many of his commanders tried in vain to calm the warriors everywhere.

The creature had black scales and a very long tail that swung back and forth, ending with what looked like blades that probably could cut through anything. Summ heard and now watched the massive wings rise and fall slowly as he took in the huge head, which ended at a thick neck, looking down at his army and those in the south. Bright red eyes, almost like flames, stared down, and within a wide, gaping mouth about the size of a frost giant's full frame, Summ could see huge razor-like teeth, which reflected the flashes of lightning as the beast roared again, making it seem as though the sky was falling upon them as it looked down at its prey, slowly circling over the field.

Blinking a moment longer, Summ got himself back to the situation before him.

"HORNS … HORNS NOW!" he screamed. The three elves wetted their lips and blew with everything they had, quickly filling ears everywhere with the sound to charge forward as it echoed loudly through the air. Upon hearing the sound, the elves lifted the banner and flags high and raised their swords, shields and spears into the air, cheering loudly as they quickly stepped forward as one and charged towards their enemy.

Hearing the elven horn, Methnorick lifted his glowing red hand up and, in response to the elves, made his own hand explode in a fiery red light, signaling his orcs to charge forward.

Quickly, the once-silent field where deer loved to roam and play erupted and shook hard as elf, orc, goblin, man and giant charged towards each other, not knowing if they would see the sun's light again or not, as the sky had already darkened from the hundreds of thousands of arrows that flew up into the air, covering the sky in blackness. The roars from both sides were quickly drowned out by the roar of the beast that flew over Methnorick, who smiled, looking north.

"This night, the elf shall end!"

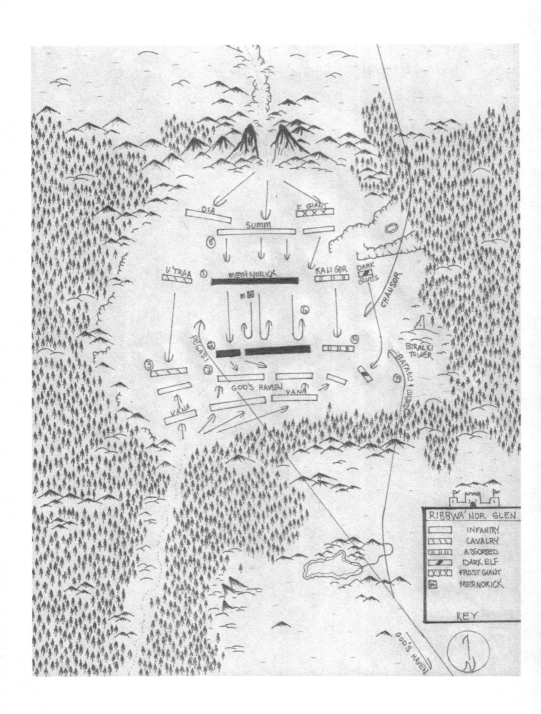

Made in the USA
Middletown, DE
22 March 2024

51463827R00159